the Night Nurse

SCOTT GILLES

Edited by Jason Letts
Formatted by Evgeniia Gurcheva
Cover design by Adam Kleinert

Paperback ISBN: 979-8-9997586-0-6
Electronic ISBN: 979-8-9997586-1-3

First Edition: 2025

To Emily.

Ecclesiastes 4:9-10

Thank you for being my other half,

and for always lifting me up.

1

Dear Chloe,

It's me, Dad.

It hurts my heart to write this.

It had never been difficult to talk with you in the twelve years we had together. Yet here I am, struggling to communicate when in truth you were the sunlight in my life.

Until you weren't. Until your light was extinguished.

You're probably thinking that beginning with "Dear Chloe" feels "lame". It seems as if you're far away when all I knew with you was closeness and presence. I'm still not ready for this change in reality, though I do know I should be, because it's the one I live in and have for almost two years now.

The truth is we need to talk. If only. Or more accurately stated, I need to tell you a story and hope you can hear it.

It's been two years. Really it's been two years, three months, and twenty-four days, but who can keep track, right?

I have to excise this story from my mind, sweet girl.

You may not believe a word of it, but every last detail is true.

It's about April 18, 2024.

I don't know what you saw that day. I don't know if those who pass from this life can continue to see its events once they're gone, but if there is a God above, I hope you saw none of what I'm about to describe.

If there is a God? Had someone told me on April 17th 2024, that I'd be asking such a question, I would have laughed at them. Winslow Miller, husband to Joey, father to Chloe, wonders if God is real? How foolish.

When you live your entire life among the sheep only to one day discover you've run headlong into a wolf, it changes you.

That's why I have to write to you. I can't continue to live under this cloud. Life and its realities are but a hazy blur these days, and the way I maneuver through the haze isn't fair to anyone. Truth be told, the haze has surrounded me for a long time now. Two years, three months, and twenty-four days if I may be precise.

"Death comes for us all." People keep bombarding me with this and more pithy little sayings like they should bring some form of comfort. As though I am not aware of it as the singular constant that's existed from the onset of life on this planet, from the dawn of humanity after the fall of man, and will remain so unless the day the good Lord returns does actually happen.

I know, I heard it.

One can only hope that the inevitability of the finite holds off until they're old and sleeping, resting from a life fully lived, weary from a fullness of experiences – not young, woken from their slumber and waiting for pancakes, their life only fractionally lived.

No one should experience a day like the one I relive every night in my dreams and every day in the moments I drift away from my surroundings. I'm haunted by visions of pools of tears, the acidic taste from puddles of vomit, and the smell of roasted meat.

Forgive me if I get my times wrong. Much of my day was spent distraught and trying simply to remember to breathe while clinging to the one rock I had left. We were trying to survive.

A lot of the details were given to me later from the few survivors who cleansed the smokey smell from their nostrils with fresh spring night air, but I'll explain that as we get there.

It feels as though that day went on forever, when in truth it lasted only about twelve hours. Perhaps less. How is a parent supposed to properly grieve when the immediate moments following the stricken incident are as chaotic as ours were that day?

Let this letter be my goodbye. No. Let it be my "see you soon." Let me not forget and move on, but accept and move forward. And if God is as real today as he was then, let my faith return. For all our sakes.

For your sister's sake most of all. That's right, Chloe. I don't know what you can see from up there, but it finally happened. You always said you wanted to be a big sister. Now you are. Down here, that means I get another shot at being a daddy.

Which is not to say I won't always be your daddy, but it's different now. I hate that, but it's true. I think the worst part is how that truth is affecting my ability to be the daddy your little sister needs me to be.

This is my attempt to put it all out there and maybe even begin to heal. The story of April 18. The story of you, your mother and I, your doctors, your nurses, a chaplain, a detective, and a man named Tom.

As well as the story of the devil who took you from me.

2

I met Tom, the Director of Patient Transport, in the cafeteria at roughly the moment you died, while your mother stood watching, helpless from the corner of the room while an array of nurses swarmed between you and her. As horrible as that sounds, and with as many nightmares as she's woken up from, I wish I had been there. Truly.

Baby, you had been so sick before we finally brought you to the hospital. Your bright baby blues that normally had a shine like polished diamonds gleaming from your chestnut skin – a color that seemed like a compromise between my chocolate milk and Joey's two percent – were dim and hidden by your sunken, malnourished complexion.

I never dreamed I'd have a blue-eyed baby girl, and neither did Joey. It turned out the father she never knew passed her the gene, and she passed it to you. Guess what, Chloe? Your sister has your eyes.

That was the thing that made it all come as such a shock. As rapid and steep as your decline had been, your rise had been its equal, characterized first by the return of that shine in your eyes. Ten days at home followed by ten days in the hospital, the tenth being the last. Doctors appointments, the emergency room, the PICU, and finally the fifth floor and that room where Doctor Collins finally used the magical H word. H-O-M-E.

In our case it actually was where the heart is and the promise of going back lifted our spirits. We were back to telling bad jokes, Star Wars puns, and laughing at your mother's use of curse word euphemisms that bordered on the absurd. Do you remember "flingin-flangin?" Lord almighty, how could anyone forget?

My best memory from our stay in Franklin Children's Hospital was one of the last. One of, not the last. The last was the worst. No, it was from the night before. You looked at your mom with those newly brightened blue eyes that were beginning to get their sparkle back and asked, "Mom, where did you meet Dad?"

Joey smiled with a faraway expression, and I could see in her soft face that she was being transported by years and miles to the moment we met.

"It was a chance meeting in a far-off land, sweet girl," she said.

"That's a fairy tale, Mom."

"It may sound that way, but it really is how the story begins. Why do you ask?"

"One day, I'll be married, and I want it to be like you and Daddy."

Your sweet, innocent face gave no room for doubting the honesty in your motivations for the question. I fought back a tear as I watched your mother do the same before responding.

"One day, you will and knowing you, princess, it will be an amazing time to an amazing man. That day is a long way off, and I frankly don't want to think about you growing up yet, little miss. You stay my baby forever."

I think you even enjoyed the smothering of kisses that followed a little more than you let on. Truth be told, Joey and I never loved each other more than we did in that little hospital room we were confined to for so long. I've learned from every card, letter, and visit from nurses and staff in the time since that something was evident to everyone who stepped foot in that room. That something was the love between our family. That you adored us, we adored you, and we adored each other.

To think of how much was robbed from us, knocked down, trampled over, and destroyed... I need a minute.

3

When we were told you were going to have an extended hospital stay, your mother and I decided we would be moving into the room with you for as long as you would be there. We were told later how unusual that can be, but that never made sense to us. We were a family. A family didn't leave. To their credit, our jobs accommodated us. Although if I'm being honest, if they hadn't then we would've dealt with it.

Joey and I had a schedule worked out between us. I did the running so she was available to the doctors when they came on their rounds, and when things settled down, usually in the afternoon, she would go for a walk to get some sunshine. Part of that running meant I was out of the room after seven each morning to visit the cafeteria in the main building across the pedway so I could bring back breakfast for the two of us.

On the morning of April 18th, I kissed your nose for the final time and walked away with your laugh echoing through the door.

I wish I had known at that moment that our time as a family had almost run its course. That once I left room 513 on the fifth floor of Franklin Children's Hospital our family would never be the same. We would never again be together on this side of heaven.

I left room 513 with you smiling through the darkness in my direction and Joey struggling to get up and moving. Those little beds, if you want to call the somewhat cushioned benches on the side walls of the room beds, were comfortable enough to get to sleep on, barely.

My shoes squeaked on the linoleum floor of the hallway with each step as I passed nurses ready to start their day shift, having relieved the night nurses of their duties. The breakfast cart stood in the corner waiting to be pushed around the halls of the west wing of the fifth floor. I could smell the pancakes and bacon you ordered the night before.

Going through the double door entry to the unit early in the morning was like stepping off a plane into another world. The acidic smell from the unit and all the bleach used to disinfect everything above and below still burned in my nose while the welcoming scent of lavender and lilac wafted in from the separate air circulation system that served the general areas of the hospital.

The hallway was lit so brightly compared to the darkened wing that had yet to begin waking up that it would take the twenty or so feet from doors to elevator landing for my eyes to adjust to the white ceiling, white walls with blue stripe running the length of the wall that matched the blue linoleum tiles in the center of the hallway floor, and white tiles bordering the blue.

Each floor of the hospital looked identical except for the color of the center tiles on the floor and matching stripes on the walls. They differentiated the floors to make each unit more visually identifiable. Down on four, where you were in the PICU, the color was green instead of the fifth floor's blue. The second floor, where the pedway was located, was gray.

The landing had four elevators, two on each side of the square space open to the hall on one side and a door on the opposite side that I never once saw unlocked and open no matter how many trips I took to the lobby or the second-floor pedway.

I jabbed a finger at the call button to go down and moments later heard the distinctive ding of the arriving ride. I stood facing the doors on the right, door set two of the pair of doors on the west side of the landing. I heard from behind and to my left the opening of door number three.

Entering alone, I pressed the floor button on the console that looked like it was perhaps older than I was and settled into the corner of the car, leaning on the rails to give a brief rest to my aching body, still tired and sore from a night of forced fetal position the "bed" forced me into. The world seemed miles away, separated by so much time away, relegated to the confines of hospital rooms, hospital food, hospital showers.

I longed for the normalcy of life that was teasing its return to our family, perhaps even by day's end if some of the doctors could be believed.

After a moment, my heart began to race. My breathing intensified, claustrophobia beginning to flare as I realized the elevator was not moving. Flingin-flangin contraption.

Standing at attention, I looked around the car hoping to see an emergency call button, a door latch like the action movies I took Joey to while we were dating, something that would let me get the attention of someone, anyone, on the outside of the closed box that would soon begin to collapse in on me like an intergalactic trash compactor while on my mission to save my princess.

That was when the chime sounded and the door opened. I looked out at the landing, my dilated eyes settling on the bright-blue 5 on the wall. I took a fresh glance at the control panel and had to laugh. I pressed the button for the floor I was already on.

I had been at the hospital for far too long.

I very deliberately pressed the button marked 2 and was on my way to the conjoining pedway. Once across and inside the main building, on the final stretch before the escalators that led to the cafeteria, I passed the chapel and gave a smile and wave to the short husky lady with the long dark-brown twists that reminded me of my Auntie Rosemarie, only a few shades darker. Thankfully, Chaplain Jenkins didn't try to pinch my cheeks when she came to the room the night before as we were getting you back in bed after brushing your teeth. We were so proud of you for being able to get up and walk around. A small thing that was so easy to take for granted until you lost it, or watched as someone you love lost it.

She introduced herself as a chaplain, though I was unsure at the time what denomination used that terminology and probably wore the confusion on my face as I cycled through the different names for preachers that I had heard to that point. We usually called them pastor or reverend, maybe the occasional bishop, but never chaplain. I thought it was a hospital title, but I could've been wrong.

She greeted Joey as she came through the door and seemed to pause when she got to you. She had a look that seemed like Siri was announcing "recalculating" inside her mind. Turning to find me and looking again at your mother, she seemed to smile. Our multi-hued family dynamic always caused a reaction, but who could hate a smile? Maybe that was why she offered it.

She told us the door to her office was always open. She seemed caring and nice. She launched right into a Christian prayer for all of us without asking if we would be offended by it. We weren't.

I never would have guessed at the time how she would end up less than 24 hours later.

4

"Are you in line, mister?"

Those were the first words Tom said to me. In hindsight, they came at just about the moment it got hard for you to get your breath. Go figure.

The voice startled me and I jerked around to look at him.

Tom was staring right through me, as though I had a hole in my chest and he was peering through at the counter behind me to see whether they had refilled the oatmeal container or not.

"No, you go on ahead," I told him. "Sorry, I lost focus for a minute there."

I'm not very tall. At five foot eight I tend to be on the short end of the stick in all my friend groups. Tom was even shorter, with a receding hairline and protruding stomach that seemed at odds with the scrawniness of his arms and legs. Judging from the tattered bundle of loose material at the bottom of his faded blue scrub pants, he also commonly misjudged his height. I couldn't say I blamed him there though.

"Thank ye kindly, friend. Ye looked like ye was somewhere else, but I reckoned I'd ask anyhow. Felt the neighborly thing to do. We could all use a bit more neighborliness in here with everything goin on around us, that's what I think. Name's Tom, nice to meetcha."

He held out his hand, and I took it as I gave him my name in response. I had to be careful not to squeeze it. Tom's hand felt like a small, dead fish pulled from the nearby river, and I didn't want to hurt the little man. I told him I had never heard the word "neighborliness" but tended to agree with him.

"I expect to be out of here later today. My girl's getting better, and we're hoping for discharge papers soon. What about you, Tom? What's got you in here today instead of out and about in the world?"

I watched as his eyes darted away from mine as he spoke. Recalling it made me as uneasy then as it still does now.

"Oh, just a little business to tend to here close by is all. Got a pickup to make in the hospital across the way. It's not the cheeriest work, but it's work that's got to be done nonetheless."

It was like he spoke in riddles no man should want answers to.

"I hope you can find some joy in it today. I'll see you around."

I grabbed my tray and started to the scrambled egg station next to where we had been standing. I didn't want to stay with Tom any longer than I had to. I didn't like the feeling that came from being in his presence. I sincerely hoped I would not be seeing him around.

"Oh, I'll enjoy it myself, friend. It's only no one else will, is all. I'll see yinz around, that's for certain."

Tom grabbed a muffin and walked off as I was left standing and staring, wondering if I'd even want to try and figure out his riddles.

I had the distinct feeling I did not.

5

The halls were beginning to get busy with the hustle and bustle of a typical hospital workday as I walked the path from your room in reverse, carrying two sacks containing breakfast. Thankfully, the cafeteria provided plastic grocery bags for such an occasion.

After a week and a half, the upward-moving escalator was finally working that morning, and I got to ride the stairs up as God intended. That was the point of Jacob's dream about the angels moving up and down on the staircase, sometimes called a ladder, right? A vision of the world's first escalator.

I again looked in the chapel as I passed by, but Chaplain Jenkins was nowhere to be seen. Another day, another family to pray over, I assumed. It was then I noticed a lone earring lying on the floor in the hall leading back to the pedway, and my mind was suddenly gone from the smell of antiseptic and blinding fluorescent lights. I was in Montana with Joey, and no one was sick. Life was great.

It was four years earlier. You were eight years old and as healthy as ever. I could almost hear your dark curls bouncing as you jumped for joy at the prospect of a weekend at your best friend's house, not showing any sadness whatsoever at being away from us for three days. I didn't like that much, but your smile always melted away any sadness, large or small. You were growing up, and visions of late-night dance parties fueled by pizza and popcorn at Aunt June's, your affectionate name for Joey's best friend and mother of your bff Crystal, had you walking on air.

We took the longer road to Montana for the weekend. An excuse to get lost in the wilderness past Missoula, where it was said all things merge into one and a river runs through it. It was there we attempted to fly-fish like Norman Maclean. It was there we attempted to make you a big sister, too. We failed at both but found plenty of fun in the trying.

The ding sounding my arrival at the fifth floor brought me back to the moment. Perhaps if the elevator had been silent I never would have come back from Montana in my mind. Joey and I would still be trying to stay lost together, and you would still be singing karaoke in Crystal's bedroom at 1 a.m., to June and Norman's dismay.

After a left turn from the elevator landing, it was only a short span to the double doors leading into the west wing. 5W for the regulars. The metal doors stayed shut and secured by a magnetized lock. That lock may have been the most up-to-date technology in the entire hospital, outside of the imaging equipment, if that. You had to press the intercom and smile for the camera before getting through, if you didn't possess an employee lanyard. I had made the trip so often that security would sometimes buzz me in on sight before I could get to the intercom, a thankful experience with both hands full of rapidly cooling cafeteria food.

That morning, the doors were left open as nurses and various staff rushed through.

I thought to myself, *There must be an emergency. Poor kiddo, I hope their parents are with them. I'd hate to be the guy who went home or to work overnight only to return to something terrible happening in his child's room.*

Chloe, you were on infectious lockdown in your room the entire time of your stay, so you never got to walk the halls of good ol' 5W like some of the other kids. One silly girl even rode a small battery-operated Jeep through the hall next to her dad. Her dad told me once she was struggling with several blood conditions, and he was worried about her making it out of the hospital alive, not to mention the divorce between him and her mother making it impossible for both parents to be together at the same time.

You'd think people could put things like that aside in those and similar situations, but they almost never do.

I digress. Passing through the double doors it was a straight shot until the hallway came to a T at a giant mural painted on the wall. It looked like it belonged in one of the books we would read before bedtime. The image of a fantasy city with erected skyscrapers around a waterfall that cut through a tropical forest. Surely it was meant to inspire kids with a sense of longing or to spark a desire to get well and reach the heights of travel to a far off land, but the waterfall always just made me want to pee for some reason.

Turning left at Urination Falls puts you on a path down the hall and past the indoor playroom and the nurses' station before reaching the final wing on the right side of the hall, where room 513 contained the two keys to my happiness on this planet.

That morning the rushing nurses and staff all seemed to be on my same path. They weren't stopping to admire Urination Falls, look in at the room of toys, or eavesdrop on the floor nurses. They were running as though word of my keys to happiness had reached them and they needed to see what the fuss was about.

When I made my left at Urination Falls, it was like someone or something inside my head pressed the mute button on the remote that controlled my sense of the world. All went completely silent except for a faint whistling noise that could have been coming from the base of the waterfall for all I knew.

When I looked up and saw the direction of the flow of hospital staff, the bags of food meant for our breakfast became a falling styrofoam container bomb heading for the blue and white floor. The resulting mess of oatmeal and eggs would have probably reminded me of the mess your dog Daisy had made on the driveway the morning we came to the hospital, had I noticed it clearly.

It was during the run to your room that I realized there were no real guidelines or mandates for the color of scrubs in a hospital. I had either never thought of it before or had simply not noticed. The flurry of people at the final right turn beyond the nurses' station was a technicolor cloud of blues, greens, and reds of every shade, from new and bright to old and faded.

I forced my way into the room full of people, expecting Joey to be standing by your bedside and you to be telling everyone, "I'm fine. It's nothing. Leave me alone and let me eat my pancake." But she wasn't, and you weren't. Instead I saw Joey - the love of my life, my rock - curled in a ball in a corner of the room. She was crying so hard she was shaking, her mouth open but no sound escaping through her thin, perfect lips.

I froze in the doorway to room 513 and heard a voice call out, "Time, 8:36." A nurse reached for your monitor to silence the long, steady beep that was signaling the absence of activity from your previously exuberant heart.

At the sudden silence, a wail began to escape through the parted lips of your mother, echoing from the deepest recesses of her soul.

6

I sat on the floor in the corner of the room and cradled my love in my arms. Joey's wails had subsided, but our sobs had not. Tears pooled on the cold linoleum floor beneath us. It felt as though we were totally and completely alone, curled up at the edge of a storm, watching ourselves from a distance. It was as if we were both the storm chaser watching the tornado wreck the trailer park on the outskirts of town and the homeowner looking at the strewn wreckage that was once all we knew and loved. You were lying still in the eye of the storm of doctors and nurses, their voices a drowning level of white noise echoing in our ears.

"This never gets easier."

"Someone radio for transport."

"Does it feel like this has been happening more frequently lately?"

"She was a kind soul. My heart hurts."

"Someone should call for the chaplain."

"Am I crazy, or wasn't she improving?"

"Transport's already at the desk. It's Tom."

The sound of that name pulled me from the storm like a foghorn billowing from a nearby lighthouse. My mind raced through the halls of the hospital until I was back in the cafeteria, staring at a man introducing himself as Tom, who said he had a pickup to make. Tom, who had something to do that wasn't the happiest but enjoyed it anyway.

That was when I realized I heard the moment my baby girl's heart stopped beating.

I threw up on the blue and white linoleum floor in the same spot where our tears had formed a puddle.

7

Chloe, your favorite doctor trio arrived for their morning round sometime in the moments that proceeded. I noticed them in the doorway standing in stunned silence. I can't imagine that part of the job ever getting easier.

My mind felt both completely empty and as though it was full of twinkling bells and cymbals. I didn't know what day it was or anyone's names. I only knew there had been a cosmic shift in the fabric of my universe.

"How did this happen? We were debating whether we were going to discharge today, said the doctor I knew as "the tall one." She was wearing a light-brown dress with pastel flowers that looked like they belonged in a decorative Easter display.

That was when I realized the docs rarely wore scrubs. Only took me a week and a half.

The shorter one had round framed glasses, shoulder-length curly brown hair held back by a mint-green headband, and a matching shirt dress cinched at the waist by a thick brown belt.

She grabbed a stack of paper towels from the sink and knelt in front of me to clean up my vomit.

All I could think about was how long it was going to take housekeeping to replace that stack. They were so bad at that. Well, most of them. The head lady was always mad when she came by and it hadn't been done. She was kind and never failed to bring a smile to our faces.

The vomit matched both her dress and her headband.

That was when I found a new emotion for an already emotionally overwhelming morning, shame. I couldn't believe I was thinking of myself after what had happened.

My eyes caught hers, and I noticed the tear rolling down her cheek from beneath her glasses.

Another level of shame, realizing you were not the only person being affected by something.

The blonde lady in the navy-blue dress, solid with tan flowers on the lower left side, got the attention of the staff still in the room.

"Okay, everyone out."

The room cleared. When Joey hit the alarm during your episode, the floodgates opened, and nurses filled the room from everywhere. Now they were leaving to go back to their morning tasks.

It wasn't until the mass exodus that I noticed the chaplain. I still don't know when she got there, but she walked out with the nurses.

Blue dress continued, "Tom will need a clear path to the bed once he gets here, and we need to speak with the parents. Someone get me the overnight chart. I want to know who was in here, why they were in here, and what they did while they were in here."

"There were only two people, the floor nurse, and someone from the IV team."

The three doctors who remained in the room stopped in their tracks when Joey spoke. Her gaze was still fixed on the floor in front of us.

Blue dress knelt down in front of us, and I saw from her name badge attached to the pocket on her left breast that her name was Doctor Collins. She didn't seem to notice the wet spot where the mint-green vomit had been moments prior to her kneeling there.

"I am so sorry for your loss. Please know that I will mourn your dear child for as long as I live and breathe, so please forgive me if my questions seem cold. However, I do not, in my medical opinion, understand what happened, and I need answers too. So take a deep breath, think back, and try to remember. What reason did your night nurse give for why an IV team member was being called in last night?"

She looked at Doctor Collins through bloodshot eyes that appeared to be dilating.

"I have no idea," she said as her eyes rolled back in her head and she collapsed away from my arms in a heap of the blue and white floor.

8

"Hi, love," Joey said, looking at me and smiling. For a moment, all was right in the world.

It didn't last.

"Where's Chloe?"

She blinked the drying tears from her eyes as if she were trying to banish them and all they represented. She slowly sat up on the small couch we had laid her on after she fainted. It may be too small, but it was better than the floor. She looked around the room at myself and the three doctors. You could see the waves of realization sweep across her face as reality set back in.

"You've been out for a few minutes, ma'am. How are you feeling?"

Doctor Powell was nice, always soft-spoken and first to be extra personable. We liked that about her.

"Everything's foggy, but I'm fine," Joey replied.

I gave her a cup of water from the sink while I helped her sit up.

Once while coming home on a long road trip shortly after we were married, Joey insisted that we take a love language quiz. "We're newlyweds. We should know what to expect from each other!"

I humored her, even though I thought it was another tactic to sell a few books. "Acts of service," she read back to me once I was done with the questioning. Who could have guessed that one? In fairness, how could a man be with someone like Joey and not want to do everything in his power to bring her joy and comfort? It was one of the only things that made sense in this world, if you asked me.

Doctor Collins, the most experienced of the bunch and a pro through and through, took Joey by the hand and looked in her eyes while passing a small light in front of her face.

"I was worried I might lose you too. Your color didn't look good for a minute, but I'm glad you're back and looking better. Now, I have to ask again. Is there any chance you remember why the IV team came in last night?"

There was worry on Doctor Collins's face. More than could be only for Joey, it appeared to me. From the look on her face, Joey noticed it too.

9

You hated all the blood draws and IVs. You got to calling them "stabbings." Every few hours for the first days, and twice a day for the last ones, it'd be "time for another stabbing."

The final night wasn't our first encounter with the IV team, not by a long shot. "They're weird, Dad. Their job is to stab kids. It's literally *all they do*."

It seemed your veins had given the nurses trouble the entire time. In that week and a half, you had three different IVs placed. The first "clotted," and the second "kinked," but in all five had been attempted, the other two were simply not successful.

You had several "butterfly" sticks, your favorite, for blood draws, and even a few of those failed. One poor nurse stuck you a good eight to ten times before quitting. Other nurses did finger pokes when they could, so many it looked like you had been playing with barbed wire.

It all seemed so excessive, but at the time it made sense. They were doing their jobs, and you were getting better! But even though you were getting up more often, your color was back, and you were drinking again, the nurses still called you a "difficult stick" and called for the IV team. "Flat veins," "rolling veins," "collapsed veins." We had no reason to doubt the word of the professionals. We were sure of it.

Until we weren't, listening to Doctor Collins and her questions.

Chloe, this was one of those parts of the story where I could get a detail wrong here or there, but know it was all accurate in the greater sense.

Doctor Collins and her team stepped out of the room with Joey and I still seated, our minds resting, our hearts hurting as we looked at the spot that less than an hour prior held the bed you occupied, our twelve-year-old angel. They took their usual spots in the hallway, where they had convened countless times over their time working together, but their expressions were anything but usual.

Doctor Collins was tracing a line from her nose to her chin with one finger, the other arm folded across her chest, rising and falling with each full breath. "Somebody give me something. Start with what we know."

"We know a little girl who had been making a miraculous recovery suddenly died this morning. We know her parents are in there wondering why their little girl is dead. We know *Tom* is wheeling her body to the morgue. We know that!

What in the actual FU.." Addison's watch sent out an alarm that stopped her mid-yell, her blonde ponytail left swaying from the remnants of her building fury. "Heart Rate Elevated" indeed.

"Enough, Addison. That isn't helpful. We all feel it, and I have no doubt we'll all be feeling it for a long time, but there are parents in that room who are looking to us for answers, and if we break down right now, they will not get them."

Doctor Collins's experience always had the ability to shine through in the darkest moments, and her team was always thankful for that.

The team all felt what Addison, "the tall one," was expressing. The frustration, the fear, the anger, all raged inside each member of the pediatric general physician team. The team also knew that Doctor Collins was correct, as usual. If they allowed themselves to get lost within those emotions they would never be able to provide us with answers. The worst part was the feeling that they may never have answers to give, regardless of whether or not they kept their composure intact.

Doctor Collins took a deep breath. "Let's try again and do this like it's any other case we're handling in our rounds. I'll start, and you two chime in with whatever you deem relevant."

She probably knew this was the only way she'd be able to handle this one. It was likely lying on her chest like a barbell she couldn't press up by herself. Lila Collins considered Addison

McCray and Indiana Powell the best doctors she had ever worked with. Together, they had been able to handle every case, large and small, tough and simple, that had come through Franklin Children's Hospital in the last three years.

"After clearing the room, a few things happened. First the body of Chloe Miller was taken to the morgue. The coroner may not request an autopsy, but there needs to be one. Put it on the checklist. Second, you both saw the physical responses of the parents. Shock, vomiting, fainting. They need to be handled with care. Thirdly, and where I'd like to focus for a moment, we learned the IV team had repeatedly been called during the night shift the past few nights."

Doctor Collins paused, allowing time for her colleagues to catch what she had just dropped.

Addison seemed to catch it first, but only by a second or two. "That can't be right."

Indiana, Indy to her friends, responded, "I agree. It doesn't sound right. Would the staff still choose to call IV in? She wasn't getting that many labs done at this point. I don't see what the issue would've been."

Indy, who sometimes went by Doctor Jones when the patient was a younger boy who might smile at the Indiana Jones callout, was the team's junior resident in the second year of her residency. She was very analytical, the one who made sure everything was tracking with the "by the book" plan for whatever was ailing the team's patients.

"No." Addison was quick to interject before Doctor Collins had a chance.

Addison was the team's fellow, having been in residency for three years now. Her experience allowed her to keep her mind open beyond purely analytical thought to explore the off book, outside the box approaches that a junior resident may not be comfortable with yet.

"It isn't that using the IV team in Chloe's case wouldn't be the right choice. It wasn't a choice that was made. Lila, when we left Chloe's room, I went to the nurses' station and grabbed the chart, which is a mess by the way. Their name wasn't even on it, and of course the board was wiped for day shift already. Anyway, I was able to read the night nurses notes. The IV team wasn't called. At least not officially."

Lila Collins, the attending physician, chose both Doctor Indy and Doctor Addison primarily because their approaches were so different. She liked being challenged. This was exactly the approach she needed, and the smile on her face was the acknowledgement of how grateful she was to have built this team prior to today.

"So we have acknowledgement that calling for IV may not have been the correct call for Chloe, though we may not know that for certain. And we have the charted notes from the night nurse that don't show any such consult took place last night. Let's get the name of her nurse from last night and each night she was here.

"Finally, if utilizing IV was unnecessary and wasn't noted as happening in the first place, answer this. Why is the mother adamant, with the father in agreement, that two people spent time in their room last night, less than six hours before their daughter, who we agree was improving, suddenly died? Two people, the night nurse..." Lila paused, knowing from experience how to utilize dramatic effect and being able to tell by the leaning in from Addison and Indy that it was working. "...and someone from the IV team."

10

Lila Collins walked back into the room that once lit up with every smile you graced it with.

The air was thick and heavy from the weight of the events from the previous hour. The space in the center of the room that once housed your bed was empty now. On one side of the vacant space sat the table on wheels that would slide under one side of the bed to give you a place to set your meals. It was now sitting alone with no one to use it.

The floor where the bed once was showed streaks from years of sterilizing mops reaching from around the sides as best as the cleaning crew could reach it. An IV pole stood in the corner by the bathroom door. On it hung a tangle of unused tubes running to nowhere, a reminder of days gone by.

We sat together on the lime-green recliner built for one. We were holding onto each other with desperation, trying to keep a grip on a hope for something we couldn't quite express.

Your mother had been readying that table for the breakfast you never got to have when she saw you in the beginning moments. You were struggling for breath. She said when you locked eyes, she finally understood what fear was and what it meant to be helpless. She talked about the look you gave her that screamed silently for help that Joey couldn't give as she tried to shake the air back into you as though you had fallen off your bike in the backyard before running to the doorway and screaming for help. That look was burned into the backs of Joey's eyelids like a poorly thought out tattoo. She was trying to close her eyes to turn the lights illuminating the moment off but she was met by that look of her baby girl, begging for her mother's help.

There was a pit opening in the depths of my soul, spreading itself deeper and wider with every breath I was able to take. I missed those final moments of my baby girl's life. I was beginning to reason with myself, looking for a way to silence the noise in my head. I hadn't had to endure those final moments, those fearful eyes, the desperation of wanting to help with the knowledge there was nothing in my skill-set of any use during the worst moments of your life.

Yet I hadn't been able to comfort you or say goodbye. I hadn't been able to hold my wife in her time of greatest need. I was absent, sheltered from them, yet robbed of them.

Like neighboring families during a storm, one of which loses everything while their house crumbles around them while the other sits in evacuated safety to return to nothing. Both traumatized, neither able to relate to the other.

So I held Joey in that chair as the team returned, attempting to understand her experience through my own, wishing they had been shared, praying their differences would never be divisive.

Two years later, it was a divide we were still attempting to traverse.

11

"Mr and Mrs Miller, once again, my name is Doctor Collins. Today, I'd like you to simply call me Lila. You know Doctor McCray, Addison, and Doctor Powell, Indiana, or Indy. I realize we have met many times, but with the events of this morning, I thought it best to reintroduce the team, and I would not expect you to hold onto those names even now, given the circumstances.

"I want you to know that we genuinely cared for your daughter. I don't only mean we cared for her medically as her doctors. We cared about her young, beautiful soul. We are heartbroken with and for you. We will not leave you to bear this burden alone simply because our patient is no longer with us. We will continue to support you.

"On that note, I must ask you a couple of questions, and then we'll leave you to rest. I strongly suggest you leave this room and get some air. Go to the cafeteria and get some food. We have some things to follow up on, and we'll come find you to update you sooner than later. Now, I have three things to ask. First, do you remember the name of the nurse from last night's shift? We can get it, but it would help if you knew."

I had to look at Joey. If either of us would know that sort of detail, we both knew it would be her. She was the yin to my yang. We each had strengths where the other had weaknesses, and details like names, dates, and times were not strengths I had.

She spoke so softly even I found myself tilting my ear toward her.

"No, I'm sorry. I do know we had her more than once. I'm not sure when, but it was multiple times."

"That's okay, dear. It helps more than you realize. Next, is there any chance you know the name of the IV team member who came into the room?"

Joey closed her eyes. You could hear the air rushing in as her lungs filled to their maximum potential. She knew a second nurse had come into the room, but at that hour we would both have to fight the sleep from overtaking our eyes, even for middle-of-the-night treatments. It was a fight we often lost.

"No, I don't. It was a man. I don't remember his name. They seemed friendly but had masks on. I don't know that I would have recognized them even if I had been able to stay awake.

"I do wish I could be of better help, but the days seem so long here. It's so hard to be present at those times during the night…" Joey's gaze drifted to the empty space at the center of the room.

"As a mother myself, I simply cannot imagine what you're experiencing right now. I do want you to get some food and rest, after one more question. Did your nurse tell you why she was bringing in an IV consult?" Lila was both tender and direct, attempting with all she had to coax a memory and response from the grieving woman sitting in front of her.

"It was always something different," Joey said and began looking everywhere and nowhere, gazing beyond the physical environment into a realm beyond what was seen and felt, "but it never made sense to me. She seemed to be improving, but once they needed blood, then it would seem like she wasn't, not really. Wasn't it supposed to get easier? It never got any easier. Does everyone have that much trouble? Sometimes they wouldn't even try. Aren't they supposed to at least try? Why wouldn't they try?"

I couldn't take it. Her voice echoed like a thousand mourners calling out in one voice.

"Thanks for being here, Docs. Really, I think we should take you up on your offer and get out of here for a little bit. Come on, babe."

I pulled your mom to her feet, gave the doctors the best smile I could offer, and exited the room hand in hand with the love of my life.

12

When Lila Collins was in third grade, her teacher asked what she wanted to be when she grew up. She placed the tip of her finger to the tip of her nose and dragged it lightly down across her cool-aid stained lips to the tip of her chin.

She imagined herself as an old lady, as least as old as the teacher who had asked such a thought provoking question. Mrs. Fletcher was almost as old as Lila's mother, after all. If that were true, she had to be closing in on the ancient age of twenty-eight.

"I think I'd like to be a police officer like my Uncle Owen. He always tells me about all the bad guys he puts away. I'd like to get the bad guys put away too. If there are any left when I'm as old as Uncle Owen."

When Lila Collins was in eighth grade, her guidance counselor began the conversation of which classes to pick to help the transition into high school by asking her what she wanted to be when she grew up. Lila didn't notice she was tap tap tapping her way from nose to chin, until she tapped a spot where a pimple hadn't yet made it to the surface. She winced from the sharp pain, which reminded her of the pain she'd been repressing deep under her surface since the previous summer. Her hero, Uncle Owen, had been killed in the line of duty, randomly shot on break in his squad car. The video he was watching on his phone was still on the screen with the "replay" icon waiting to be touched. A video sent from his sister of his favorite niece winning her latest academic contest.

"I want to be a private investigator, like Nancy Drew. PIs don't get targeted by random bad guys. They don't even know who they are."

When Lila Collins was a sophomore in college her academic advisor looked up from his computer screen where he had been admiring her high test scores across the core set of classes she had been taking. He noted the absence of a major, a minor, or the evidence of a path of any sort. He asked her what she wanted to be when she grew up. Lila ran a finger down her nose to her chin. "I think I want to try for med school, sir. There are too many bad guys in the world. At least I can help fix the good ones."

Doctor Lila Collins stood in the room that up to very recently held one of her favorite young patients in a long time. Ms. Chloe Miller. She stood in front of the two doctors she handpicked for her personal team with her arms across her chest, and one finger absentmindedly moving from nose to chin as it had a thousand times before.

Her breaths were long and deep, filling her lungs to the point of no return with each breath. Doctors Indy and Addison gave glances at each other with each breath deeper than the last, silently wondering if their boss was going to be okay, or if this was one case too many and she was in danger of hyperventilation and fainting the same way the mother had earlier in that very room.

Lila let her hands fall to her sides and after one more lung clearing breath addressed the room.

"This may have been a random event, one of many I've seen over the years and one of many more you'll witness in your careers. However, I don't think I'm alone in the feeling that the events of the past few months, including this event today, seem to be something more. Doctor Rothbottom owes me a favor, and I'm going to ask that he take our rounds this morning.

"Addison, make sense of those notes from last night, and get the nurse's name. The staff can't be so inept that it isn't logged somewhere, for God's sake. Once you have it, look back and see which nights she had Chloe's room. She was only on this floor a few nights, so look at PICU too.

"Indy, look at the IV team. See who was on call since Chloe was admitted and counter-reference to see if you can get names for who saw her or who could have seen her if it wasn't charted.

I'm going to go to the body, if I can track down Tom. I'll look into the autopsy and talk to the medical examiner if I have to. We should know by day's end whether this was a bad break or something more. Stay in touch."

The three doctors agreed to meet by dinner in the cafeteria to compare notes before separating and going their own ways.

13

The air pouring into my lungs until the muscles burned from the stretch felt different while standing in the doorway of the west wing of the fifth floor. It was as if the world outside was burning, the smoke being spread through the ventilation system until it found its way into my mouth. The only respite from the acidic taste was the radiance of your mother. Her light may have been dimmed but her beauty shone, still.

My hand found the crevice in the center of her lower back as I guided her through the double doors, the same way it did fifteen years earlier on our very first date.

Back then, I was only twenty-two and thought I was going crazy. Either that or I was in love. Crazy seemed more likely. Love at first sight was a concept spoken of by children and romance novelists, not rational adults, but there I was doing every trick in the book to manufacture closeness with this beautiful being so that maybe she would discover feelings similar to the ones igniting and burning through the forest of my mind.

Fifteen years later, she still did, as much as it turned out she had during that first date, the same as me. She still felt the warmth and electricity of that touch inches above her waistline now as she had then.

Now when she looked at me, she saw the face of a broken man desperate to hold himself together.

The last time I walked this path, mere moments and an eternity ago, you were alive. Your final smile still warm in my eyes. This time, your body was somewhere in the bowels of this old building, that smile decidedly colder in my mind.

I was frozen in the door when Joey took my hand in hers and placed her lips on the back of my hand with the gentleness of a drop of rain gliding down the petals of a rose. She drew me forward, and I felt my feet begin to move, pulled from the rocks of grief. One step and then another as I attempted to regain the feeling of how it was to walk this familiar path with a family still intact, knowing with each step I was replacing that old life with a new one in which my family, the world built around me for twelve years, was in fact broken.

Standing in front of the elevator with teardrops forming in the corners of my eyes, I hoped Joey wouldn't notice for fear of what door they would open. I only wanted to be strong for her.

Vulnerability was never one of my strengths, but there would be plenty of time to exercise that part of myself now.

14

On the other side of the pedway, the pain inside was bubbling in our bellies like a pair of volcanoes beginning their swell to an inevitable eruption. The magnitude of the event was palpable and took our full thoughts to quell on our travel through the halls.

My vision tunneled. I had little thought to my surroundings outside of Joey's presence and the occasional coming or going or a group of docs in the halls, each with their own tragedy of the hour.

Joey stopped. We were at the door to the chapel, and something inside had caught her attention.

"Excuse me," Joey called out through the slightly opened door into the office on the right side beyond the chapel doors.

Beyond the cracked door were the sounds of shuffling paper, a muted slam, and the clank of metal on metal. My guess was someone doing paperwork was being interrupted, they quickly put the papers in a drawer and went to stand, the abruptness causing the wheels of their desk chair to knock over a nearby trash can.

The door swung open to reveal the chaplain, one hand on the door and the other reaching to correct the upturned metal trash can.

That was the first win I'd had all day, and I'd be lying if I said it didn't make me smile.

"How can I help..." Chaplain Krystal Jenkins straightened her fallen can before facing the doorway. Her solemn expression at once came alive with a jolt as though the brass knob had been triggered by a small taser.

"Oh my dears! Come in!" With a flick of her stocky arm the door was flung open, nearly resulting in a chair meeting the same fate as the can, as she began rearranging furniture to make room for us.

"Oh, do come in. I stopped by this morning but had to leave the room when... Well, I left when the good doctor cleared the room. I'm so glad you found my door. Oh hunny darlin, I'm so sorry for your loss." She grabbed Joey in the biggest bear hug her little arms could muster. She didn't even let go to bring me in. She waved me in with a gale-force wind created almost by her sheer will.

Talking to Chaplain Jenkins in this situation was like grabbing an electric fence at the side of a country road then trying to pull away. The magnitude of the way the little woman approached her job as a comforting member of the clergy far outweighed her physical stature, and she was unrelenting in her displays of compassion despite what I felt was an obvious sight of wanted nothing more than to get away and forget our compassion-inducing situation for a few minutes.

She went on for the better part of ten minutes, talking and listening, preaching and waiting for a response. She went on about the brokenness of the world from the fall in the garden to the redemptive work of Christ on the cross. She talked of forgiveness of sin, the importance of the blood, and the resurrection of the dead.

She started to talk about the blood again until she maybe began to sense the realization that this may not be the time.

Finally, she said, "Listen, I don't tell many people this, but I liked your little family the moment I entered your room the first time. I run a small group here in the hospital with a couple of hospital employees. It's a chance for encouragement, compassion, and a little forgiveness in a dark place. We have a space away from the darkness of the hospital where we can relax in a safe space.

"If you're up for it, I'd like you both to come. Sometimes the others meet up after their shifts without me, but we always gather for a few minutes before shift change in the evening. It lets them prepare for the work to come. Come back here by

4:15—make it 4:00. It takes a minute to get there from here. We'll walk down together."

No one talked about the moments after a loved one dies. We didn't know what was expected of us, what would come next, when we'd have to talk to whoever. We really didn't think there would be a closed door meeting with strangers in a back room somewhere. She seemed to gather that.

"I'll wait for you until 4:15, then I'll go on by myself. How's that? But I do hope to see you later."

She gave us the second bear hug of the morning, though it was softer than the first, like a small child hugging a well-loved teddy bear with a head that was prone to falling off when hugged too tight. After a farewell, we were off, out of the room, and heading in the direction of the escalators.

We planned to make the meeting by 4:00, though the circumstances surrounding it would be much different than first described by Krystal Jenkins.

15

In the cafeteria, the business from the morning shift change had been exchanged for a handful of businessmen, a few visiting parents, and a table of nurses crowding around a laptop who probably should have been in lab or office instead, judging from the way they were glancing around the room and shushing each other when the laughs got too loud.

I had little time or attention for the others in the large room. I was too busy looking at your mother.

I traced the sharp outer edge of her creamy white face with my eyes, lingering with each memory-inducing inch. It was a task I could perform forever. The soft indention above her high cheekbone where I would rest my forehead and breathe in her flowery scent. The angled point of her jaw under her ear that would cause an audible exhale when kissed. Even the small scar on her chin from when she was about your age and was introduced to the ground by her falling bicycle. The wispy streak of hair that extended in front of her ears that she always tucked when she was thinking intently, golden brown and largely straight with the slightest curl. I knew from the moment I saw that slight curl, in light of the dark nap that I keep shaved close these days, that my daughter would have the most beautiful Curly Sue hair.

I was right too. You were the perfect mixture of the two of us.

My gaze stopped to rest at Joey's light-brown eyes, her mothers eye's, which shimmered with the slightest flecks of gold like a magical pond that could be stirred up to reveal the secret to life. I had spent countless hours lost in those shimmering pools and can attest to their life giving powers. When I waded in them, I could live forever.

The impending storm bearing down on the periphery of our lives was palpable and threatening us in every direction. We could both feel it, the mist clouding our eyes and the waves grew taller in the surge heading for our shore, but in this moment, we felt safe within the barriers of the bond we had shared and grown for a decade and a half.

Joey put down the plastic spoon she was using more to stir the watery oatmeal with enough brown sugar to bake a batch of your favorite chocolate chip cookies than to actually eat and took my hands in hers. Her little hands were cold and trembling. I closed mine around hers.

"Winslow, how do we survive…"

She couldn't quite finish.

She buried her face in the tangle of our hands and filled the voids within them with her tears. If her tears were plaster, we could have formed a mold around our hands like one of those mail order kits we saw in those gift magazines you liked to look through at Christmastime.

Her chest heaved with each sob, as if her soul had been torn down the middle, separated into two halves, each under a ballistic assault barrage of heavy mortar fire from the other side.

I knew from nearly twenty years spent with your mother the best way to comfort and calm her was from a "silent ministry of presence," which was the fancy term the pastor's wife used in the marriage seminar we attended early in our marriage, until there was a ceasefire in her soul. Under the circumstances, I wondered whether that call would ever be made.

Chloe, cards on the table, I also wondered if I was able to be the man she needed. I never felt anything similar to the pangs of soul ripping warfare like Joey, until that day. That day, I could feel the floor of my mortal being breaking apart and a fire from deep within the recesses of my very essence was seeping through the cracks. I wondered whether I would simply burn from within or if the trenches would be able to close and heal in time to carry on with some semblance of normalcy, if normalcy could even exist in this new uncharted world.

From deep in the shadowy alleys hidden away in the back of my mind echoed a reminder of the message given by Pastor Eugene at our wedding in the little country church in Joey's hometown. She had long desired for her wedding to take place in the nearly two-hundred-year-old log cabin church that her ancestors built and attended for generations. The old bell tower even rang out its chime at the conclusion of the ceremony, fulfilling her childhood dream.

Pastor Eugene officiated a beautiful service in front of our family and friends. The outside of the log built church had been damaged by a flood a few months earlier. The rains came and the creek rose, but though the outside showed damage, the structure was still sound.

Pastor Eugene stood behind a decades old pulpit made of hand-hewn pine from the neighboring woods and ministered to the ending of our individual lives and simultaneous beginning of the new life we had as two parts of a new whole.

In the presence of God and our colorfully eclectic families, he read from two passages of the Bible, which was another in the line of questions my mother had for why we didn't use a black preacher. I assured her our children would be dark, but if white was good enough for my wife, it was good enough for my preacher. She relented at the idea of grandbabies, fanning the heat from her face at the thought of being a GamGam with the pink silk hat she had commissioned for the wedding, even if there would be a little cream in the mocha.

First, Song of Solomon, chapter eight, verses six and seven. "Place me like a seal over your heart, like a seal on your arm. For love is as strong as death, its passion as enduring as the grave. Love flashes like fire, the brightest kind of flame. Many waters cannot quench love, nor can rivers drown it. If a man tried to buy love with all his wealth, his offer would be utterly scorned."

Then, Ecclesiastes, chapter four, verses nine through twelve. "Two are better than one, because they have a good return for their labor. If either of them falls down, one can help the other up. But pity anyone who falls and has no one to help them up. Also, if two lie down together, they will keep warm. But how can one keep warm alone? Though one may be overpowered, two can defend themselves. A cord of three strands is not quickly broken."

When we returned home from our honeymoon in Maine, we walked into a living room full of wedding gifts. My new in-laws thought we were crazy for booking a cabin in Maine in January, but Joey not so secretly hoped we'd get snowed in while we were there so we'd have an excuse to extend the trip and get an extra week or two off work. "Due to nature, there was nothing we could do. It was an act of God!"

One of the packages awaiting us in our little living room in our little starter home - fresh white paint on the siding outside, fresh white paint on the wainscoting inside, and enough room for cuddling beside the old radiator while more white fell from the sky outside - wasn't especially large, but it was fairly heavy. An anonymous giver had made or commissioned two wooden plaques, pine to match the old pulpit, each with one of those two passages from the ceremony etched into them. It was exactly the sort of thing a young country bride squealed over and couldn't wait to get her young country husband to hang on the wall that transitioned from living room to kitchen.

Over all the years we've been married, and through all the changes in decor brought about by HGTV and grocery store checkout magazines, those two plaques always remain. They had been looked at and read, silently and our loud, countless times during the last sixteen years, fourteen at the time.

In the cafeteria, your mother's sobs finally began to subside. I was still upright, tiny streams of dried tears visible as faint salty streaks winding their way down my brown cheeks. My hands intertwined with hers on the table between us while Joey's head was face down on the brown and white entanglement of fingers and palms, her hair cascading down and splaying across the table like a hill covered with brown wheat, the sun dancing through it in golden reflective streaks.

We were an island unto ourselves in a cafeteria of increasingly sparse patronage, as the time grew further beyond the morning shift change and the kitchen staff emptying the stations of the breakfast offerings while preparing for the upcoming lunch rush. The small crew moved about seemingly unbothered by our downtrodden occupation of the table. They had likely seen enough dejected couples pouring out their sorrows over a hot counter service meal to have become somewhat desensitized to the sight of crying spouses consoling crying spouses.

I spoke loudly enough for the sound of my tear-scratched voice to be heard under her wispy blanket of golden auburn hair, yet softly enough that the old man two tables over trying to conceal his tears with the morning edition of the Wall Street Journal could not.

"Place me like a seal over your heart, like a seal on your arm. Love is as strong as death," I said, my voice beginning to break.

Taking a breath, I continued, "It's passion as enduring as the grave…"

I couldn't do it. I thought of a gravestone bearing the name of the little girl whose name I had suggested, a rhyme of the abbreviated pet name I used for my beloved, Josephine, the woman I loved from the moment I met her inspiring the name of the girl I would love from the moment of her conception.

My mind began to race with the unforeseen necessities of the day. Would we have to call a funeral home? Would we have to buy a grave site? Would we...

"Two are better than one..."

It sounded like her voice, but not quite. It was raspy, worn from tears, sobs, cries, and screams. All taking their toll as a sort of penance.

"Because they have a good return for their labor. If either of them falls down..." Joey lifted her head to meet my gaze, our misty eyes meeting over our interlocked fingers, fresh tears beginning to well up and fall fresh over cheeks recently watered, streaming down well established pathways still clearly seen.

"One can help the other up."

Smiles, for the first time since 8:36.

Tears forming waterfalls running into the corners of the smiles, but smiles all the same. Familiar smiles between lovers and friends unfamiliar with the newfound depth of shared trauma no one would wish to share, yet sadly in this life so many do.

In unplanned unison, like so many times our hearts had aligned to speak the same thoughts, we finished the passage.

"Though one may be overpowered, two can defend themselves. A cord of three strands..." Our voices strained to finish at the thought of our recently cut strand. "…is not quickly broken."

"I love you, Mrs. Miller."

"I love you, Mr. Miller."

"What do we do now?"

"We exist. Our cord is frayed but unbroken. The seal on our heart has tears, but it is not torn. It's dark, but the sun still hangs, and the world still turns. Most of all, I have you, and you have me. Let's go sit in the sun somewhere. Maybe we can come back for that small group later. Or maybe we stay gone…"

We got up, our hands still together as we walked through the doors to the hospital. We started walking and probably could have walked for hours.

I wished we would have.

16

Doctor Addison McCray was a superhero on a mission to find out why a girl with heroes and aspirations of her own was gone.

Addison had tracked down the charts from your stay in the hospital from the very beginning, including the notes the various nurses had made during their shifts in your room. She took them to the office she shared with the other two doctors and spent her morning going through them, making notes of her own and tracking everything.

Even according to Addison's notes, it was clear you were improving. The charts made that crystal clear. She knew the reported IV consults, though Indy was checking on those details, and she knew the names of the nurses who had been assigned to you over seventeen twelve-hour nursing shifts, the last of which was only your nurse for an hour before...

There were six nurses over those seventeen shifts. Circled on the page was one name that stood out to Addison. One nurse who took an extra shift and was moved from the fourth floor PICU to the fifth floor on your final night. Claudia O'Dell.

17

I've learned that most of the staff in the hospital, doctors included, arrived thirty to sixty minutes before their shift began. They arrived and went to their floor, their station, or their office, but some, including Lila Collins, made a stop at the cafeteria first. Her routine was so unchanging that everyone who knew her knew her routine: Get to the hospital, go to the cafeteria for coffee and a snack, a granola bar, preferably with chocolate chips, but vanilla chips were acceptable. That was most days. Some days, when she was rewarding herself or feeling the pressures of the job more than usual, it was coffee and a donut. It was a habit she was trying to break but with no success.

Lila thought dating a policeman, something she thought she would never do given the pain in her past from losing policemen who were close to her, would present a problem in breaking the morning donut habit, but she learned pretty quickly that Whitey shunned stereotypes as much as Lila did. It was one of the reasons she found herself falling for him.

Once she had her snack, it was right to work. It was one of her longest habits and dated back to middle school. "You have to fuel your mind if you want it to run properly." It was that habit that was primarily responsible for the fact that, until the morning of April 18th, Lila Collins had never been in the basement of the hospital she had worked at for so long.

From the elevators in the lobby of the hospital the lowest accessible floor is LL, one floor under the first level. LL, the lower level, was where the emergency room was. The ER took up most of the lower level, that and the imaging lab. It was the lowest Lila had ever been. She never had a need to visit the morgue or transport bay, until now.

When Lila left her team after the instructions to split up she went to the employee elevator in the west wing. The west wing contained room 513 where she and her staff's mornings had been stopped in their tracks and turned upside down before being shaken and turned around a few more times for good measure. She pressed the lowest button on the panel, stepped back in the elevator, leaned against the wall, closed her eyes, and took a deep breath. It wasn't even eleven in the morning yet, and she was already facing mental exhaustion. The anxiety of the morning was building in her head a bicycle tire with the air nozzle stuck on the stem and long, even pumps steadily coming with no end in sight.

When the car stopped and the door opened, Lila stepped out and took a long look around the familiar environment of the emergency room. She reached back into the diminishing space between the closing elevator doors to keep them from shutting her into the undesired space and stepped quizzically back in. Convinced she had pressed the wrong button, her head was swimming in the potential outcomes of the day which all seemed to be competing currents desperate to catch her in their undertow and drag her out to sea. She faced the wall panel on the right of the closed door.

She needed another coffee and probably a cream-filled long John.

Taking inventory of the panel of buttons, she scanned the bottom row. There were a pair of buttons. On the right: a 1 for the first floor, where the lobby was, as well as the cafeteria and, hopefully, that cream filled long John. On the left: LL, lower level, where the ER was housed.

She was thoroughly and completely confused, kerfuffled even, to quote a certain creamy white lady. So much so that she stood and stared at the panel while the doors closed, then opened, and closed again. Lila blinked herself back to the present and pressed the 5, thinking that maybe she would have better luck if she started over.

Back on the fifth floor, she got out to think. When Tom would come to grab a body to remove to the basement, where would he go? The morgue, she knew, which was in the basement, but not on the same floor as the ER and the Imaging Lab, so there must be another basement. The question of the day would then be, where was there access to another, presumably lower than the lower level, basement?

The fifth floor consisted of a single central hallway with the general elevator landing in the center and east and west wings on either side. Within each wing was a staff elevator used to bring patients between floors without clogging the central elevators, where the families might be, with sick or injured kids on oversized hospital beds and IV poles. Lila Collins stood in the west wing of the fifth floor and ran the layout of the floor in her mind, trying to locate a space where another elevator with basement access could be.

Like most hospital employees, Lila had never even considered the existence of a morgue in the hospital. The job dealt with the living. Once they were no longer living, it was typically "on to the next," and you kept moving. She was smartened up during Covid by a funeral home director she was dating at the time. He had fallen behind and needed extra room to get his "work" done, which meant doing it at the hospital when needed. She assumed he meant using the surgical ward, but he said there was a morgue in the basement, and he could use it for storage, embalming. It even had the ability to do cremations. The hospital was so old, he said, that it had features newer hospitals didn't have because originally, and for decades, it was all done there. It would have changed when she was a kid.

Going to the east wing was a failure as well, the panel in that elevator was identical to the west wing elevator. Lila's stomach growling was as much a signal of her growing frustration as it was a signal of her mid-morning hunger, which she decided was an easier fix than the problem that had her stumped. Knowing the pedway was closer to the west wing than it was the east, she again walked the length of the hallway and entered the west wing though the same double doors used that morning by two parents besought with grief. She thought about her suggestion to them and hoped she would see them once she got downstairs.

Lila pressed the call button on the staff elevator again. She would go to the familiar second floor this time, use the pedway to the main hospital, and visit the cafeteria for a fresh coffee and whatever Danish was left in the case, though she knew what she was hoping would be there. Hey, if Whitey was there, they could share mid-morning donuts. That made her laugh. Whitey hated donuts. What kind of cop hated donuts?

When Lila looked at the panel for the button with the 2, she was struck by a feature she hadn't noticed previously. At the bottom of the panel were three circles the same size as the floor call buttons, each with a key slot that could be turned to a desired function.

The one on the left was labeled "inspection" underneath. It had two functions, off and on. It was turned to on. Lila reasoned this would turn the elevator function as a whole either on or off so workers and inspectors could check out the inner workings of the car, or the shaft the car rode in, safely.

The center circle was outlined in red, or had been once, it was quite faded. She wondered for the first time about the age of the elevators in the building. Off and on were present here as well, the circle labeled "Fire." She didn't have any good ideas for how this one was used, but since it was turned to off, she hoped that was the safer of the two choices.

The circle on the right intrigued her. It was unlabeled, or if a label once existed, it had long since worn off. Where the prior two had off and on, this had differently marked functions: "LL1" and "LL2." The west wing elevator was set on LL1. Lila quickly thought of the east wing elevator. It had looked identical to the one on the west wing, but was it truly?

Lila was back in the east wing elevator before she was aware she had made the decision to go there. Pressing the call button, she paced backward and forward, her arms crossed at her chest, her right finger as familiar as an old friend, tracing a well worn trail from her nose to her chin.

The door opened with a ding, and Lila jumped inside, turning to look at the panel beside the door. The three circles existing at the bottom are just the same as those from the west wing elevator. The one on the left showing on, and the one outlined in red, less faded here, she noticed, turned to off. When Lila looked upon the circle on the right, it was not turned to LL1 as the one on the west elevator had been.

This one was set to LL2.

18

Across the pedway from Krystal's office, over in the children's hospital, Indiana Powell had one job to do, and she planned to do it exceedingly well, in the honor and memory of the little girl who had reminded her of herself at twelve.

At this point in her day Doctor Indiana Powell was off to the office of the head of the specialized intravenous therapy team, or "IV team" for those of us who wish nothing more than to avoid regularly saying words like "intravenous."

It had been rumored for weeks that members of the IV team had, for some reason unknown to the rest of the staff, been making unauthorized and undocumented bedside consults to the rooms of sick children during the night shift. But without proof, they were only rumors.

The office for the head of the IV team was located on the lower level in the hallway between the imaging department and a pharmacy lab. On a good day, the coffee cart would come by while the CT room was in use and skip them on their way to Doctor Kirschner, the head of the IV team.

Gregory Murray, who ran the CT machine during the day shift Monday through Thursday, always got an extra bear claw from the cart. On the days Greg couldn't answer the call from the cart lady, Doctor Kirschner was all but guaranteed to get one of the few bear claws she stocked in the limited space on the cart. Those days were his favorites, except one day last month when Mrs. Kirschner came to visit her husband one morning and found him with a mouth full of bear claw, which his own doctor told him he couldn't do anymore.

Doctor Kirschner's good morning turned into a bad morning before his first decaf coffee was gone.

Indy always thought red was a tacky color choice for the lower level, since the main component of the floor was the emergency room, but she didn't have time to focus on it this morning as she power walked to Doctor Kirschner's office. She knocked on the door jamb of the half open door and let herself in.

Doctor Kirschner sat behind his desk with one hand holding the handset of his hardwired hospital landline telephone next to, but several inches away from, his right ear with his right hand while rubbing his eyes underneath his rectangle framed glasses with his left.

He looked like he had been awake for days or had done days' worth of critical thought, which for ten in the morning, could be said for most department heads throughout the hospital.

Indy stood and waited silently, giving the elder doctor space to work through whatever crisis he was currently dealing with. Once doctor Kirschner looked up and saw the waiting doctor, no taller than his granddaughter who was in the sixth grade, he sat up straight in his black ridgeback executive office chair and softly spoke into the handset, "Yes, dear, I have a doctor in my office in need of a consult. I'll call you back, dear." He hung up the phone.

Looking at Doctor Indiana Powell, the sixty-one-year-old Doctor Kirschner sighed and said, "Apparently we're out of eggs again, and I can remedy the problem from here better than she can from our dining room... Have a seat, Doctor."

"Indy, Doctor. Indiana Powell. Junior resident, second year." Indy spoke clear and precise with the same voice she used at Kaiser Towers, the nursing home her grandfather had called home since her grandmother passed away three years ago.

"Indy, hmm?" Then the elderly Doctor began quoting Short Round's admonitions of Willie Scott in Temple of Doom. The hysterical laughter from Doctor Kirschner nearly sent him out of his black ridgeback executive office chair. The sight of the gray-haired doctor laughing at a mis-quoted Indiana Jones line with the same fervor as a twelve-year-old in a 1984 theater sent Indy into a fit of laughter equaling that of Doctor Kirschner's. She had met many doctors in her years of schooling, interning, training, and working, but none made the first impression that Doctor Kirschner made.

Indiana Powell had a new favorite doctor.

The spectacled elder statesman of the IV team gathered himself, wiped the tears from his tired eyes, and addressed the young doctor seated in front of him, "My, I haven't laughed like that within these walls in God knows how long. Many thanks for indulging an old man this early in the morning. Now, how can I help you, Doctor Indiana?"

Doctor Kirschner sat and listened to the young woman sitting in front of him in his small office on the lower level of Franklin Children's Hospital as she explained a theory shared by her immediate supervising fellow that seemingly put into question the integrity of someone or someones on his IV team.

"Allow me to summarize the theory you have presented to me, Doctor Indiana," began Doctor Kirschner. "You believe the rise in pediatric and adolescent deaths over the last five months is due to one or more rogue members of the hospital IV team, acting perhaps in cahoots with one or more members of the hospital nursing staff, performing undocumented acts on children during the auspices of the night shift. Is that an accurate summation of the information you gave me?"

Indy measured her response carefully. She needed Doctor Kirschner's help and knew if he felt insulted or accused he may not offer it.

"Essentially, Doctor, yes. I know how it sounds. You've worked hard to curate this team, and here I am intruding into your private office uninvited and making accusations off of assumptions against someone on your team, but the fact is we feel strongly in our work as primary doctors for these kiddos.

"When you objectively feel like your work is accurate and something comes along to fly directly opposite of everything you've seen over the course of treatment, then in the wake of evaluating what went wrong, you come across a theory, uncomfortable as it may be, that potentially explains everything, you *owe* it to your patients and their families, hell you owe it to the science of health care itself to test that theory the best way you can, because damn it, sir, that's how this works."

Indy knew at that moment she went too far. She braced her hands on her knees to stand up and exit the room before Mount Kirschner blew and leveled everything in its wake, namely Indy and her career.

"I agree."

That smacked Indy like a sucker punch from her blind spot.

"I'm sorry, Doctor, could you repeat that?"

Doctor Kirschner laughed softly, like her grandfather during his favorite *All in the Family* episodes.

"Doctor Indiana, you speak with the passion of a doctor new enough to the profession that you can still use the stethoscope you bought in your medical school's equipment room. I miss having that level of passion. I'm two years from retirement, Doctor. The only things I have passion for anymore are my mystery novels and the bear claws my wife says I can't eat. If you say there may be an issue with my team, and you need to use the scientific method to determine if your predictions are backed by data that can lead to an analyzed and accurate conclusion, then that's exactly what you have to do. For the profession and for the children. What else is there?"

Doctor Indiana Powell rode the elevator back up to the fifth floor feeling like she had won an important battle in the war against dying children. She never felt so alive. Doctor Kirschner was in the process of alerting every IV team member of their need to check in before their next shift.

He assured Indy he would be as tactful as he could. It was a promise he *fully intended* to keep.

19

In the basement of the Franklin Children's Hospital, there existed many hallways that hadn't been used in many years. At the end of one of those hallways was a room that, if stumbled into by a lost hospital worker, would appear to be a storeroom for old storage shelves. Behind and through the maze of those shelves was a doorway cut into the century-old limestone block foundation walls that led into a room forgotten to time and construction projects, which had been found by an overweight little man named Tom, the head body transport team member in the hospital.

Three nurses, two being members of the IV team, sat alone in the room. They had spent roughly an hour or so discussing the events of the previous nights shifts, and all the drama that went along with being a nurse on the night shift, before drifting off to sleep for several well earned minutes while awaiting the arrival of their friend, the chaplain.

Breaking through the silence in the dusty old room was an alert tone from the hospital-issued Vocera messaging device.

Vocera was capable of both two-way radio calls and incoming text-based messaging. It combined the best of both hands-free two-way radios and the old school pagers that were being phased out with the retirement of the older doctors who still didn't like things like iPhones and Fitbits.

The male nurses only realized they hadn't turned their devices off after the alert. Richard Mercier and his bald yet bearded coworker, Edward Falcone, both groaned at the sound of the message they already knew would be from their boss, Doctor Kirschner, the only doctor they personally knew who still used the text-based feature.

Unclipping their units, they read the message at the same time before quietly switching the devices off. Richard's face had turned a similar shade of red as the flock of hair that sat unkempt on his head. The pair unconsciously mimed each other's reactions: mouths agape, staring first at each other, then at Claudia.

"IV team, be advised there is an investigation underway by a team of primary doctors in the hospital looking at recent child deaths and the possible correlation of IV team consults. Please be forthcoming with both myself and any doctors who may be calling on you imminently.

Doctor Kirschner."

The sound of silence filled the room.

20

Your mother and I, hands still joined, waited as the light at the crosswalk changed from stop to go, not that it was necessary at eleven in the morning on a random Tuesday in April. Once the morning rush of traffic around the hospital had cleared out, there were fewer vehicles on the road than people around it, and we were the only people within eyeshot.

It felt as though the weather outside had failed to get the memo about the dreadfulness of the day. Whatever storm clouds were present inside, both the building and our hearts, were absent outside where the sun was shining and a warm breeze was blowing through the cool air. There must have been a food truck parked around one of the corners. The smell of Southern barbecue was in the air, which should have felt rather foreboding in hindsight. In the moment, it was mouthwateringly sweet in a way that can bring a different sort of tear to the eye than had been so familiar so far.

We had been downtown before. You would remember it. We had good times here. We would've passed the hospital going west on Capitol Drive toward the Museum District, the city's peak tourist area, perfect for a day out with two brainy girls. How'd I get so lucky, huh? We would go to the Natural History Museum, the Austin Art Gallery and Museum, and the children's museum. They were all on the west side along with that pizza place you liked, Gwens, and the coffee shop that makes those smoothies.

Instead of taking a right out of the hospital, we turned left, heading east on Capitol Drive, wanting to get as far away from other people as we could, for as long as we could. Where there were people, there were conversations. How are you today? What's new with you today? Been up to anything lately? Witness the death of your only child yet today? You have? Care to talk about it?

Your mother and I did not want to have a conversation with anyone other than ourselves.

We crossed Capitol Drive and turned south on Pine, where we passed an old, rundown parking lot surrounded by a falling down chain-link fence. There were patches of green growing from inside the cracks in the pavement, and a broken broomstick was in the middle of the lot. Probably a nice place for stickball, but there were no kids around at that time of day.

Surrounding us on both sides of the street were old brick buildings, long deserted as the growth of the city had moved west, abandoning many of the old buildings that once had been part of the thriving epicenter of the city.

I found a mostly spherical rock on the sidewalk and began kicking it along their path. I watched the rock skip and jump on the broken sidewalk while maintaining a mostly straight line and thought about the way our lives had been tracking lately. A month ago, our little family was sailing smoothly through life on a line so straight you could use it to lay brick without one of those fancy new laser plumb lines. Then our line started skipping and jumping all over the walk, and here we were.

We were one fewer now, and I was sure that hole would never fill in, but the sun was still in the sky, the world was still spinning, and our line was invariably still on the course it had always been on, albeit broken and messy.

As we approached the next stoplight where Pine intersected with York, we stopped and stood, looking out at the different directions and wondering which way to turn on our mind-clearing walk. I kicked the rock in front of Joey with the deftness of a professional soccer star or a teenager with a heavy hacky sack.

"Winslow is looking for the assist. He hits the pass to Joey, which direction will she choose to send the rock of destiny?"

Joey smiled, squeezed my hand, and looked left then right. Closing her eyes, she brought her foot back and with a smile whispered, "Boom." She let her foot go with all the might she could muster, years of aerobic kickboxing group classes going into that one kick.

The rock left your mom's right sneaker like a rocket in desperate need of one of Elon Musk's engineers to troubleshoot its guidance system. It shot off to the left of where we stood on the corner of the sidewalk facing crosswalks to their front and to their left. Once it hit the ground, it hopped farther left before coming to rest diagonally across the intersection, in front of what appeared to be either an old storefront church or a mission shelter for the homeless.

Joey shrugged and tugged at my arm, heading across the crosswalk first to their left, then to the right, coming to rest in front of the Weary Sojourner Mission. Joey, in the first true display of affection that day, gently touched her thin lips to my cheek, sending a cascading wave of shivers from my head to my rock kicking feet. Together, we went inside.

21

The Weary Sojourner Mission looked like a country church out of a 1960s sitcom, with the exception of the iron bars on the outside of the five-foot glass panels in the double doors at the entrance.

Going through the well-worn doors, you entered into a single-room church with seating broken into two sides, each side having five rows of pews covered with purple upholstery that looked like it was from the 60s too. It smelled more like the backroom of a small-time casino than a church, with the sweet aroma of wine wafting in from the back mixing with the vanilla from the wall plugs on either side of the room and competing for front stage with the mold and mildew coming from the areas of the space that hadn't been well cleaned in several years.

The space could have easily fit five more rows on each side. Instead, there were two large racks of folding chairs against the left wall and several folding tables stacked against the right wall.

We announced ourselves to the open room and made our way to the front, taking note of each picture hanging crooked on the wall.

Every few feet on the wood paneled walls, there hung pictures in frames of various sizes and styles, some as small as 4x6, one as big as 9x11. Each framed picture showed different smiling kids from twelve to eighteen, all with the same man in a black button-up shirt with white collar, black round-framed glasses, and a cross necklace that hung past his white collar. The pictures covered a wide span of time made evident by the varying levels of gray in the hair and wrinkles around the eyes of the man.

When we got to the front of the room, we sat in the first pew on the right and simply sat. Each of us felt the weight of the day like a backpack turned the wrong way so the weight settled heavy on our chests. We were sitting under that weight, eyes closed, hands clasped on their laps, when a voice spoke from the shadows in the front corner of the room where the stage stopped and disappeared into the unknown areas beyond the stage where the congregation wouldn't gather.

"You two in trouble? Don't tend to get random couples in here this time of the morning' 'less they're in some form of trouble."

We recognized the old man, old to your mother and I but too young for the Social Security Office to be writing checks, as the man in the pictures. The deep Texas accent hadn't been evident from the pictures, which surprised Joey, the surprise itself a surprise. Why would a picture suggest any accent at all?

Joey stood first, then I followed her lead. I had been caught off guard by the sound.

"We're sorry to intrude, sir. No, no we aren't in any trouble." She looked to my face for confirmation feeling like that wasn't entirely so.

"No, no trouble, as trouble goes, I suppose." I picked up where Joey dropped off. "Though I must say we aren't exactly chipper either."

"Nah, I wouldn't s'pose so. Chipper couples don't find themselves in places such as this at times like these."

The collared man was wheeling a small wooden cart from the back. On the top of the cart was a tray, and on the top of the tray were a couple dozen little cups, stacked in pairs. I recognized the cups from the church they had attended a few years prior as communion cups, used for taking the Lord's Supper.

"For a place that doesn't get non-troubled couples at this time you sure have quite the helping of communion cups there, mister..."

"Creed. Jim Creed. Call me either, call me pastor, call me that ol' sumbitch," Creed chuckled at the sudden widening of the couple's eyes at the last of his suggested names. "That's the fav'rite of the neighborin' colored boys from around the way here. I let 'em call me whatev'r comes out, colorful or not, s'long as they keep comin'. A lil color a speech never hurt anyone. For some of 'em, it's a door they think keeps'm safe. S'all right by me, like I say. Whatev'r keeps 'em comin'. Cain't reach 'em if they ain't within' reach."

He handed us each a double stacked cup.

"Cup on bottom has the cracker, top has juice. Used wine 'til it got right obvious the kids came for the taste. Got no interest in leadin' 'em to drink outside these walls. Figur the good Lord can bless 'em with juice just as well as wine. He made both."

Something about the phrase, "He made both," sat in my belly like a yeast roll that hadn't finished expanding yet.

"We're here from the hospital. Our daughter died today."

Joey surprised herself when she blurted that out. Was he sure that wasn't wine?

My eyes stayed on my wife while I spoke, "We were on a walk to clear our minds when we found your building. The doctors said to take a day while they look into it. We're not totally sure what 'it' is, but they said it, so we're here. We figure tomorrow will be hard, with morticians and funeral homes and whatever else..."

"So today is to get prepared. Well, that's a good way to be, I hafta say."

90

Old man Creed had a directness to his voice, his speech pattern coming like a well-swung bat, but all the same it was gentle on our ears. The bat landed softly. We figured it could come hard when it needed to.

Creed suddenly stopped his morning tasks and turned towards maybe the first mixed race couple to occupy two seats on the front row in his little storefront church. I still wonder if that was true.

"Which hospital you say you was comin' from?"

"Franklin Children's Hospital, sir."

Joey's voice was beginning to waver, the weight coming back onto her chest with a vengeance.

"If they lookin', they need to know where ta look. Y'all go back an find yer doctor, the one doin' the lookin'. You tell 'em you know what got yer little girl. You tell 'em it's the same one been gettin' all the young'uns these last months. I read the papers, I hear the talk, and I know the devil once'st I see 'em. The devil's in that place. He was here once'st, and I know he's there now. You tell 'em they lookin' for Edward Falcone. Tell 'em Jim Creed is sure of it."

22

The blood drained out of Claudia's face first, until her tanned skin began to match the white patch that existed in a slash across her face. She began seeing dark spots like the room was suddenly years deep in a leprosy diagnosis when her hands and feet got cold from lack of 98.7 degree blood, which was rapidly retreating into her core. If she wasn't seated already, she may well have passed out on the cold concrete floor, creating a Claudia-shaped spot clear of the dust and grime currently settled where no man, or Tom, had cleaned before.

"I... We... Guys..." Claudia was slowly watching the dark spots shrink into nothing, the room's leprosy healing like it had touched the hem of Christ's robe. "I knew it. Jesus, guys, I..."

If swear words could be collected like kibble in a measuring cup, Claudia at this point dumped the cup into the bowl of the room, where they spilled out and scattered along the ground to be trampled and crushed underfoot later.

Her blood rushed back to the extremities where it belonged at the same time her body dumped a rush of adrenaline into her system like a busted Louisiana levee after Hurricane Katrina, and if Edward and Richard hadn't been as quick to their feet as they were, she would have destroyed them like a suburb in Saint Bernard Parish, I *gar-on-tee*.

The two men approached Claudia like circus-keepers approaching one of the lions under the big top: defensive posture, weight on their heels, arms extended and holding a stool and whip. Their eyes widened. If left to her own fit of rage at this moment, the lion would leave little left of the keepers.

"Claudia, take a breath," Richard said. "Let's talk this out. That's what we do here. We talk things out."

"Yes, listen to Richard, Claudia," Edward said, stronger than Richard. He wasn't the type to hide behind any stool. He would wave his electric prodding stick at the lion, as ready to strike back as the big cat was ready to strike.

"Talking, that's a strength of yours, girly. Let's do that."

The look Claudia shot at Edward when "girly" came across his lips made even Edward take a step back.

She took turns aiming the raging fire flowing from her eyes alternatively at the two men. If she couldn't pounce, she could burn them down.

"I told you both," she growled, "to find another way. You want to stick people, find a practice lab, or go to the university. There had to be—"

"Another way, yes, you told us." Edward was taking the point in responding to Claudia. There was never a confrontation Edward Falcone was afraid to handle head-on. This was close to being the first, but it wasn't.

He continued, "And we told you, girl...Claudia, we had a job to do. It's getting pretty obvious you still don't fully realize the work there is to be done."

Edward stood firm near the center of the room like a statue welcoming your tired and your poor. He only needed a torch and tablet.

Richard paced, sensing the need for calm in the space between Claudia and Edward, "We were trying to find a place. I had a lead on a good place, a cadaver lab where we could work on pokes, but they turned us down when Edward went to check them out. We even started poking each other some, but we couldn't keep stickin' each other unless we wanted to show up to work with what looked like track marks up our arms. We couldn't do that, could we? What was the harm, he—"

"WHAT WAS THE HARM HERE?"

Richard knew it was the wrong thing to say as it was spilling out, and Claudia confirmed that thought immediately. The white patch that slashed across her face was as red as the wildfires that had swept through California last fall. If the guys weren't careful, it would burn them down where they stood.

"What was the harm in calling you two into dark rooms to practice sticking kids in the middle of the night? I didn't know. Does that make you feel better? I didn't know. It made some sense, sure. A few harmless pokes for the benefit of all those future kids who would get better pokes from practiced guys. But then...oh, but then, guys, then when the first kid...you said, 'You're being paranoid, Claudia. It's a coincidence, Claudia.' I should've stopped it with the first..."

Claudia fell in on herself. She managed to stay upright, still on her feet, but she crouched to the floor, her knees in her chest, arms around her knees, her face buried in between. She shivered and cried, cried and shivered, her rage morphing into a fountain of sorrow.

She felt like she was drowning.

Richard knelt beside Claudia, the odds of her lashing out now seemingly diminished, and put an arm around her quivering shoulders.

"Claudia, I know you feel like the world is on fire or something." He looked up to Edward as a way to ensure he had his back in case he set Mount Claudia back into eruption mode. "But nothing is going to happen here. Coincidences, that's all. What we've been doing is safe. We've cleaned all the syringes, made clean pokes, nobody saw anything, nobody will be coming."

Slowly, Claudia raised her head, sniffling the loose snot back into her nose in the absence of tissues, tears filling her eyes and running over the edges like above ground pools after a hard rain.

"If it was as clean as you say it was, there wouldn't be a pattern of kids being brought to the basement. It was wrong. It was immoral, I knew it, and I did nothing. You made a mistake somewhere. How you cleaned the old needles, using them too many times, something, I don't know, but it killed kids, and now someone knows and is coming. They're coming."

Edward felt something inside him begin to stretch tighter than he'd felt in a long time. He thought it might snap.

He looked down at Richard and could see something changing in him too. Maybe no one else could, but Edward was from the streets. You didn't survive on the streets, inside the homeless shelters, without learning how to read the wings of impending danger. Richard was smiling at Claudia, but Richard was not happy.

"It's going to be okay, Claudia," Richard said in his softest, most charming voice. "It is. No one is coming. No one died from you letting us come practice our craft. The cleaning process worked. The needles didn't get overused. Everything is fine."

Richard looked up and met Edward's eyes. He raised his eyebrows and nodded ever so slightly at his friend.

"Yeah, girly." Edward felt no danger from Claudia. Not now. "Everything's a-okay."

Richard and Edward helped Claudia to her feet and back to the folding chair under the "Never Give Up" poster taped to the limestone block wall. The rage that burned inside her moments ago, which turned her white patches to flaming red like iron fresh from a fiery kiln, had sapped her of what energy had been left after her twelve-hour night shift that ended hours ago.

The news of the impending investigation bore a hole through her soul that allowed all the feelings of doubt in the plan put forth by her friends that she had stuffed back and locked away to come pouring out like water through a hole in a dam that she could no longer plug. She knew she shouldn't let her friends from the IV team come to the rooms of sick kids during the night shift to practice their sticks and pokes.

"They'll never know, Claudia. If anyone asks, tell them you couldn't find a vein when doing lab sticks. No harm, no foul."

Except there were both harms and fouls. When the visits started coming more often, and done without official calls and documented clearance, the guys couldn't use new equipment anymore. New equipment would have to be scanned, after all. They said the old needles were clean. They said there was no risk of using them too much, no barbs, nothing to cause more harm or damage the veins, no risk of infection, no risk of clots, no worries, girly. But worry she did. She knew they should too.

"Let's take a break. Hit the head. Tom's not here yet. There must've been a delivery to make. Krystal's not here yet. Hit the stalls, come back, talk it out. Once Krystal's here, maybe leave some details out. Come on…"

If Edward had a point, it was that they did all have to pee. They quietly left the room and maneuvered through the maze of old storage shelves in the room behind the room and split off to different spots to find a bathroom and take a breather. When they came back, they figured they could decompress.

Claudia was sure they all had blood on their hands.

23

Lila Collins pressed LL and waited, standing as far from the door of the elevator as she could get. She eyed the round keyhole marker, which bore the markings L1 and L2 and wondered if her hunch regarding them was correct, that L1 was the first lower level, the only lower level she had been on, the one which held the emergency room, imaging, and various offices. If true, that would mean L2 would be the second lower level, right?

That made logical sense to Lila, after having not been able to find a way to the basement she theoretically knew existed. Having never been to that level, she had no idea what to expect once the elevator car stopped.

The bell dinged, and the doors opened. She hadn't realized that her hand now rested in front of the lower portion of her face, her finger now on her chin.

The bell sounded when the indicator read LL and the doors to the elevator opened. Lila realized she would only know if the L2 from the keyhole had changed which level she was taken to if she would open her eyes.

After a deep breath, the pilates instructor from the class she took on her non-hospital days called it a "cleansing breath" meant to expel the negative energy from within, Lila opened her eyes and stepped off the elevator before the doors closed behind her.

It took Lila's eyes a moment to adjust to the lighting, or lack thereof, in the hallway she found herself in. Her nose recognized the new-to-her environment first. The musk, the dust, the cocktail of mildew and bleach so old and faint that the mildew was overtaking it. It all tickled her nose in a way that caused a similar tickle in her gut that she neither cared for nor wanted to last very long at all. She had a feeling very few doctors, nurses, or staff of any kind other than the little man who ran the transport team had seen this space in quite a long time.

Lila was most certainly not in Kansas anymore, Toto. Gone was the bright fluorescent lighting. Gone was the calming but slightly outdated tan wall paint on the hallway walls. Newer hospitals used a steel gray these days. The tan was already a relic of renovations past. Gone was the brightly colored wall runner, different for each floor, matching the brightly colored linoleum tiles running in the middle of the hallways, bordered by white tiles, each floor having a different corresponding color scheme.

Light came from individual bulbs in hanging fixtures spaced twenty feet apart running down the hallway. The walls were a strange paneling, made of thick textured plastic that would be a nightmare to disinfect in today's modern, post-Covid, sterilized to the moon and beyond world. Her footsteps rung out on the wood floor, swollen with years of moisture seeping up from the concrete below, which was worn and dirty to a degree that made it known to Lila why the change to linoleum tile had been implemented.

The air was thick and cold, stale like it hadn't been opened to the world above it in years. She looked behind her as she walked down the old hallway toward the darkness ahead of her and noticed a collage of footprints in the dust on the ground. Even the housekeeping crews had long forgotten the basement level of the hospital.

Who in the world even had a key necessary to turn the elevator from L1 to L2? Was there anyone other than Tom the transport guy?

"Okay, Lila, get it together. You have a job to do."

Oh how nice, she thought, *now you're talking out loud to yourself.*

"What a change of pace from the inner monologue."

Yep, and now you can run your thoughts multi-channeled like a good home stereo system, she thought as she switched the output of her thoughts yet again. She was deciding which to stick with.

"Might as well use your outside voice. It's too quiet without it."

Stopping to shake her head and chuckle, Lila took another cleansing breath and continued down the dank, forgotten hallway.

She walked down the hallway slowly, taking in the appearance of every sight from a bygone era of the hospital. The fixtures, the signs, the hardware on the doors, everything screamed...1980s? 70s? She thought the hospital had its first renovations in the 90s. How long had it been prior to that since anything had been made new?

Lila peered in each door she came to. Most opened to empty rooms, some filled with boxes, some with metal desks and rolling carts, some with shelving units or gurneys, all covered with many layers of dust and fallen debris from the ceiling above them.

At the first hallway intersection, Lila turned right, leaving a line in the dust on the floor with her foot as a breadcrumb so she would hopefully not get lost down here. She tried not to imagine the day when her lost body was discovered by some future ancestor after having been lost to the ether of the bygone basement. However, with each turn and corridor, Lila felt more like a child lost in a maze at the fair. *Sir, have you seen my mother?*

"That's enough of that. You are a respected pediatric doctor. You run the best team in the best hospital this side of the state. You are not a little girl anymore, you are not lost, you are Lila Collins. Hold it together. You have a job to do."

Another pep talk or two and she may even start to believe it.

Lila was discovering lots of signs that no one from maintenance or housekeeping had been in this basement for several presidential election cycles, the most disconcerting being the abundance of burned-out overhead light bulbs.

"Why not do this in the dark literally? The whole thing is in the dark metaphorically anyway. I can't even get the other administrators to take this seriously, and we're talking about dead children for God's—," Lila stopped when she walked face-first through a giant cobweb.

"If I get out of here alive, I'm going to have a talk with someone about the state of this basement. This is absurd. We're an award winning hospital for crying out loud, old enough to remember both the country's centennial and bicentennial celebrations or not," Lila said while picking silk web from her lips.

The corridors were getting darker the deeper she got into the maze of the basement. Whatever light fixtures were hanging had been stripped of their bulbs.

"Who in their right mind would take out the... Tom."

Lila found herself in the midst of an epiphany. She stopped mid-corridor and slowly spun in circles, looking for some clue to confirm to her whether or not she was on to something. She hoped she was, if for no other reason than it would get her out of here faster. It seemed faster couldn't come fast enough.

"Tom, the only person with a reason to still come down here, because of the morgue. Tom transports the dead to the morgue. Why does Tom do that himself? Doesn't matter. Tom comes down here, no one else does, no one to change the light bulbs." Lila's speech cadence was picking up steam as her hypothesizing ran downhill. The volume of her voice was running in the inverse, straight uphill.

She had no idea how loud she was becoming or who could hear her.

"Tom needs light in the morgue. What easier way than to strip old bulbs that still worked and use them where he needs them. Where is the God forsaken morgue?"

Lila began rushing through the hallways looking in every door that opened for any sign that would point to the morgue, hypothesizing out loud to herself as she went.

"Find the morgue, find Tom, find Chloe, get answers. Answers, what kind of answers are you even going to get? This isn't a police station. I should've called Whitey. Lord, why didn't I call Whitey? Lila, you idiot, you're dating a police officer for goodness sake. Never mind, anyway, what am I looking for when I find Tom? Chloe's body, obviously. I can call the medical examiner and start a perfunctory autopsy myself. This is all so crazy. Did one of our staff actually do this? Do I believe that? It looks like it. Why doesn't anyone else believe it? It would help if it wasn't just us, but they'll believe soon enough. I bet Addison and Indy have some answers on the nurses and IV team who saw her. I'll find Tom, find Chloe, call Addy and Indy, get the names, call Whitey. This will all get settle—OOF!"

Lila Collins went down to one knee, unable to get the breath back that had been driven out of her by something hitting her in her abdomen, off center on her right side. Her eyes opened wide in the darkness of the hidden corridor, grimacing while searching for air. She tried to find the cause of whatever had delivered the blow to her liver that had left her body in shock. On one knee and unable to draw a breath, she felt her arm and head being grabbed by what felt like an animal escaped from the local zoo.

Now she couldn't breathe or move. She was trapped in a bearhug of a snare and had never felt more vulnerable. Lila was lifted into the air by her head and arm with an ease that made her feel like she was a kid again, flying through the air headfirst on the swings pretending to be Wonder Woman.

Wonder Woman never went headfirst into a wall though. Not as far as Lila could recall, as best she could try before the world went dark.

***

Her body went limp after the first impact. The second cracked her skull like a ripe cantaloupe dropped from the grocery cart on the parking lot pavement. The third splattered bits of Lila Collins's brain matter and cerebral fluid on the floor, pooling in the freshly made hole in the broken tile on the wall, and scattered on the hands and arms that had held her lifeless head and arm. Hands that now reached down and shut off her Vocera device. Hands that grabbed her hospital issued name badge that read "Lila Collins, M.D." in big, bold type.

In the darkness, she hadn't known she had entered one of two men's bathrooms on the west side of the basement. She didn't know she was two hallways over from the morgue that held the body of Chloe Miller, which Tom was currently entering into the system. She didn't know she was around the corner from the room used as storage for old shelving units that hid the entrance to Tom's living quarters. She didn't know that her assailant was on their way back to that room where their two colleagues had already returned from their bathroom breaks.

Lila Collins would never know these things or who was responsible for the deaths of the children from the last five months in Franklin Children's Hospital, not in life at least.

24

Indy rode the elevator up from her lower level meeting with Doctor Kirschner feeling fairly proud of herself. Not only had the impromptu meeting with the senior physician gone better than she had hoped, but he was in the process of urging every member of his team to be responsive to requests to talk to her, Addison, and Lila.

She hadn't pre-read his outgoing message but felt confident he would be as discreet as he had assured her he would be. The last thing any of them wanted was to alert any potential evildoers. Indy chuckled at the word but thought if it didn't apply to a potential child killer, then what would it ever apply to?

The elevator doors opened on the fifth floor, and Indy took a direct path to the office the team worked out of. She had planned to page Lila and Addison once she got in the office to see how their tasks were coming and when they could meet back up. She still needed to go over the assignment logs to document which members of the IV team were on call which nights, but she hoped Addison had made at least a little headway in narrowing down when the potential undocumented activity occurred.

She was considering the possibilities of some amount of the cases prior to Chloe's having been documented. Would it be possible they were documenting the IV consults as a way to hide in plain sight and Chloe's case was the outlier? This was beginning to feel less like a hospital shift and more like a Kinsey Millhone Mystery. *P Is for Pediatric Homicide*, available in hardcover, paperback, or e-reader.

Indy found Addison already in the office.

"Hey, girl." She winced at the casualness of her voice in that moment.

Addison barely looked up from the stack of papers strewn across her desk before updating her friend, "Indy, check this out. I've spent the last hour tracking a nurse named Claudia O'Dell. According to the record logs kept by the head nurses in charge of scheduling for the fourth and fifth floors, Claudia kept a busier schedule than most nurses on staff, not totally abnormal by any stretch, but with as many shifts as Claudia was working, I feel confident we'll find a correlation between the patients under Claudia's care during her many night shifts and the names of the patients who have died these last few months.

"Including Chloe Millner, we've had thirteen pediatric deaths in the last five months. Claudia O'Dell had been the night nurse on at least one night for all thirteen. There's no way that could be a coincidence, but we need more. We can't run to the president of the hospital with a stack of timecards yelling, 'I have the murderer of all those kids no one thinks were murdered!' That wouldn't go over well at all.

"Anyway, there weren't any other patterns that I could see as far as nurses go. If someone on the IV team is doing something to the kids and using a nurse to set up their time in the rooms, Claudia O'Dell seems like the only choice."

Addison paused to silence her watch. Another high heart rate alarm, shocking.

She continued, "Of course, it's possible they weren't using a nurse. If they were using tainted needles, they could wait for consults, but that would raise two problems. First, we run labs on almost all of these kids. I don't know for sure that the basic labs would pick up a foreign substance, but wouldn't they? So put a pin in that. Second, that would mean every consult was documented and charted, and we're going off the assumption that there was an undocumented consult last night."

"It could mean they were getting desperate. Or even bloodthirsty and cocky, willing to take new risks," Indy added.

"It could, but then how did they get in the room? They would still need an in, someone to call them in. I know that sounds like a Stephen King vampire novel, but it's true. And Chloe's mom said the IV team member was there with the night nurse. If the uncharted consult was new, if it was desperation or eagerness or pride because they hadn't yet been caught, the night nurse would still have to be involved in this case. Since this particular nurse was also a nurse on staff for all the other kids before their deaths, we still look at her first...right?"

Addison was borderline frenzied as her watch alarm went off again. Indy noticed the alarm also sent a notification to Addison's Macbook and reached down to close the box for her worked-up friend.

Indy had heard about Addison's athletic past – she held every record in her high school's record book – but had never seen it actualized in any way beyond preparation. She prepared like she was scouting the other team with every patient.

This was different. Addison was intense. She hadn't been this locked in since the first half of her senior night. That night cut short when her younger brother was killed outside in an accident. The event led to her becoming a pediatric doctor and now, years later, she was back to that younger, ultra-competitive Addison. Indy wanted nothing more than to turn her loose on whoever was responsible for this, but it had to be directed in the right place.

"Addison, I think you're onto something, but if this Claudia girl pulled a night shift a few hours ago, we probably have some time before she's back in the hospital. Let's take a few minutes and go over the IV team logs and see if we can get that list whittled down, see who was on during those shifts and go from there."

Addison took one of Lila's cleansing breaths. She had to know Indy was right but also would have known she needed to get out of the office and into the fight.

"Tell you what. I'll leave these logs here, and you go over them and find that pattern. I need a breather. Let's meet back up in an hour. I'll come back here after I go for a walk. Who knows, maybe Claudia never left the building. There are Murphy beds in the back lounge for a reason."

Addison left Indy in the office to compare the IV team call logs to Claudia's schedule over the last months.

At this point in the day, Lila Collins was nowhere to be found, but we were pretty sure she was gone by then, killed by the same person responsible for what happened to you. If that part of the timeline was correct, it would've been clear which doctors were the ones looking into the child deaths from Doctor Kirschner's memo. Doctor Collins's team was well known to the nurses on staff in Franklin Children's Hospital.

If Lila was discovered looking in the basement for information, which evidence shows was where she was attacked, in a bathroom between the morgue and Tom's room, it would've been assumed her two team members were probably somewhere upstairs looking at schedules, time clocks, charts, and God knew what else.

And if they somehow knew no one beyond her team was looking at this, then they also knew the makeshift investigation died with them...right?

25

We sat in the church for several minutes past Jim Creed returning back to wherever he had come from. In the silence, we looked at the statue of a suffering Jesus on the left side of the stage. I couldn't tell if someone had cast the Lord out of a metal or carved Him out of stone and, horror of horrors to purveyors of art, painted the results. Raised streams of blood flowed from the crown of thorns that appeared to pierce the crafted head.

Joey wondered silently what the kids Creed got to come into the church would think about the grotesque imagery and if it helped or hurt his cause to reach the lost. We talked at length in the days that followed whether if that had been the first thing she had seen in a church setting she would have stayed or run away screaming and trying to forget the sight before she fell asleep.

I simply continued to wonder about the process behind making the statue. It may have depended on the age of the piece or whether it had been a gift or if Creed had found it...and where would you find something like this anyway? Abandoned church? Fire sale? Flea market? Surely Creed wouldn't mind if he walked up and got a closer look, right?

"Winslow?"

I was snapped back into the reality of the moment by the question. I turned and gave my wife my full attention, though from the wrinkle in her nose and the half-cocked way her head hung while looking blankly ahead, I wondered if I had her full attention or if she was still forming her thoughts from somewhere else.

"The doctor asked us three questions. I have tried so hard to forget them. I've tried to focus on you, on us, on the chaplain. Okay, I wasn't focusing on the chaplain. I didn't want to hear anything she had to say, not being rude, but I didn't. I was focusing on her hair. Winslow, I loved her hair. I could never pull that off." Joey's train of thought drifted. "What did she call that? Braids? Twists? Do dreads come that thin? Maybe I can ask your mom the next time we see her. When would they go to Pennsylvania again? Oh! They'll probably be coming here..."

Oh, how I loved your mom's tangents. You were quite similar to her in that way.

"Sorry, hun, three questions. The nurse, the IV guy, the reason for the IV guy. Isn't that what she asked?" Joey finally stopped staring into nowhere, coming back from wherever her mind had been and her eyes met mine.

"I believe so babe, but to be honest, as little as you were listening to the chaplain, that's about how much I was listening to Doctor Whatsername. I was still worried about you, Joey. I thought I was losing you too. I still..."

I had to stop and gather myself. I was standing on a ledge and felt myself teetering like I was looking over the side of a skyscraper.

"I still don't know what they said."

We sat a minute more, our hands carefully holding the other's like they could shatter and scatter the broken shards across the floor of the church, shards lost in the carpet to cut again and again when found by future bare feet. After a minute, Joey broke the silence again.

"It was three. I don't know the name of either nurse. I wish I did. Edward Falcone? That's what Creed said. Was that the guy's name from IV? I know we had the girl before. There was something about her face. She always had her mask on, I'd assumed because of the contact precautions, not that anyone else followed them, but there was something poking out from under the top of her mask. I think she had that skin thing, that condition where your hair goes white in spots. It can happen on your skin too, and I think maybe she had it on her face. The only other time we would have had her would have had to be in the PICU. Can they move between floors?"

"Yes." I surprised myself with how fast I answered, but I did know it. She had told me. "I don't remember her name, but we had her in the PICU and commented on it that night in the new room..."

"When she walked in! I saw that little bit of that color change on her cheek and, Winslow, the curls. She had those curls of hers pulled back in a ponytail! God, Winslow, her hair was gorgeous. How could I forget that hair? I was so jealous. Babe, would you love me more if I had hair like that? Do guys think about hair the same way women do?"

"Some guys do, but I like your hair, Jo. It's long and straight with a little wave. I like it that way. I thought you knew. Remember when you got—"

"THAT PERM!"

We yelled out the finish to my sentence in a way that best friends so often did then fell into each other in laughter.

"You hated that perm," Joey said and snorted.

She only snorted when the laughter was dramatic and genuine. It embarrassed her more than anything else she did. Chloe, I had made it my life's mission since our second date, when I heard it for the first time, to make my future wife snort as often as possible for the rest of her life.

I sat for a moment, before hitting her hanging curveball with a corked punchline with all I could muster. "You're flingin-flangin right I did."

Home run, folks. Drive home safely.

Joey erupted with laughter, finishing with the biggest snort I had ever heard.

We sat afterward gathering ourselves and discussing Doctor Collins's three questions for another few minutes before rising from the front row pew and walking out the door, walking in the direction of the Franklin Children's Hospital.

We never wondered where Jim Creed had gone and why he hadn't returned during our uproar. We had been squalling like Pentecostals waving flags to a heavy drum beat and Hammond B3.

An ambulance from Franklin Hospital passed your mother and I on our way back, but we had no way to know who it was for. His warning was in the forefront of our minds and the reason for our return to the hospital despite our desire to keep walking in the opposite direction.

Once we walked up the three steps from the sidewalk to the sliding double doors leading to the main lobby of the hospital, the air seemed to shift from the warm spring breeze to a cold wind from the darkest winter. We stopped, frozen in place like we had taken two steps into fast setting cement.

We simply could not bring ourselves to take another step. Something was blocking the door. Something we could both feel but not articulate.

Simultaneously, a gate opened above our hearts, and a flood rushed in, filling every chamber until it was so heavy in our chests our knees sagged under the immense weight. The sorrow was finally flooding in, and we were unable to keep the gate closed anymore. Our legs stopped being able to hold our weight as the mass of the entirety of our lives had suddenly bore down on us while on the front sidewalk of the hospital.

In vacuumed silence similar to a walk in deep space, we began to collapse in on ourselves like dying stars. Somehow, we managed the four steps to our right to the wood slatted bench next to the concrete ashtray where the incoming smokers would sit and finish their cigarettes before entering the hospital.

Barely able to expand our chests enough to take full breaths, your mother and I clung to each other as the overflow of our sorrow and remorse began to spill out of our eyes, watering the ground beneath us.

26

In the basement, the trio had regathered after the bathroom break intended to calm the nerves of the group, which had learned a trio of doctors from upstairs were unofficially investigating the increase in pediatric deaths since the pact.

The nerves had not calmed.

In early November, Claudia, Edward, and Richard had sat together in Claudia's hatchback in the hospital parking garage after returning from Chaplain Jenkins's apartment. They had not yet met Tom. This was the first meeting at Chaplain Jenkins's as a trio. Edward had invited his new friends days ago after mentioning them to Krystal Jenkins. They would carpool once a week to the small group meeting from the work garage and return back. The trip would take an hour out of their day, and already they were hoping to find room in the hospital to move the group meetings.

Edward was the first to breach the subject. While he attended nursing school, the college had a cadaver lab the students could use to practice their sticks and pokes, a room he used generously during his time there. Richard chimed in with his own collegiate exploits in the cadaver lab.

The problem today was that Franklin Children's Hospital was not the size of the bigger hospitals in the bigger cities or even one of the large university hospitals with the state-of-the-art instructional facilities. All that to say, there was no cadaver lab at Franklin Children's Hospital. Nor was there the artificial cadaver lab found in a school with a large donor base.

Edward said he could feel the need of a practice facility with each passing day as his highly tuned skills seeped from his pores like oil from a hole in the line of a once finely tuned automobile that was years from its last tuneup. Richard agreed that was exactly how he felt.

Claudia's counterpoint? They were running multiple lines and installing multiple ports every day during every shift. Maybe in their minds they were slowly but surely losing their touch, an inevitability since once they were practicing hour after hour and now were only simply doing the job, right? They weren't taking into account these were live patients they were working with and on, that each stick here was worth one hundred on a cadaver, or at least that was Claudia's argument once they put forth their strange and highly unethical query, but they wouldn't hear it.

They couldn't. She wouldn't, couldn't, understand. But she had to—she was their only choice.

Three weeks before that fateful discussion in Claudia's car, Edward and Richard had devised a plan to get their reps in. Who would balk at a star player staying after practice to get more shots up? Surely no one they knew.

They had decided first to lift as many needles as they could from the supply room that held all the tools of the IV trade. They wouldn't need much. Edward knew a way to find more.

His years on the street and in the homeless shelter had shown him there were places to go to get all the needles you would want. The city would provide them for all your intravenous drug use needs, no questions, no waiting. Anything to keep a druggy from dying on the streets, anything but actual care. Care was too expensive these days, but needles so they could use them clean? That could be done.

The second part came in the privacy of their apartments, away from the prying eyes of decent and moral people. That was where Edward and Richard would practice their intravenous punctures on each other. Four free arms, no waiting. All the pokes they could handle and then some.

There woud a problem with their plan that they had overlooked, a problem that didn't exist with the drug user population, who only cared about the syringe push after the needle stick. What could Edward and Richard, two health care professionals on a specialized unit, not do that the homeless user in the shelter didn't have to think about? They could not go around with track marks on their arms. That would be a big no-no from administration, folks.

They told this story with all the doe-eyed wonder they could muster to their twenty-two-year-old nurse friend as though they were the victims in this crazy trade. "It's perfectly normal to practice on each other, Claudia. Don't you think we should be practiced up when you call us in the room in the dead of night? Well, don't you? Why do you hate the children, Claudia? Why call an unpracticed IV unit member to do an IV poke? That's just cruel for the kiddos. How could you? Morals? That's the morality pull, that you hate kids. Why, Claudia? Why?"

It should not have worked.

Claudia should have walked out of the car and away from her friends, but she hadn't had friends in so long... Maybe they were right? What was the harm in wanting to be sure of your skills? Hadn't she practiced using her stethoscope on herself? Her sphygmomanometer? Sure, she wasn't stabbing herself, but would she if she didn't have the option of calling IV?

Claudia's thoughts stopped. The car was silent, the air stale in her nostrils. This didn't feel like the end of the conversation. That was Act 1. This was intermission, and no one was coming with a snack cart anywhere she could see. The feeling of the actors changing their outfits and practicing their lines before the curtain pulled away for Act 2 to commence was so strong Claudia could feel the lights dimming as Richard started to speak again.

"We've come up with a plan to be able to practice on live arms — to hone our craft, Claudia, for the children — and not get anyone in trouble."

He spoke with both caution and brevity then waited for the next speaker to enter from stage right.

Right on cue, Edward spoke with conviction and passion, "Long term, the care improves, the kids get better faster, and no one ever has to find out how."

The play took a dark turn. Claudia was terrified of the how.

The how consisted of a pact between the three nurses. The night nurse and the two IV specialists. Claudia would identify kids who would potentially need the services of an IV consult. Kids who were needing labs drawn regularly, with times during night shift on the chart. Kids with nightly labs were already getting stuck, though the nurse would do it herself.

Preferably, the nurse would pull from the IV, if they had one and if it was bleeding back properly. If they didn't have one already, the nurse would use either a finger poke or a butterfly poke. A finger poke was great for labs that only needed a smaller amount of blood. If multiple vials were necessary for the required labs a finger poke wouldn't do, it would have to be an IV or a butterfly. The nurse would do the butterfly if it was needed, but if the stick was difficult they could call for an IV consult.

All the guys were asking Claudia to do was to call for IV on nights when they were on call, even if the consult wasn't needed. If the parents were asleep or not paying attention or absentminded, absent altogether would be the easiest, then Claudia could proactively call the consult in. Otherwise — only on the rarest of occasions, rarer than rare — Claudia would have to poke the kids first then claim she couldn't get the stick and needed a consult.

Problem number one came quickly. If one nurse was consistently calling out for help, surely someone in charge would wonder what else she was incompetent at. Claudia couldn't have that. She liked this job and wasn't going to risk getting fired for incompetence.

Problem two: What if there weren't that many kids who fit this bill? The guys had an answer for that. "Claudia, friend, bring us in anyway. It's the night shift, parents sleep. No one has to know."

"Nope, no way. That would never work. And, oh my God, that's immoral, guys!"

Claudia protested with a level of disgust so strong the guys almost felt bad, but their own convictions were warring with Claudia's morals on the battlefield of children's veins.

Again, they played on the future need of rockstar vein pokers. A few extra pokes wouldn't be so bad in the grand scheme of things, but actually there was one problem. "If we come in for an 'unofficial' consult, we won't be able to gear up from the supply closet. It's not an actual issue, but we figured we'd tell you ahead of time, before you start asking."

Richard spoke with the surety of a professor at large. Claudia, a simple schoolgirl who didn't yet get it.

"Well, where in the world will you get what you need?"

Claudia's eyes were wide, so wide Richard thought if he tried he could see halfway around the orb itself.

The solution was simple, my dear. They would sneak out what they could and reuse it as much as needed. They would sanitize it themselves. The studies all showed what was fine to use on medical equipment, even intravenous equipment. This wasn't the 70s. There were actual studies now. It'd be fine. Plus, these kids were getting labs already, so if something showed up, they'd get treated and be fine. How many times could you reuse needles? Why, over and over again, or course. Clot risk, schmott risk, Claudia dear.

On and on they went, around and around the logistical minefield playing on their friend's sense of friendship and kinship. With friends like these, who needed serial killers?

The first death was two weeks after the experiments began. "Coincidence," both friends claimed when Claudia told them after her shift.

After the second, Claudia came to them nearly hyperventilating. "Wait for the lab results. They'll show it was something else entirely."

The third came announced with a white patch-faced girl mid-anxiety attack. "Watch the autopsy show no sign of any foul play. You'll see. The greater good will be accomplished."

Time after time, there were no calls for inquiry because of lab results or autopsy reports. Sick kids were dying, but reasons could be plentiful. The word Claudia heard most, clotting, could be from medication complications, bedrest, steroids, lots of things that weren't overused needles.

Why would anyone be looking for overused needles anyway? There was nothing on the chart to suggest that was in the realm of possibility, but she knew. She would go home and do her own google searches. Read her own medical journals.

Overuse of a needle could result in microscopic breakdown of the needle, which could tear the walls of the veins, which could lead to clot risks. Clots could do damage in grown bodies. Clots were killing in small ones. But surely it was all coincidental, until it wasn't.

They were coming now. Someone suspected, maybe even someone knew.

Claudia, Edward, and Richard sat in Tom's room, Claudia still livid, her fury not resigning. Not at all.

Sensing the heat coming off Claudia like a chemical bomb about to explode, Richard spoke, "Tom and Krystal will be here soon, surely. Once they finally show up, let's cut the meeting short and go beat the bushes a little bit, get ahead of the storm. It's only a couple of docs. Convince them nothing is wrong, and we all go home and get some sleep."

Claudia was not convinced. Something was wrong. Something had been wrong and was still wrong. She knew it and knew they knew it, even if they still wouldn't admit it.

Edward moved to the space between his friends and reached for a hand from each of them. Edward was strong, tough, even feared, but that fierceness was felt differently with his friends. He was a protector, and with him they felt safe.

"Remember what Krystal talked about at the last meeting? No man knows the day or hour? Well, we can know the season, and this is the season of harvest. We are the harvesters. We're a team, together. We can't forget that."

Claudia looked at her two friends, unsure of what Edward meant. By the look on their faces, it appeared they knew, so she smiled and let it go.

Edward extended a hand to Richard and Claudia, who met his with theirs, and they vowed to make it through the day, together. Then things could change, maybe even back to the way they had been before the pact.

27

Tom was standing under fluorescent lights in the cold morgue, breathing the moist air and looking at the closed door of the steel refrigeration unit that was no longer empty. The light reflected off of the door and into the little man's eyes. He grimaced and turned away, rubbing the spots out of his eyes. Little did he know that as he was closing the door on another young life, the skull of Lila Collins was opening in a bathroom three hallways away.

Tom started toward the door of the room of tile and steel before turning back to the little door. His instructions when learning the morgue transport job had been to always lock the doors that held new bodies. They had to protect the dead until the time of pickup by either the medical examiner or one of the town funeral parlors. When his narrow eyes beheld the lock in the handle of the steel door, Tom had a flash of a frightening memory shine behind his eyes.

Had he turned the lock in the elevator back to L1 before bringing the corpse to the morgue? Surely he had, but poor Tom couldn't remember for sure. He thought of the meeting happening this morning in his room. It was possible he left it open for the nurses, but surely not, since he had made his new friends keys of their very own. The only new keys made for the elevator basement switch in decades.

Tom looked at his watch. He hated to make his friends wait. He lived for so long without the sort of friends who came willingly and treated him with kindness. Was anything worth the choice to spend more time apart than was totally needed? It was with great displeasure and duress that Tom made the decision to run back to the elevator and double-check. After all, if the wrong people came to visit, they could be the kind of friends Tom had in the cornfield of his childhood. While he missed those friends, he did not miss the scars they gave them.

Tom hadn't run since high school, the last time he saw his cornfield friends. Tom thought about those friends intermingling with his new friends. Tom ran.

***

Upstairs, Addison left the office where Indy was now looking over the time logs of night IV staff. She took one last glance through the crack in the door at her coworker and friend and allowed the door to close.

She stopped in the restroom with the realization that the sudden pain in her bladder meant she had gone the entire morning without relieving herself. If she wasn't careful, she'd end up with a bladder infection, and wasn't that just what the doctor ordered after this crazy, messed-up day? She wondered aloud whether anything could be worse than that.

Drying her freshly washed hands, Addison backed out of the door and started toward the staff elevator. She was heading in the direction of the offices by the imaging lab on the lower level. There was an administrator with an office there who could have valuable insight into the IV team. Doctor Collins had made introductions for her team with doctors in positions of oversight in various departments in the hospital for times like these. "In times of hardship, it's always good to have wise counsel available." Addison was grateful for the leadership Lila gave her and fully intended to utilize it.

She entered the elevator and pressed the button for LL. She didn't notice the switch marked L2.

***

Downstairs, Tom got to the elevator moving as fast as his little legs could move and pressed the call button. He hoped to switch the call back to L1, if needed, and run to the meeting before his friends left his room. What was the point of a secret room if you couldn't enjoy it with your friends? It was the fort he always wanted with the best friends he could have asked for.

As the elevator approached, Tom heard the faint sound of his phone going off in the distance. He instinctively grabbed for his pocket and found it empty. Tom began to pat himself down like an officer in a traffic stop that was beginning to go wrong. Finding no source for the ringing sound he shouted the type of swear word that would make Joey proud. "Son of a biscuit! Where'd I leave it?"

The morgue? The bathroom? He knew he had it when he got downstairs, but he could not account for its whereabouts now. He knew he could leave it and let the sounds of Lynyrd Skynyrd — "Sweet Home Alabama," a sweet home here indeed — ring out in the silence, but what if it was one of his friends? Oh, what if it was the chaplain? Once again, this time while the coming elevator was midway from the fifth floor to L2, Tom ran.

Minutes later, the only evidence of Tom being the skid marks in the dust on the ground, the doors opened, their light illuminating the many layers of dusty footprints as well as crusty old animal droppings where the wall met the floor. Addison looked outside the elevator doors like she was looking into a dream she had never experienced. Was she even still in the hospital? It looked like the version of Franklin Children's

Hospital that would exist within the Upside Down back in Hawkins, Indiana.

She looked again at the call button, LL. That was indeed the same button she had pressed hundreds of times before. It always led her to the familiar setting of the emergency room. Today, though... she simply did not know.

Addison stepped out of the elevator and looked left down the dark hall, with its dirty wood floor and rough plastic-paneled walls, then right at a near mirror of the left with perhaps fewer of the overhead single fixtures working than on the left. The doors closed softly behind her. Did the hospital have a basement she didn't know about? She took one step, then another, her eyes adjusting to the darkness and her steps mingling with Tom's. If you didn't know better, one look at their steps in the dust, and you'd think maybe they were dancing.

***

Tom had reached the morgue in record time, record for Tom, and grabbed the phone from the workstation bench in the middle of the open room. Looking at the screen through spider web cracking on the glass, Tom did not have the surest hands in the hospital. He thought for a fleeting moment to return the call from his ailing, elderly mother before remembering why his lungs were burning alongside the stitch in both sides. He needed to get to the elevator quickly.

He then remembered the strip of latex-free polyester in the pocket of his dirty blue pants. He could feel it burning a hole in the pocket of pants that needed no new holes. It would be a detour to get to his room, and he may get distracted and forget the elevator entirely, but he had to get to his closet.

After sliding to power off his phone, Tom ran, or what he considered running anyway. To an all-seeing eye, Tom would be mildly hastily meandering through the hall, but to Tom he was moving at break-neck speed. He entered the room he called home to find it empty. The part of him that was devastated was overshadowed by the part that was relieved to have a free shot to the closet without having to explain. Maybe he beat his friends there after all, which meant he still had time to get to the elevator. So, once more, Tom "ran."

He thought often about the darkness levels in the basement, which he considered his own private quarters. Casa de Tom, if you please. He thought of going to the local Costco or Sam's Club and getting a few cases of light bulbs — even LED's perhaps, for their longer life and energy efficacy — with which to brighten up his hallways, but he never did. Truth be told, Tom liked living in the darkened halls. The fewer people who could see you, the less they had to use against you. That was the lesson of Tom's life up until now.

When finally he reached the elevator, Tom again pressed the call button.

When Tom was given his first job on the transport team twenty years ago, he did his job with all the gusto of a man on a mission. A mission to move. Within a year, everyone knew who Tom was. Within ten, everyone forgot, or wanted to.

Tom said he never noticed, but he did. When the position at the top of the transport unit came available, Tom was the only one with experience who actually wanted the job. When he mentioned in his interview that he wanted to manage the team but take all the deceased transports personally, he was given the job. What better way to give everyone a break from Tom while keeping his work ethic in hand for the beneficiary of the hospital patients than to give him a raise and a job that kept him in the basement half the time.

No one went into the basement. That was ten years after the last office moved out of the basement level, and that was ten years ago.

When Tom was given a key to switch the elevator from L1 to L2, no one realized it was the only key still in existence. Maintenance tried for months to get Tom to give them a copy so they could at least try to keep up the level in case admin would want to give a tour or bring in an architect to renovate the space, but they never got their key and after a time stopped trying. It was Tom's baby until someone forced his hand.

Tom's hand was never forced. New keys had finally been made two months ago when his new friends, the nice male nurse, the male nurse who talked nice but had evil in his eyes, the girl with the two-toned face, and the curvy brown chaplain, all wanted to be Tom's friends, and he raced to make them keys. But only if they'd switch off the level when stepping off of whichever elevator they used to ride down. No one else could know. He didn't want to get in trouble and had it too good. Now Tom turned the key back to L1 and returned to his room.

Back to where his friends should be by now.

***

Addison crept through the dark, dirty basement. She traced the tops of moldings and shelves and stared at the amount of dust her finger would pick up with all the disgust of a mother in her teenage daughter's bedroom right before a stern talking to about cleanliness. It was next to godliness. This place must have been vacant for a very long time, and very far from godliness.

Turn after turn, corridor after corridor, room after room, Addison felt increasingly lost, like she was trapped in one of the pyramids of the kings. Lost within the maze of tunnels meant to trap grave robbers looking for the final resting place of the pharaoh and the riches entombed with him.

So many rooms that were once offices or operating rooms in a bygone era - or three - now existed only as storage rooms, themselves having not been touched by outside hands in years.

Addison heard a sound break through the silence. She had thought she heard music faintly in the distance when she first got off the elevator but that had stopped with her first steps, something traveling through the ductwork perhaps. Then she believed she heard the familiar ding of the elevator door, but had since heard no sounds of humanity, the ding coming from the recesses of her mind like phantom phone vibrations in her jean pockets when buzzing flip phones were a thing in her teens. Now this, a different sound. A door closing or something dropping. She was sure of it coming from up ahead.

She reached yet another turn in the hall, its walls intermittently containing doors closed and locked all in the darkness of the hall with one singular light flashing away in the center of the long hall. Addison tried the handles of the doors, relieved with each locked response, until seeing one at the end of the hall, up by the next junction, slightly ajar.

She pushed the door open, the bottom of the door hitting a fallen rolling cart leaning cockeyed on three legs, one had gone missing. Oof, this place was decrepit. What a sorry shadow of what the hospital once was. No wonder no one came down here. It would take a major renovation project to get the forgotten level up to the relative newness of the upstairs.

She pushed ahead into the room and flicked the switch on the wall in vain. She knew from the prior expired lights in the halls and rooms she had seen to this point that it wouldn't turn on anything, but when she flicked the switch up a loud *POP* went off above her as the old light. Decades old? Older than Addison herself? The bang startled Addison, making her appreciate the trip to the bathroom she took before coming down here, or who knew whether she'd still have dry panties right now.

Gradually, she pressed on into the room, her eyes adjusting to the darkness. Surrounding her were old desks, a matching metal cart like the one in the doorway, and a few old metal shelving units with boxes and old trays on its shelves.

Addison crept closer to the shelving unit to her left and looked at the tray in front of her. Were those...blood collection vials? The small ones the nurses would use for the smaller samples needed for labs? Why were there so many, and...were they used?

Addison picked up one of the vials. Her eyes were adjusting to the darkness after being down here for several minutes now, but the label on the vial was still hard to read. She reached for her phone — *Dummy, you've had a flashlight this whole time. Wake up* — and turned on the light.

Devyn Samuels. That name was familiar. She picked up another vial. Emerson Paige. That was familiar too. Oh God, oh GOD, these kids died recently. Addison's heart started to race in her chest. Her breath coming in gulping waves she picked up vial after vial, each containing a label with the name of one of the children from the hospital who had died in the last five months.

She looked to her right and saw another shelf. As she approached her breath, a moment ago a storm of uncontrollable gale forces, stopped at the sight of a box labeled "Weary Sojourner Mission."

She opened the box, looked inside, and immediately turned and vomited on the floor of the dark room. The box brought the realization that she had stepped into her worst imaginable horrors. It was filled with vials the same as the ones on the shelf, the ones of souvenirs of dead children. What then were these?

To her left, she saw several sitting on a third shelf. Her hands quaking, she lifted one and saw the name of a nurse she recently learned, Richard Mercier. She saw Richard's name on the list of IV unit members. Next to it the name would have made her vomit if she hadn't already. The chaplain, Krystal Jenkins.

Behind her, she heard the sound of glass breaking. A vial had fallen and shattered on the ground. If she had been able to read its label, she would have seen the name Chloe Miller on a vial that had not yet made its way to its resting place among the others..

However, before she could turn fully around, she was struck in her left temple by a force carrying the seeming mass of all humanity behind it. Addison McCray spun like a rag doll in a tornado, her head whipping at a speed beyond that of her body, her neck fracturing at the force. On the ground and unable to move, she lifted only her eyes at the source of the great hit that had felled her and saw a man holding a pipe.

She heard a voice from the end of a long open tunnel echo in the distance. "I really wish you wouldn't have come here, but as the lightning cometh out of the east... Hmph, I guess it is time after all."

He swung the pipe again at her head, and the lights went out for the final time for Addison McCray.

28

Eventually, Tom entered his room, his home, and greeted his friends. His smile faded when he saw they were not all there. The chaplain hadn't yet arrived, and only two nurses were present.

Tom was startled by a hand on his shoulder. He felt a familiar squeeze, fingers that dug into the soft tissue surrounding Tom's bony shoulder in a way that made him wince, but he said nothing about the pain. From behind him, a voice sounded too friendly to be fully believed.

"Hey, Tom, glad you made it! Tell me, how did that delivery work out this morning?"

Tom was surprised to see Edward come in from behind him. His face asked a question that his mouth did not. Where did Edward come from?

"Went right as the mail, friend. As you'd said it wud."

Tom's wide eyes caught Edward's before dropping to the floor. The transports were getting more frequent, and Tom wasn't sure, but he thought Edward was starting to know they'd happen before they happened.

"Transport? What transport? Did it happen again?" Claudia clasped her hand to her mouth as the tears already swelled to the point of spilling over. "CHLOE? No, Edward…"

Claudia doubled over and collapsed in a heap on the cold floor, clutching her head, and violently sobbing.

29

The way to an elevator with L2 access, if you had a key from Tom, from the office of Chaplain Jenkins was down the hall from the chapel toward the lobby, down the escalator to the lobby, left at the door and down a hall that led toward the main hospital administration offices. It was one of two elevator shafts in the main hospital with access. For anyone but Krystal Jenkins, the walk from chapel to elevator would take three minutes. But Krystal considered herself a people person, meaning that she stopped to talk to people no matter how much of a rush she was in. The retail clerk in the gift shop across from the clerical offices, the greeter at the second-floor welcome desk, the security guard on the escalator, and the greeter at the first-floor lobby help desk all got special, personal greetings from the sweet chaplain on a daily, sometimes hourly, basis.

As she was set to start from the help desk to the hallway that approached the administration offices, Chaplain Jenkins glanced out of the glass doors that led out of the main entrance way of Franklin Children's Hospital and did a double-take when she saw your mother and I collapsing in on each other like dying stars on the concrete bench outside the hospital.

She would have known she was late to the meeting in the basement, but like I said, she was a people person and couldn't help herself. She stood frozen mid-step, not sure which direction to go, but only for a moment. What was the purpose of the job if not to answer the call of a couple in the middle of a breakdown on the worst day of their adult lives? What would be the point of mentoring someone like Father Thomas, another member of the hospital clergy team, with lessons on empathy and the ministry of presence if she wasn't able to drop everything to lean into those things herself?

Chaplain Jenkins pivoted and went toward the all-glass double doors that served as the main entrance to the hospital. The space that formerly housed an atrium had been removed, and now the doors exited directly outside. The walk went ten feet to a semi-circular drive used for drop-off and pickup, each side branching off from the main road. It wasn't ideal, and the newer hospitals would sit back farther from the road, allowing for a full roundabout for easy access, but not this 150-year-old building in this 150-year-old part of town.

On either side of the walk from the drop-off point to the main door were concrete benches, two on each side. One on the left had a new black coat of paint, leaving the others, white paint chipping off to show the bare material underneath, as eyesores waiting to be loved, each with concrete pillars for cigarette butts to get twisted and smashed to their final resting place. The presence of two such stands wasn't enough to keep the edge of the ground from concrete to mulch and grass to be littered with stray used butts. Apparently a building meant for health care was an optimum place for the smokers of the world to unite and gather out front.

We sat in a puddle of ourselves on the first bench to the right. Chaplain Jenkins walked over and sat next to Joey. She brought her hands together in her lap and lowered her chin to her chest, her gaze following suit until she had little choice but to look at the cigarette butts on the ground. She would have had to close her eyes to keep from counting the first dozen, then the second, and so on.

I said, "We went for a walk to clear our heads for a while. We've never been here, ma'am. Not 'here' here, but here...in this situation. We weren't sure what to do or what came next. One of the docs said to take some time, that the clerical stuff can wait til tomorrow, what with autopsies and..." My eyes grew too heavy to remain open. I sighed and continued, "Autopsies and whatever else they're planning to do to our baby."

The chaplain spoke softly, "Winslow, you don't have to say anything. You can—"

"It's okay. I don't... It's fine. We were doing okay and walked a while. We stopped in this little church not too far from here. After a word from the preacher there, we wanted to come back and talk to one of the docs. If there's time, we could go to your meeting later, but really we needed to come tell them something we heard."

"Okay."

Chaplain Jenkins was well versed in that part of the ministry of presence that was allowing the bereaved to talk about whatever wanted to spill from their grieving mouths. Sometimes, Chloe, when given space in the conversation, it was best to do some talking yourself. Not to teach or speak anything of deep meaning, but to give time and space for the one in pain to process what they were feeling. Krystal was good at holding court in the space of allowing time to process.

"I reacquainted with a young man recently. 'Young man...' He's my age, but hey, I'm young too! Not even thirty yet, heyo!" Krystal chuckled to herself. "This young man had something bigger than himself hiding in his eyes from the moment we first met. He had something special. You could tell he was more than the man you were looking at. He had a purpose, a mission you wanted nothing more than to join, to contribute to. Then we got separated and lost touch. Until later on. Met him again here, matter-of-fact.

"Anyways, long story shorter, we'd talk in a group setting about the job. I meet with a couple of nurses here in the hospital on the regular, as you know. This young man had more to his story that he wasn't telling the group. I knew it as well as he did, so I asked him to meet solo, and he agreed.

"Comes from the wrong side of things, had a hard upbringing that affects him. Had some big events happen that left him confused and unsure for a long time. We feel like this is a new lease on life and a chance to lean into what he had been unsure of. He's done some stuff, but who hasn't? He still makes some choices we don't understand, but he means well and wants to do the best he can to fulfill his calling.

"Our solo meetings took a turn, and now, well, you don't want to hear any of that. Point is, this man lost everything a couple times, and he's trying to...not necessarily make things right but keep living so others can make things right, through... I'm rambling. Let me tell you what it all comes down to.

"The sun rises, Millers. May not feel like it, but it rises. Every morning. The good mornings, the bad mornings. And when it does, you gotta move. Forward, backward, whatever. Don't let nobody say backward isn't okay. Sure you don't want it always that way, but movement is movement! It's the sittin' and stayin' that ends us."

Chaplain Jenkins found herself worked up, so she ended the unintended pep talk and resumed her sitting and listening.

"What's his name?"

The question rose softly as if it was a wisp of smoke from the ashes of the pale girl sitting in the middle like the major key of a piano nestled in between its sharp and flat black keys.

Chaplain Jenkins lifted her head and tilted her ear toward the white lump also known as Joey. "What's that, Joey honey?"

"The young man with the rough past who's trying to move forward. He works here? What's his name?"

"Oh that." Krystal lifted her gaze toward the clouds the way a lover does when remembering a forlorn moment stolen in a forbidden moment of time.

She smiled and said, "His name's Edward. Edward Falcone."

30

Silence, thicker than the humidity in a Louisiana summer.

As you can by now imagine, we were suddenly aware. Awakened from their depressed stupor like a foghorn had gone off in our ears. We exchanged side glances with the movement of a pair of mating sloths in the zoo that can hear the lions from across the span of the African-themed habitat.

Very slowly, Joey turned toward the chaplain, who had said the very name given as a warning by old man Creed back at the mission. Something about a "troubled past" seemed to correlate with his warning of "the devil" in the hospital.

The chaplain sat staring off into the sky with a satisfied smile on her face. Joey knew that face. She wore it many times thinking, well, to be frank when she was thinking about her husband when she was alone and feeling the memory of my touch.

I still catch her looking that way. I'm afraid I've allowed this all to take its toll on not only me but on us. I fear that the memory of my touch is coming with more distance than it ever should. But then, that was part of the purpose of all this, wasn't it? To heal the living, even if we couldn't heal those gone, however much we wish we could.

She caught my eyes once again and opened hers as far as they would open, hoping I was receiving the signal she was putting out.

I sat up and cleared my throat, bringing Krystal back to the present.

"Chaplain, thanks for coming out and checking on us. We do need to go find one of Chloe's doctors though. Someone at the mission had a message for her."

Joey stood with me so quickly it was plain she saw a few fleeting spots in her vision. Not so many as to stop her though. There may not be so many available to have made it possible to stop her from completing the task Creed set us on.

"Oh, okay, hun." Krystal stood alongside us, looking startled at our sudden mobility. I'm sure we had shown no sign of doing so since she had walked outside.

"I can go help you find her if you—"

"No, that's okay." I stopped her before she got all her words out. I knew when I did that I needed to slow down.

"I'm sure you're a busy woman, with so many hurting inside here. We can handle it. You've done so much already. Thank you."

"Okay, well, you know I'm always here if you need me."

Krystal began to walk inside in front of your now upright and alert parents then stopped and turned back to Joey.

"What was the name of that church you said you stopped at? I'm curious if I know it."

Joey's face hardened. She didn't like the follow-up Columbo question.

"Wayside Sojourner Mission. On the corner of Pine and York."

She stared into Krystal's eyes, searching for meaning behind her reaction to the name of the church. She had to know if there was more there or if this was a dead end.

"Wayside? Old man Creed, probably?" Krystal's face shifted through emotions as fast as she could understand one and control it toward another.

"Well, darlin', y'all better go and find your doctor. Tell her whatever it is you need. I do have a meeting to get to. Don't forget my offer later, four o'clock. I'll watch for you both. Maybe you can bring the doctors too."

Joey and Krystal locked onto each other's eyes, each wondering what the other knew and what they thought they knew. The collective heartbeats racing in the space in front of the main doors to the hospital stood a chance to shatter the glass doors if they didn't break and go their separate ways.

Which we did. Each was on a mission to let it be known that each knew something about the other that neither thought would become known.

31

Downstairs, Edward had started toward Claudia when Richard put his hand on Edward's chest and pushed him back.

"Stay there, Edward. I've got her."

He bent down on one knee by the girl he had first seen at the hospital job fair back in August, the one whose protective shield had recently begun to come down enough to be comfortable around the group with nothing covering her face, and put his arm around her hunched shoulders. He could still smell the coconut-scented conditioner she had washed into her hair yesterday afternoon.

"Claudia, it's..."

She squirmed and shook his hand off of her shoulder as though she had felt the slither of a snake making its unwelcome appearance across the top of her scrubs.

"No! Don't you tell me it's alright, Richard! You don't get to do that!"

Claudia's eyes gave the appearance of someone both hurt and betrayed, widening farther still with each passing moment as the fear of the possibilities of what would come next grew.

Richard froze and held his hands out to show to Claudia he was both innocent and harmless. Claudia was buying neither.

Her eyes rapidly shifted from man to man to Tom. An onlooker may have wondered what Claudia was having withdrawals from.

"You will all stay where you are. I need answers. You promised me the consults were harmless. Even with the rash of deaths, which I should've seen and taken to the authorities, but I didn't, and that's on me, but you assured me..." Claudia was trying with the might of a thousand men to not break down into full hysterics. "You assured me it would stop. But look at you. You know what's going on. You know what you've kept to yourselves. Edward, Krystal's on her way down here. You know she is. You better talk fast."

Tom had been standing like a chameleon trying to blend into the wall until the mention of the chaplain's name. That brought beads of sweat to his palms and saliva to his tongue. His pheromones were going into overdrive as sweat ran through his thinning black hair, cutting lines across his forehead. The room filled with his silent desires for the curvy, braided, midnight goddess who always knew how to smile at ol' Tom.

The point he was getting stuck on, and didn't know quite how to verbalize yet, was why Edward would need to finish talking before she arrived. Oh yes, arrived in *his* home. For a moment, the world faded away, evaporating from his vision like vapor on a summer's day.

32

We knew we had to get to Doctor Collins and her team as quickly as possible.

We didn't know why, but something was wrong. This morning our only child, our first-born baby girl, had suddenly died. You had been sick but were getting better. Doctor Collins and her team had begun to present the idea of going home before passing out of the blue.

The good doctor had sat both with us and her team of doctors while questioning us about the nature of your final night alive in the hospital. The mention of the IV consult had noticeably upset her and her team, and though we pressed about the specifics, they gave no details as to why they were so intrigued.

At the mission down the street, the old pastor Creed gave us a powerfully vague warning about the devil being in the hospital. According to Creed, the devil was Edward Falcone, who the chaplain had named as a young nurse with a troubled past who was trying to keep moving forward, a young man she appeared to think of in a romantic way. If there was a connection between this troubled nurse and your final night...

We began to walk faster as we went through the possibilities in our minds.

33

Indy sat at the desk she shared with her best friend in the world, Addison McCray. It was at this desk they spent countless hours figuring out the secrets of medicine and life. They shared every detail of the others' life story and had planned to share a part in each other's lives for as long as they lived, until long past the time they'd spend as little gray-headed ladies shuffling the halls of the fifth-floor rocking babies and advising the new doctors and nurses.

Early retirement wasn't something they were looking for. They loved it there. They loved the job and loved doing it together. They were grateful for Lila Collins for including them on her team and were fully intent on keeping it together for decades, helping the world one sick kiddo at a time.

That day she was pouring over the schedule logs for the IV team from over the previous five months, looking for anyone working on the dates Indy had written down as the dates Nurse Claudia O'Dell worked.

There were several names that popped up intermittently on the page. The IV team didn't always work the full twelve-hour night shift, but there were two who stood out for the listed dates — Edward Falcone and Richard Mercier.

Falcone had worked for the hospital for several years. According to his file, he was a member of the IV team at its inception three years ago.

Richard was much newer, his record only showing eight months on file for his employment here.

What Indy found interesting was that while most IV team members had intermittent shifts that overlapped with the shift worked by Claudia O'Dell, some combination of Edward, Richard, or Edward and Richard were on call every night Claudia worked for the last six months.

Indy was deep in thought processing that information when a knock on her door startled her.

34

Edward told Tom to sit down. Claudia sat in the corner tucked into a ball next to the only other door in the room, a closet filled with Tom's entire life gathered in boxes piled six feet high. She spotted a small black and white stuffed penguin and, pulling it out of the closet, held it close to her chest. No one in the room knew about the patch on her belly, the one that matched her face, but if they did, they'd be able to note the irony of the two-toned penguin nestled next to the two-toned Claudia.

Tom whispered under his breath as he took his seat in the opposing corner on a small stool he found in the stone walled room adjacent to the morgue, the room with the old cremation oven dug into the old gray stone walls, low enough that only he could hear himself — not that it was on purpose. He was simply afraid of the atmosphere in the room. "Mr. Penguin, if you only knew how lucky you were right now."

Tom noticed the absence of eyes looking in his direction and decided to finish the thought in his mind anyway.

"Only the chaplain would be a better place to nuzzle your head on a day like today."

Richard shifted his weight in his spot where he had knelt by Claudia until he sat cross legged on the floor. He knew the extent of the situation he had gotten himself in, at least he thought he did, at least ninety percent or better anyway, but he did not know, could not know, exactly what Edward was going to finally confess to Claudia.

Richard was absolutely sure the chaplain didn't know. In all their meetings together, from when it was the four of them until it was the five of them, he had never known Edward to say much at all in a forthcoming way to the chaplain. It seemed he didn't want to let the chaplain into his life much at all.

Edward looked around the room and addressed his friends, the group he had spent the majority of his time with over the last several months.

Everyone except the chaplain, with whom he had spent the majority of his time away from the group with, a fact the group did not know.

35

Indiana Powell lifted her glasses from her nose and set them to rest on her headband so she could rub her eyes, tired from screens and forms filled with names and numbers, as she stood from her desk chair. The office was small, freshman dorm room small. Lila could put a desk in the master closet in her house and have more legroom than this office. But still the door knock rapped a second time before Indy could get to it.

She opened the door. The small glass window was frosted, and she hated never knowing who was on the other side of the door. We had to be a sight for sore eyes standing there exhausted as though we had run a marathon or two already that day. Emotionally, we had. The day had not been kind to us, and to Indy it looked like we had been running, crying, or both. Indy stepped to the side and motioned us into the tight room.

"Come in, guys. You're in luck. There are exactly three chairs in here, and I'm alone at—"

"Do you know Edward Falcone?"

Joey interrupted the small, spectacled doctor before she could finish her invitation.

A look of shock spread across Indy's face. It had taken her and Addison all morning and several cumulative hours to get the name Edward Falcone revealed in this case, but here were the grieving parents bringing his name to the doctor. Maybe they should've included us instead of sending us away.

"How do you know about Edward Falcone? What have you two been up to this morning?"

Your mother and I filled Indy in on our visit to the cafeteria. We talked about the Weary Sojourner Mission and old man Creed's warning about the devil of Franklin Children's Hospital, Edward Falcone. We casually blew by our breakdown in front of the hospital on our way to telling about the conversation with Chaplain Jenkins, the insinuation of a relationship with someone in the hospital that was around her age who had a troubled past, Edward Falcone — so in love she didn't think to omit his name to the grieving couple — and the reaction she had at the mention of the mission and conversation with old man Creed.

"So that's where we are. I'm guessing from the lack of color on your face that we connected some dots for you. How about doing the same and talking us through what you know," Joey said to Indy with enough surety that the conversation to this point felt like the inverse of the conversations usually held between doctor and parents within the walls of the hospital.

"I don't know that you need to be this far—"

"Take off the kid gloves and be real with us!"

I lost my cool and interrupted Indiana. I didn't feel great about it, but it happened.

"We're adults here too, doctor. Yes, we lost our daughter this morning, and maybe we should be curled in a ball down in the chapel or the parking garage or the bar down the street, but we're not. We're here. Doctor Collins told us to meet back up with you guys later, and we're here and we know stuff, and we're pretty sure there's stuff you can tell us too. Ten minutes ago, we were a mess, and now we're here, doing this. Let us help you, and if something is wrong here then maybe, we can help you bring it out."

A tear formed in the corner of Indy's eye. "You're right. Both of you. This is a terrible day full of terrible things. I wish I could take it all away for you but I can't. If you need to be in this right now, I'll be in it with you."

She showed us the shift logs for the nursing staff they used to find Claudia O'Dell, followed by the shift logs for the IV team they cross examined with the knowledge of Claudia's night shifts to single out Richard Mercier and Edward Falcone. Before she could edit herself — she was on a roll now, all downhill and picking up speed — she even laid out her and Addison's theory that someone from the IV team, likely Richard or Edward, was using some nurse from the night shift, likely Claudia, to get into the rooms of sick kids to do unofficial sticks and blood draws, and something about those sticks had been harming kids, perhaps leaving a wake of deaths behind them.

That was the line, and Indy crossed it.

"Deaths, plural? You think this is bigger than Chloe? How is that possible?"

Joey's jaw was on the floor, and my head was firmly in his hands, shaking while I moaned to myself in an audible drone that I'm sure made me sound like an AM radio caught between stations.

Indy suddenly realized, after looking up from the stack of papers to the occupants of the chairs in her office, the couple who were not Lila and Indy but rather a pair of parents who just lost their daughter, that she had gotten caught up in the gravity of the situation and said more than she should.

"Look, there have been several deaths in the wings of the hospital over the last few months, more than usual but not so many more that anyone beyond Lila, Doctor Collins, has been suspicious. But we think this may be something bigger than... It may be big, and we need to figure it out. We didn't know if we'd even get this far, but it looks like, between what Addison and I have here and what you may have gotten from that preacher, we may be onto something. I'm not sure where Lila and Addison are, but if you're in, I'm in. We'll find them and figure this out."

As your mother and I sat processing what we had just heard, a sound broke through the silence from the direction of Addison's Macbook, sitting open on the desk behind Indy.

Indy sighed dramatically.

She rolled her eyes at herself. "Girl, get your heart rate in check so this thing can stop going off. This is the third time in half an hour. Cleansing breaths."

She spoke aloud to Addison in an Addison-less room while reaching to turn off the notification on the Macbook. It wasn't the first time, and if Addison could've figured out how she got her smartphone notifications to go to her Macbook, she would have turned it back off.

When Indy saw the gray box on the screen, she froze. Her eyes grew wide, her breath dropped to a dangerously shallow rattle, and her heart rate soared. If she had a smartwatch, it would have pinged the alert she had anticipated seeing on Addison's computer, the one she usually saw multiple times a week. "Heart Rate High."

Instead the words in the gray box read, "S.O.S. Fall Detection." It was followed by another alert ping and another new notification box while Indy sat frozen in her chair, "Low heart rate." Each box had multiple boxes behind them. Had she been so into her work that she didn't hear any of them until now? Indy's heart dropped into her stomach, and she felt the color leave her face.

If Indiana Powell had a smartwatch of her own, the alarm would be sounding again, "Heart Rate Dangerously High. Girl, chill." She thought her heart might be about to burst. Something bad had happened to Addison.

While she sat staring at the boxes on the screen of Addison's computer, a knock on her door yet again startled her back to the present. The door opened, and her eyes fell first on a gun holstered against crisp pressed black slacks, then up to a gold badge, then farther up to a face she recognized but wasn't sure why. The world was spinning. People didn't look like themselves when they were spinning.

The man with the badge and gun opened his mustached mouth and spoke, "Hi, I'm looking for Lila Collins. My name is Officer Arthur L. White. Maybe Lila's mentioned me? She calls me Whitey."

It took Whitey repeating himself three times before Indy heard his question. She was thinking about her friend.

36

Chloe, a few days after April 18th, we got an anonymous letter in the mail, though by now it's clear who sent it. Allow me to copy it down here, it sets the table for what's coming.

```
Dear Miller family,
You must have lots of questions
following what happened in the hospital
basement. To be honest, I do too. I feel
like there is information you should
have as you work through and process
everything. I know I'll be thinking
about it for the rest of my life.
Not long before you arrived in the
basement, Edward Falcone gave what I can
only describe as his "final sermon." I
thought I knew Edward. I called him a
friend, but I guess he was good at hiding
his true self. If you want to know what
```

I think, I think Edward Falcone was a mask. Maybe not for all of his life, but at some point it became that way. A mask worn by… I shouldn't try to inform you. Make your own judgments. I'll do the best I can to transcribe them exactly as he said them. God above knows I'll never forget them. They're burned in my mind, etched into the very folds of my brain.

They will color in the missing pieces of what happened. I hope you can find the answers you need in them.

My friends, fourteen-year-old Edward Falcone lived in a house at the end of a cul de sac outside of the city.

My mother had not worked outside the home for as long as I had been aware of things like "work" and "stay at home moms." When I was in the fifth grade at Saint Francis Elementary, I overheard my homeroom teacher, Ms Ferber, a lovely lady with horned-rim glasses who always wore long dresses and smelled like coffee and flowers, talking to the guidance counselor about my home life.

To tell you the truth, I had felt pretty special that people as important as teachers and counselors would talk about my life outside of school while they were at school. That conversation was the first time I had heard the word "depression." It was the first time I heard postpartum too, but it was a strange enough word that I didn't remember it well enough to think about later.

My father had always worked outside the home. It was a simple fact of our family, a part of the fabric of our tapestry. My father would leave the house before I ever got up and began moving. Before Cheerios and Sesame Street, before Super Grover was ever on the scene, later when I entered school before the bus stop, before toaster strudel, my father was long gone. It was simply how my world worked.

That fact held true until a random day midway through one summer's break when my mother got a phone call sometime after lunch. Not one random day, a Thursday. Not sometime, 12:32 p.m. I can see the numbers on the microwave clock still, fifteen years later when I close my eyes. More so even than the death of my father four years beyond that, the accident was a juncture in time for my life, beyond which nothing was the same.

When we were able to bring my father home from the hospital two months later, everything had changed. The family dynamic was off. The household didn't run the same at all. I was forced to grow up at fourteen years old at a rate most in this century wouldn't experience for another four years. This wasn't 1944 or 1776—it was 2009, when a fourteen-year-old boy in America should be able to be simply a fourteen-year-old boy.

Through it all, for my mother and for my father, I picked up my big-boy pants and carried on. My father's lawyer, a shyster in poorly fitted suits purchased from the discount rack in the secondhand store and whose ties seemed to all have mustard stains under the clip, got him a settlement check for his injury that should've provided for the family for years to come. What it didn't provide for was the new drinking habit my father picked up along with his new opioid prescription habit.

Watching her husband in bed instead of going to work for the first time since she had known him, watching him wash his pills down with a beer, then with beers, then with vodka with the beers filling the interim between dose times, took a toll on my sweet mother. Watching her baby boy stay home when school resumed in the fall and watching him bike to his job in town instead of board the bus to freshman year broke the back of the camel that had been weighing her down in the depression she had fought since after I was born.

In the months leading to my fifteenth birthday, I would leave in the morning to bike to the local Speedway gas station, and when I would return home in the afternoon, I would walk through the door to the sounds of my father yelling obscenities in the back bedroom, fueled by his favorite cocktail of vodka and a handful of Vicodin, and the sight of my mother in the recliner in the living room zoned out in front of Dr. Phil. What a sight, friends. I would often think to myself that if any family deserved to be on Dr. Phil, it was this one.

At fifteen years old, the Falcone family lived in the homeless shelter on the ground level of the old National Bank building.

One evening back at home, one of the final days in the little house at the end of the cul de sac, I answered a knock on the door to find another middle-aged man in another poorly fitted suit and tie. His tie had a pale-yellow stain front and center between one of the blue and red stripes that I thought was either leftover from the man's lunch or a grease spill of whatever generic hair tonic he used to get that slicked back look the TV preachers my mother used to watch always had. Spotted ties seemed to be an omen for our family. The man informed me over the yells from the back bedroom and the way-too-loud Jeopardy episode my mother was staring at but not watching that my father's bank account had run dry, and there was no longer any money to pay the housing costs, the mortgage, the utilities, nothing. Within a week, the three of us were on the street and an auction for the belongings in the house was being advertised on every telephone pole and street corner in a five-mile radius.

As it happened, I had heard about the homeless shelter from an elderly man who came to the Speedway three weeks earlier driving a 1991 Mercury Marquis, who could forget such a wood-paneled marvel of a thing, who took one look at the teenage boy pretending in a man's world and thought there was a pretty good chance he was homeless. Only a few weeks off, pretty good guess, mister. Try that discernment at the county fair and win a stuffed Yogi Bear, complete with *pic-a-nic* basket. Ha.

I drove my parents like a cowboy on a cattle drive through the streets of town until we were walking through the doors of the shelter, tails tucked between our legs like the ancient Isrealites seeking food and asylum in pagan Egypt. My father spent his days sleeping and his nights going through withdrawals from the booze and pills he no longer had the funds to procure while my mother sat idly by not knowing which day of the week it was or why her house looked like the inside of an old bank. Only, where were the tellers, and what was that smell?

To get away from the sights, sounds, and smells of the shelter, I would spend my days at the Speedway. I kept my week's pay, always given in cash from

Red, the owner, who thought a little tax evasion was his best gift to give a young homeless boy, in a plastic zipper bag at the bottom of the backpack I had brought as my only reminder of home. One evening, I almost lost that backpack in an incident that forced me to grow up the rest of the way. Apparently, I had more to go through but didn't know it at the time, until there was no more childhood left in a life that had all but snuffed it out over the last year.

I was walking back to the shelter from my job at the Speedway. It was two miles from the old downtown building and I would have preferred to take my old silver Redline bicycle, a relic of a better time that I had snuck — snuck being a relative term since it was difficult to sneak on a bicycle with Wade Boggs baseball cards clipped to the spokes — out of the yard behind the house before the property had been closed on by the bank, so I could get back sooner, but that had been stolen and stripped for parts the week prior. I wasn't sure, but I thought he saw one of the rims, without its tire, leaning bent on the side of a parking meter near the corner of Candlearia and Monroe, the tattered Upper Deck card stuck between two wire spokes, the clothespin long gone.

I would walk at what I heard referred to as Edward Pace most days, Edward Pace being similar to Hawaiian time, I suppose. You get there when you get there. That was alright with me. I had my backpack on and was running through the events of the day. Not the actual events of my real day, mind you, but the events of the day had my life turned out anything close to normal. In that day, I had spent my time before class started by kicking a hacky sack around with my stoner buddies. I could smell the weed wafting off their breath. Making out with my girlfriend between third and fourth period, I could taste the strawberry lip gloss on my tongue, and scoring a hat trick during soccer practice, I could feel the sting on my legs from sliding across the rough-cut grass on the school's practice field.

It was a good, solid day that came screeching to a halt when I looked ahead of me and saw two men in their… Thirties? Twenties? Who could tell? They were coming across the road up ahead, right in position to intercept me and my backpack between the taxi parked by the covered meter ahead and the tinted glass storefront of the King's Ransom pawn shop. I began to veer off to my left and into the street before having to come back to my right when the two men ahead had matched my trajectory.

When I was thirteen, my father had taken me into the backyard to teach me a lesson on how to take care of myself. He had taught me how to throw a punch — thumb on the outside, break their nose not your thumb — back when I was eight, and the bully on the playground kept tripping me in the mud by the left foul line of the makeshift baseball field beyond the swings.

At thirteen life's problems that could be solved with violence were often more intricate, and he thought I should know. I remembered the lesson while approaching the two men. "If you have to fight your way through a crowd, Edward, you find the guy closest to you and take him out before anything else can happen. Boom, now you have fair numbers."

I thought about that. I could hear the gravel in my father's voice that came from years of drywall dust and no mask, which were for superheroes and cowards, son, and if the hero needed the mask, he was probably a coward.

The men looked bigger than me from a distance. Up close, they were not. I balled up my fists, and I swear to you I saw them start to laugh when I did so. The men spread out, putting distance between themselves to better corner me between them. It was a smart tactic, but the shorter man, the one in the

Dodger hat, made a mistake. He started speeding up. He was five steps closer to me than the taller guy in the red and black New World Order shirt. I saw one opportunity to get off that street with both my backpack and my health. When Dodger Hat looked to his right to check on his buddy, I launched my right hand at the side of the man's face and put every ounce of my roughly one hundred and thirty-five pound frame behind it. When the fist struck the man between his temple and his ear, his consciousness didn't stand a chance. He was a speed bump on the sidewalk before he had time to tell his friend to speed up.

The force of the leap fist-first through the man's face sent me careening off balance into the taxi. I rolled to my right and looked up at New World Order Shirt, who was temporarily rather statuesque looking at his unconscious friend. My shin found the frozen man's favorite appendage and temporarily made the man an Irish tenor. Pavarotti, who?

I ran as fast as I had ever run. I felt myself losing speed and ducked into the first door I came to. I knelt over, grabbing my knees, and tried to force oxygen back into my body so I could keep moving toward the shelter. Gradually, I sat on the floor and put my head between my knees so the dark spots would hopefully go away. When I looked up, I saw I was in some sort of church building. An older man in a roman collar was watching me. I thought I saw a smile on the man's face.

I began to stammer, "Hey… Hi, sorry, I uh…"

"You got in a fight and had to stop to catch your breath?"

The old man had his right eyebrow in the air and was holding a tray of some sort.

I responded, "Uh, yeah. How'd you know that?"

I leaned back on my arms as I responded to the older man while wondering what had given me away. I had heard tales of preachers who knew things about people from my mother and her TV preachers, but my father always said if they knew so much about people then why did they always have a team of their own people with them moving around the room, and why did they insist you close your eyes while they talked about you? 'It's all sleight of hand. They don't get paid as much as Copperfield, boy.'

"Your knuckles are bleedin'. Right hand too. If that ain't a fightin' wound, I'ownt know what is."

The old man set down his tray and welcomed me to his church, the Weary Sojourner's Mission.

At sixteen years old, I had quit my job at the Speedway — with nowhere to go and nothing to do, who needs money, it made you a target — and now spent my days with old man Creed at the Weary Sojourner Mission. I was one of a handful of teens who regularly came to Creed at the mission. Days at the mission consisted of cleaning both inside the building and outside the building, whether it needed it or not. Vacuuming the carpet, power-washing the sidewalk, painting the trim, polishing the communion platter. Creed believed in teaching through working, and young Edward Falcone was the hardest worker Creed had seen in the mission in years. At night, Creed would lead anyone who came in, mostly teens either with nowhere to go or somewhere bad to avoid. Either was fine with Creed as long as they came. He would teach us kids about taking communion and what it meant to eat the body and drink the blood of Christ.

At seventeen years old, I was Jim Creed's second in command at the Weary Sojourner Mission. Creed wasn't getting any younger and had wanted for years to develop someone in their youth into a leader for their peers who could relate to them closer to their level. I fit into that desire like a round peg in a round hole. The kids respected me, and I loved being respected. Creed would lead the groups when we met in the evening up to a point, then he would let me take over while he watched from a distance.

The rest was good for his soul, almost as good as seeing the progress from the tough young man living on the streets. I spent as little time in the homeless shelter as possible. Watching the mental declines of my parents as they struggled with their current lots in life was more than I could bear. When I wasn't sleeping behind the pulpit at the mission, I slept in broken down cars or behind dumpsters in closed alleys. Life was hard but good.

During this season, I was becoming passionate about God, passionate about the mission, passionate about the scriptures Creed had given me, and passionate about helping my parents get back in control of their lives. But first was God, and foremost, with utmost importance, the blood.

I was halfway through my seventeenth year when Creed gave me enough slack on my reigns to have full control of my group of peers. If you had asked any of them, they probably wouldn't have told you I was only seventeen. My facial hair had started coming in two years prior, and I had the kind of beard thirty-year-old men were envious of, full from my cheeks to the bulge of my Adam's apple. I spoke with the command of one of the elders a church would normally employ, instead of a seventeen-year-old homeless kid.

Talk of my run-in with two members of the local street gang had apparently spread far and near, and to my surprise they only tried one time to get revenge for what my punch had done to the face of Marco McCollough, or Dodger Hat as I knew him. Only one time until a sunny Saturday later that year.

I had asked my main group to meet me early on that Saturday morning to do some upkeep on the outside of the mission. Creed had used similar means early in our relationship. What reason would I have to not heavily lean on our experiences together as I began the process of building relationships with my own crew?

I sat on the sidewalk waiting for the first ones to arrive just after sunrise. I had been eager to play the mentor role that morning and as a result I hadn't slept much. I was getting the kinks out of the water hose used by the pressure washer, a relic that seemed as old as Creed himself, if that was possible, when the three men rounded the corner behind me heading in my direction. The two men who had tried — miserably failing was still trying — to mug me on the sidewalk in front of the pawn shop were back, and this time they brought a friend. Dodger Hat spotted me before I was done with my water hose. He bent down in the street and picked up a stone.

My hands were wet and tired. I raised my head to wipe the water with my shaggy morning hair when surely my eyes deceived me. If you couldn't trust your eyes, what could you trust? Here it was, a sunny Saturday morning in front of the mission, where I had been learning how to grow from and through my circumstances and find redemption and atonement, atonement being the principle that had been speaking to me the most in that time. And what did my eyes see? Surely there were no flying stones in this part of the world. It wouldn't even classify as an unidentified flying object if my eyes were telling an accurate story. If true, that was a clearly identifiable stone.

I remember that feeling of confusion still when the first stone shattered my nose like a windowpane. Blood, so much blood, poured onto the sidewalk.

The blood makes atonement…without the blood, there is no forgiveness.

The record player of my mind had begun to skip from the force of the stone, replaying the messages from Creed that had smashed into my hardened pride like stones into an unsuspecting nose.

John foreran Christ's first coming. Would one forerun his second?

The three men were on me moments after the first stone found my face. They kicked me and struck me with their fists. They followed intermittently with the occasional stone. They wanted a point proven, and what better way than by a mild stoning outside a church?

Moses was like a God to his people. Who was like a God to the people today?

I knelt on the concrete sidewalk. I did not feel the rough edges cutting into my knees and hands. I was not aware of the contusions left by strikes and stones on my back and legs. I saw only the red swarm overtaking the gray ground as my blood spilt and the pool expanded on the earth like a tidal wave sweeping inland.

It purifies, it contains life, it purifies, it contains life.

A message came together in lines, snippets, and quotes. A message for an hour, whether this one or one to come I did not know but truly it was to come.

Jesus, son of man, son of God, son of David.

There was a roar in the distance of my mind. Another storm approaching beyond the hills on the horizon line that you know are coming for you though you have yet to see them. I heard the sound. The men did not, their own sound drowning out the world around them until one by one they felt the vengeance that came once what had been sown in violence and pride was reaped with holy anger, vengeance, and wrath.

Seven teenagers, coming to wash windows and paint trim around the door, not with blood this time, had turned the corner and seen their Creed, this one a peer whether they knew his age or not, on the sidewalk staring at his blood on the uneven concrete, watering the weeds coming through the cracks and spilling into the gutter.

One by one, blood was spilt by the men who had endeavored to send a message. One by one, they ran. One by one, it was decided no further messaging was needed. My blood had been let upon the earth, and I could go my way remembering it.

I shall ever remember it.

With my world on fire and bathed in blood, I felt alive. I felt like the apostle Paul caught in the blinding light on the Damascus road. Where Paul had been blinded by the light of the world emitting from the presence of Jesus, I had been blinded by blood.

He makes all things new. By the blood.

I knew in that moment, as through a voice flooding the world with its words, the same voice that had called Paul was now calling me, giving me a message for an hour when the same blood that had saved the world once would save it again. Once the blood shed for all, and now all would shed their blood. The first coming of the Christ and the second. It all made sense, perfect and complete, and it was my calling. I was as sure of it then as I was sure of the new bend in the bridge of my nose, to tell it to the world. Soon, they would understand.

Slowly, I rose to my feet under the guiding hands of my peers. I saw the world through a filter of bright-red blood. The hot sulfuric smell of the street, the acidic odor of spilt cleaning supplies, the moist morning dew burning off the grasses in the fringe of the city, mixed with the metallic burning in my nose. The bright copper in my mouth gave weight to the words weighing on my tongue before being spoken to the crowd. This was my moment, given as a gift by God to lead to repentance, to atonement, by the example of the shedding of blood.

"My friends…"

I spoke through the dripping blood smacking on my lips and gently spraying from the percussive sound, the image of Christ on the cross flashed in my mind, driving a rod down my back to stiffen my resolve as I delivered what was my own Sermon on the Mount.

"How often have we spoken of blood during our meetings?"

Oh, how my eyes must have grown wide like an addict taking his initial hit, my mind exploding with dopamine, pathways being built like superhighways through my subconscious in a moment.

"Blood, it purifies…"

I could feel myself begin to pace, moving person to person, meeting their eyes with mine, my steps leaving red footprints on the ground, the increased passion of my speech projecting a red mist in the air, accentuating my words with literal visual aides.

"Without the shedding of blood, there is *no* forgiveness, isn't that right?"

I was moved to pause and stare into the depths of the souls of each one in attendance of my righteous proclamation until a soft murmur of agreement began to gently wave through the space.

"The very life itself in our flesh is in our blood, in this…"

It was as if I was outside of my own body now, watching as I lifted both hands and wiped them down my face, covering both palms in bright red like a painter squeezing crimson pigment from his roller using only his hands, before raising them to the crowd.

"This blood makes atonement for our lives! Those men, those men…"

The red tracks made from the soles of my shoes began to extend into the street as my righteous gesturing extended to the men my friends had run off.

"Shed their blood by your hands…"

With no thought given to the state of his own hands, the Edward I watched from within and without began laying his hands on each member of the group, leaving his mark on each chest firmly ensconced in the message.

"...have provided atonement for them by their blood on this ground. I STAND IN YOUR PRESENCE FULLY ATONED!"

And I lifted my eyes toward the heavens and sprayed forth fresh blood into the air like a fountain. I paused as it rained again upon me, feeling every drop fall fresh.

"You, my friends, can have this atonement. We can be purified together. Given on the altar, our blood making the way for all. Tonight."

I felt my voice grow soft.

"Tonight, we atone, once for all, by the blood. Leave here. Come back tonight ready. Make a straight highway through the wasteland for our God!"

I turned and began to walk away from the Weary Sojourner Mission. No one spoke. They each simply turned and went their ways.

Old man Creed was a creature of long-formed habits, and as his protege I knew them all. On Saturday nights, the old preacher would leave the church for his only night away for the week. When your mission was to reach the young and lost, you learned the young and lost were otherwise occupied on Saturday nights. Repentance came knocking on Sunday. For years, Creed took full advantage of the habits of the young and lost and used Saturday nights to get away, usually at the casino on the river on the other side of town. He liked the buffet almost as much as he liked the cards he had been playing since he was a child in the barracks in North Carolina. If he couldn't save the lost on a Saturday night, maybe he could take their spending money so they couldn't make any more poor decisions.

I, however, was inside when the group of seven came back at sundown. They knew there was nothing more special, nothing that needed to be attended to that night than this. The building was dark except for the soft flicker of candles leading up the center aisle and across the front of the stage. In the space between the stage and the front row pew rested a long, slender table.

Back when the mission was an early-era pentecostal church the people would line the walls and spill out the door, sweating in their three-piece suits and fancy dresses. The solid table with the hand-carved legs was a gift from a wealthy attendee and used in the front, in the space between the stage and the front row of pews, to hold a pair of silver chalice cups filled with communion wine, one on each side of the table each flanked by a matching silver platter topped with unleavened bread. In the days since, Creed had used the table along the back wall to hold everything from tracts to bowls of chips and dip for parishioners in attendance at various addiction groups or youth groups of various ages. That night, it held seven small plates, each with a knife and a shot glass-size mason jar with a sealing lid.

I stood in front of the long table with hands clasped behind myself. They could surely see a face that was serious. Stern yet gentle, I eyed each one as they made their way to the front pew and stood around me. The silence was as thick as the blood that had pooled under my face on the sidewalk earlier that day.

"My friends," I said with the first smile they had seen that day, "tonight is the greatest event of any of your lives until now or from now on. The world is broken, and we are all separated from God. Is that not what we've been told? That all men need redemption? Need atonement?"

I began to move. I walked down the line, meeting the eyes of each of the seven as I spoke. The faces spoke of confusion, but they spoke also of longing. They wanted to understand. Heads nodded as I spoke. Lips parted as if to speak in agreement or acknowledgement yet refrained. It seemed as if the moment was due a level of reverence none of the seven had experienced before.

"Today, I understood the message I was given, and tonight I will give it to you. *You.* You are the chosen ones. You are the firstborn, the ones who atone.

I was put here for a purpose, even old man Creed speaks of my purpose. Isn't that right?"

I spun on my heels to look across the line of teenagers as they all nodded in agreement. I could feel the building of excitement as holy fire began to bathe me yet again. Yes, this was a time ordained. They'd all heard Creed's affirmation of my purpose as their mentor. He did deliver them to me so I could lead them, didn't he? Oh, yes he did. He certainly did.

"Now you will atone as I have atoned."

I beckoned each to come to the table, each to their own tray with a knife and cup. They looked one to the other with… Fear? Anxiousness? If any had turned to leave, perhaps all would have followed. No one turned, none left. Ordained. As each of the seven settled into their spots the resolve of each hardened like Pharaoh's heart.

I stood on the opposing side of the table from the seven as they came into position. Watching the faces of the group settle into the moment like a child once afraid of the dark settled in his bed as his eyes adjusted and he began to see.

Tonight, God, we will all SEE.

"Peter, how fitting. You shall be the first to atone. And on this rock, I build my church, isn't that right? Hold out your hand."

The young man brushed his red curls from his face, extended a trembling freckled hand, and peered through scratched lenses in glasses bent by schoolyard beatings at the man who stood before him with the crooked nose who was holding an old steak knife.

I placed the serrated edge of the blade on the meat of Peter's palm, just beneath his thumb. Peter's eyes grew wide and he glanced to the side quickly to see if everyone else's knives were serrated. From a glance it seemed he was the lucky one. He closed his eyes and turned straight ahead, giving his unseen focus wholly to me.

I spoke softly, as if Peter were my only intended recipient. He leaned in to hear the special message meant especially for him.

"Without the shedding of blood, there is no forgiveness of sins."

With a jerk, I pulled the blade toward myself. The serrated edge tore at Peter's flesh. He felt each saw-tooth tear further into the meat of his hand, and he wondered surely if it would affect the use of his thumb. *No matter, if it brings atonement, he can have both thumbs*, the young man surely thought as he began to bleed.

The blood first dripped, missing the cup and leaving splatters on the silver plate like a preschooler trying to impress mommy with an art project on her favorite serving platter, then with each scalloped edge the blood began to pour. It filled the cup on the platter then began to run over to the platter itself.

"It is the blood that makes atonement for the soul. First the atonement for the one, then the one can pursue the many. Your cup overfloweth. The platter be filled for the work toward the many."

Peter began to whisper, "My cup overfloweth. My platter be filled for the work that is to come."

One by one, I worked my way down the line of the seven. First Peter, then Bruce. Diana. Kenny. Sky. Matt.

I stood before the seventh and final member of the group. A short, thick girl seemingly my age, her dark-brown skin matching her hair, short and nappy, teased in small twists coming out of her head like stalagmites. The original seven. Soon there would be more followers. More atoned. I could feel it. The world was broken, but they would heal it. They would bring about the new world, coming down from the new heaven. All by the blood.

"And now the work will be completed in you, and you all will go forth into the world to bring—"

The sound of the opening door did not break the silence of the moment. The slamming of the door moments later, after Creed had heard the final words from Matt and the newest words from his protege, was loud enough to wake the dead.

"Edward!"

If the slamming door didn't wake the dead, Creed's booming voice might get them out of their graves.

"Would you care to explain *this* to me?"

Creed hit the switch that turned on the fluorescent lights and walked up the center aisle, taking in the scene as he went. Lit candles were snuffed out with a pinch of his fingers, each one causing a grimace I could feel in the muscles of my face as though Creed were smashing June bugs between his fingers. The seven began exchanging glances with each other then looked to me, my focus solely on the approaching Creed, then to Creed, who was likewise focused on me. As the old man approached the group of seven, six clasping hands that still bled with pressure meant to stop the flow, they slowly began to part, leaving nothing standing between mentor and protege other than the old table with the hand carved legs.

His eyes fixed on his disciple, Creed called out to the group, "You all are free to go. Try to not drip on my carpet. Go get stitches, say nothing about where you got those cuts. Stay away from this place. Stay further away from that man."

Peter took a step toward Creed while the other six started slowly away, calling Peter until he came to them as they went. Creed likely never saw the seven again. I went more than eight years before reuniting with anyone from the group, the time becoming more apparent each day of having not yet come. We had been given a taste of the coming glory.

When the final member of the group left through the front door, Creed took his final step up to the table that separated teacher from apprentice.

"Edward, you have to know what this looks like. The lights off, the candles, the table set with, are these my platters? And my cups, filled with… Edward, is that blood from those kids?"

Creed placed his wrinkled hands on the edge of the table and did his best to take it all in. The plates, the cups, the knives, most of all the blood.

I spoke softly to the man who had become a father figure to me, "Creed, you know as well as I, the world is broken and that the people need to atone."

I looked the old man in his pale-blue eyes and thought he looked a decade older than he had yesterday.

"Atone?" Creed's face drew in on itself and contorted in confusion. He was as yet unable to see the picture, to understand. "The people need to… Edward, the world is broken, sure. From the fall.

But people don't atone. They repent. There's a difference."

I felt my face harden at the words of the man I was now realizing was broken himself.

"Blood brings atonement. Blood brings forgiveness. Have you shed your blood, Creed?" I smiled through the pain I felt at my mentor, the man who was hardening his heart to the truth of the hour.

Creed's eyes widened, his nostrils flared, his heart raced to levels dangerous for a man of his advanced age as the arteries in his neck bulged with each beat that pumped the blood he needed to give through his old body. His hands, worn and calloused, stopped resting on the table. They grabbed the edges with the force of a much younger man.

During times of extreme duress, the surge of adrenaline could cause great feats of strength, like mothers lifting cars off of their children. In this moment, Creed wasn't gripping a car, only a heavy piece of furniture decades old, its legs and adornments hand carved. He lifted and flipped the table, not off of his child but directly at the man who until this moment had been like a son to the old childless preacher.

"This is insane, Edward! I don't know who you are right now! This has no basis in the scriptures. It has no bearing on anything logical or moral. What you're doing, what you've done here… You hear 'blood' and think of yourself? You're worse than the snake handlers, poison drinkers, and self-flogging idiots," Creed cried with a disdain in his voice that frightened himself.

"I don't think of myself. I think of the lost. All those who need to shed their blood for their atonement."

"That's not… Where do you… No, what you're talking about isn't only not real. It's criminal!"

The rage that had filled Creed was quickly emptying from within him, leaking out of his old, cracked vessel as the tears also leaked from his face.

He trembled as he stood, yet he stood firm.

The rage, the righteous anger, simmered inside my gut like a pilot light waiting for the right infusion of fuel to ignite it into a fury capable of launching into the stratosphere.

"It would be criminal not to continue the work that was started tonight. It should continue, and it should continue with you. You need to atone."

Creed looked at me with indignation. I knew the hour that had begun that night, the message that was to go out from me. From me to souls like Creed. Though perhaps he was too far gone, too much life lived to be pliable, too far gone for atonement to take hold.

"Edward, leave. Never come back."

I staggered at the command.

"I have work to do."

"You have work…" Creed chuckled through the deepest hurt he had felt in his belly in years, maybe ever. "The only work you have to do is on yourself, son.

It can't happen here, not after this. Go, or I'll send for the police."

Creed turned his back to me, and I saw fear in his eyes. He seemed to be afraid of what I may do when he wasn't looking. He truly was lost to think in such a way. He went to lift the table, but it was too heavy for the old man to lift. He would typically get help from visitors when it needed to be moved. Lately, he relied on my youth and strength. He stood and faced the cross in the back corner of the stage.

"Go."

I stepped toward Creed, who was watching me from the corner of his eyes, though he kept his back to me. Inside, Creed may have been bending, but he never broke. I bent down, took hold of the table, and stood it upright. Again, I stepped toward Creed, stopping close enough for the old man to feel my hot breath on his neck.

"I'll go, for now. But you know what happens to those who never atone. You brought me out of the darkness. I'll bring you to the light. You. Shall. Atone."

I backed away from Creed, spun on my heel, turned, and walked out of Weary Sojourner Mission for the last time.

On the day of my eighteenth birthday, I walked back into the homeless shelter for the first time in a long time. I had two hopes that morning. That I would find my parents and have a long talk with my father and that I would find they had gotten past their issues and left the shelter on their own in search of a second-chance reboot of their adult lives.

I had spent the weeks since my fallout with Creed occupying whatever abandoned building I could find a corner to hide from the world in. I meditated on what I knew was right. The world was broken, the people needed to atone, atonement was by blood, hence to heal the world I needed the people to give their blood for atonement. The hour was at hand, but was it for that time, or was there to be a time of waiting? My own half hour of silence?

Creed's words, his face, his posture, all stayed in the forefront of my mind. Surely he wasn't right, not on that night. He had been right to teach me about the fall of man, the separation between God and man, the need of blood for forgiveness and atonement. On those counts, he had been correct. But to treat me as he had on the night with the seven? That was the wrong message from my mentor. My father. No, I had a father, and his name was not Creed. That was what I needed, to find my father. He would listen to the truths I now knew. He would atone, he would assist me in healing the world, he wouldn't throw me out and break the bond between us. My father was better than old man Creed, the sinner and hypocrite.

I entered the shelter and walked the familiar space that spoke of my toughest times. The times when I had lost everything. My home, my belongings, my friends, all gone when my family had been thrown from our home. My belongings still in my drawers, on my shelves, on my floor. All gone. My friends hadn't bothered to find me. Some friends.

The farther I got inside the shelter on the way back to the areas curtained off for space between families hurting and in need of room, I realized this space also spoke of the toughest loss of all. This was where I lost my family. My poor mother's mind had all but gone, and my father's was close behind. They were as broken as the world around them.

I got to the families' unit, formerly a series of conference rooms adjacent to a ballroom all in the former bank, and went to the curtained off section I remembered as the last place I saw my parents. The hope that they had healed was forefront in my mind. Maybe they didn't need me after all.

There sat my poor, sweet mother, dead-eyed and silent sitting in the corner with an orange and brown crocheted blanket that looked like it had been knitted in the 70s by an old lady who today was long dead. Next to my mother, lying on a cot, was my father.

"Dad? Mom? It's Edward."

My mother lifted her head, but her eyes remained as blank as they were when I walked in. Her gaze lowered back to the floor.

I walked over to the cot and sat on the edge, placing my hand on his father's chest. I let it linger on the Van Halen logo on the old XXL shirt swimming over my father's gaunt body, feeling the slow but steady rise and fall that displayed my father's breathing.

"Dad? It's Edward."

I sat with my hand on my father's chest for what felt like hours. I kept my eyes closed while I remembered life before the accident.

When I was eleven, my father had come home from work while the sun was still up, and I was in the street playing baseball with five friends and a dozen or so ghost runners. When my father got out of his work truck, still white with dust from his hair to the laces in his boots, he set his lunch bag on the tailgate and came into the street. For the next hour, my father came alive like I had never seen him. He threw perfect pitches to us boys. He dug out ground balls like the best New York Yankee ever had. He ran the bases, even bounced off third — Mrs. Brown wasn't happy about the dad-sized dent in her new Buick — on his way to score after the longest hit us boys had ever seen in person. If there had been a fence in the street, even a Green Monster, it surely would have gone over it. It was the last time I ever saw my father so active and full of life.

The only other time I saw my father come home while the sun was still up, he smelled like the bottle of warm beer I had stolen from under the bench seat in the back and shared one day with the boys behind Cory's dad's shed. My dad needed to atone.

I opened my eyes and removed my hand from my father's chest to leave. When I did, my dad opened his eyes, and they met the eyes of his son. He thought he was dreaming. He reached up with both hands. With one, he touched my face, and with the other he pinched his own cheek. It hurt. He was awake.

"Edward?"

"Dad."

My dad and I sat on the roof of the former National Bank. I had said that I wanted to talk, and my dad could hear the seriousness in his son's voice, "I know a place we can go, son."

The walk up to the roof was tenuous. I wasn't sure my dad would make it up the stairs to the top floor when the elevator stopped one floor below. The final metal stairway to the rooftop was rickety. Each step would squeal and squeak in a new pitch from the previous step. Finally, we had reached the steel door that would exit into the sunshine on the top of the old building. It was held shut by a chain so thick I thought trying to break through it would have been my dads final act, but when he pushed it open, I was surprised to see the length of the chain was sufficient so as to allow the door to open enough for a child or slender man to squeeze through.

If this had been five years ago, there was no chance my dad would have fit through the crack in the door. It brought a tear to my eye to see that the injury, the drink, and the time spent in this shelter had allowed him to waste away to the point of being able to fit through the opening in the door easier than I could.

We sat on the roof and spent several silent minutes staring at the open sky, crystal clear and blue as far as the eye can see. A flock of birds sailed from the north in full V formation, and I caught a glimpse of my dad, a tear now in his eye, as he watched the birds sailing by.

"Dad, do you ever think about death?"

"Son, with the life I have, death is all I can think about with any sort of hope. Before this morning, I thought all I had was this wretched place, your comatose mother, and this shell of a body."

The broken man turned his longing eyes from the horizon line where the last of the birds had disappeared and looked at his son.

"Until now, knowing you're here and you're safe, death was all I had to look forward to."

My eyes met my dad's. The moment we shared with the sun on our shoulders and breeze blowing down the collars of our shirts was the last happy moment my dad would ever know.

I lowered my eyes as my resolve began to harden.

With a shallow breath, I spoke low and firm, "Dad, we both know the life you've lived. How can you be hopeful at the thought of death until you know you've been forgiven? Unless you have shed blood for the atonement of your soul?"

The eyes that met this time were not the same eyes from moments prior. Mine were once again blazing with the fire of purpose, and my dad's…had the shock of the sudden spilling of every bad thought he had ever had about himself and his life that he had stored away in a barrel in the storehouse of his mind, now tipped over and spilling out, staining the redemptive moment he was having with his son like blood - blood - on a plush white carpet.

Tears welling up in the lids of his eyes, my father measured his reply, "I know I was never a great dad. I did things I wasn't proud of then and am not proud of now. I also know that I'm not a learned man when it comes to these things, but what you just said… Edward, it isn't right. I've asked for forgiveness. There's a man here who talks to people. I've talked with him some. I've made my peace. But…shedding my own blood? It's 2016. That's cult stuff. Who have you been talking to?"

I could feel my father slipping away. I lost him once, after the accident. I lost my second father a few days prior when Creed couldn't see the light and threw our relationship away. Now I was losing my father again. I had to save him.

I stared straight ahead, but not at my father. My eyes could not look upon him now.

"The good book says that under the law, everything is purified with blood. Without shedding blood, there is no forgiveness. Life is in the blood, and blood makes atonement for the soul. The scriptures were shown to me by a preacher near here. He showed me what I now know is apostasy, he told me the time of shedding blood had passed, but one day not long ago I came under attack. While I was down on the ground, my own blood being spilled from within me, turning everything I saw red, tainting everything around me with the taste and smell of metal, the words of God entered in like a flood, and the words of the book came back to me, and I remembered the words of the prophets, 'Behold, I will send you Elijah the prophet before the coming of the great and dreadful day of the Lord, and he shall turn the heart of the fathers to the children, and the heart of the children to their fathers, lest I come and smite the earth with a curse'…"

I turned my attention to my father. I locked my eyes upon those of the man who sired me, who raised me. The man was slipping away again. I was determined to bring him back.

"The voice told me the hearts of the fathers returned to the children during the life of Christ. I am here to turn the hearts of the children to the fathers, the original fathers, the founders of the faith, the ones who wrote and believed in the blood for atonement. It is time for the world to turn away from the curse of unbelief through the atonement and forgiveness spoken by the fathers. By blood. It's time to redeem the world. Together, we can make a difference. Creed was too far set to believe. What we need… Dad, we can start with the children and through them save the world."

I smiled. I knew from the tears rolling down the face of my dad that this child had reached the heart of that father. It was time. I reached out for my dad's hand.

My father did not take my hand. He stood and slowly, like a man decades older than his actual age, moved away from his son.

Softly he spoke, "You shouldn't have come here. You scare me. You don't know what you're saying…but if you believe these things, and it looks like you do, then I need to go. You need to go. Don't come back here. I have no son."

He turned and bent back through the chained door, returning to his wife, who never knew he had gone. Not until four days later when he had returned to the rooftop.

When the police came up to the roof that day, they found a Gideon Bible with a page torn out. Circled in a jagged red line - no pen was found in the area or in their curtained space, but it was never tested for blood - on the page containing Malachi 4:5-6 were the phrases, "Elijah the prophet" and "smite the earth with a curse."

Eight years later, I graduated from nursing school. I had not pursued the atonement of the world in eight years. I hated my father, but through my hate I still missed my dad. I knew my calling but had felt it wasn't the right time yet. If my father and my father figure both rejected me, it must not have been time. The spirit of Elijah was upon me, of that I was certain. When the time was right, I would turn the hearts of the children back to the fathers, and their blood would atone their souls. I would redeem the world.

On the day of my graduation, I was approached by an older man named Doctor Kirschner. He had been told of my skills with intravenous ports and the ability to draw blood from tough veins. I had a knack for blood. Who knew? The doctor was starting a specialized team in a nearby hospital that would do nothing but hard-to-get blood draws and the toughest IV patients. He offered me a job on the spot. The hospital? Franklin Children's Hospital. Children. This was my sign. It was almost time.

I worked for two years with the children who came to the hospital. So many children in need of forgiveness. So many who needed to atone, but I had no opportunity to lead them back to their fathers. No chance to take their blood for any purpose other than official hospital business. Until last summer when a new colleague came to me with a proposal, a pact to use our friend, the night nurse with the skin condition, the mark upon her face, to get us in the rooms of the children unofficially.

Richard wanted practice, which I thought was pathetic. I saw the opportunity, however. The chance to begin the work. To draw the blood without packing it for the hospital. I could take some for myself to watch over. For the sake of their souls. To prepare the way before the dreadful day of the Lord. To save the world.

My decision was solidified the day I was introduced to the hospital chaplain at the small group with you, my friends. This would be the group that would save the world. I have never been more sure of anything.

37

Sorry, Chloe, people like Edward were the people I always aimed to protect you from. If I had known, if anyone had known... You could imagine how the others in the room that day reacted to hearing that... I wouldn't give it the dignity of calling it a sermon.

Richard seethed. Claudia's face was void of expression, except for her mouth, which was gaped open like a cave awaiting the emergence of the creature that lived within. Tom was lost, still stuck at the late mention of the chaplain.

"Why wud yer decision be solid meetin' the chaplin, Edward?"

From the darkness beyond the dark void of the doorway behind Edward came a figure like a spectral from the shadows, a spectral short and plump with twisted curls. It wasn't plain how long she had been there, her skin and hair hiding in the shadows of the storage room between Tom's and the hallways that led there. Chaplain Jenkins walked into Tom's dimly lit room and placed her hand on Edward's shoulder.

"So you finally told them, hun?"

Edward smiled at the woman who was a whole head shorter and bent down to kiss her, his crooked nose turning to press into hers. Claudia's eyes widened as her mouth closed, Richard's rage lowering to the dirty ground to give way to shock, and Tom picking Richard's rage off the ground, dusting it off and claiming it as his own.

"You was the girl?"

Tom spoke softly, alternating his gaze between the woman he had lusted over for years and the man he thought was his friend. "You was the last girl who didn't bleed or whatever, wasn't you?"

Chaplain Jenkins spoke to Tom as she always did, like a gentle-hearted teacher speaking to an elementary school child who would understand more the slower she spoke. If he had understood the concept of condescension, his mood would have risen from rage to outright hatred.

"Yes, Tom, I thought about that night for close to ten years. Something about it stayed with me. A few years after that night, I was diagnosed with ovarian cancer, and that's when I knew God was punishing me for not being able to atone for my forgiveness.

"After I achieved remission through surgery, I entered seminary. I figured that would be the easiest way to learn where I'd gone wrong. I hadn't seen the young man from the mission since that night. I took this job because it felt like the right thing to do. The day Richard introduced me to his friend Edward, my world shook, and I knew what was true. We met in private to learn and grow together. He helped me atone. I helped him decide how to proceed."

Claudia rose from the ground and looked at the woman she had been entrusting her deepest thoughts to for the last several months.

"I trusted you, and for what? So you could use me to help him with whatever this is?"

"Claudia, think about what I have been telling you..." Chaplain Jenkins looked around the room. "...since we started our group? The world is broken. People need forgiveness. And the blood sets you free. All that was left was the message of atonement. It wasn't time yet. But from the sound of things, time is shorter than we thought. Edward, I think the time of the harvest is upon us. That's why you gave them all the full message now, isn't it? You feel it too. Time to make them ready for the reaping and the work to be done."

"How could you? You have to know this is crazy!" Claudia paced by the wall opposite Edward and Krystal Jenkins while Tom stared at the floor, his head shaking back and forth like he was in a silent conversation with the floor and he disagreed with everything it said.

Richard spoke up, "This is insane. I'm leaving."

Edward shut the door to the room and stood in between it and the group.

"No one is leaving. Not yet."

The chaplain stood by Edward's side, her hand in his hand.

Chaplain Jenkins spoke, "We are saving the world, one child at a time. The time has passed to turn the hearts of the fathers. Theirs have been hardened. If we are to save the world, it is to be accomplished through the hearts of the children. Through their atonement, by their blood. Turning their hearts back to the fathers of the faith. But there's been a problem that Edward and I have been discussing. Claudia, you and Tom haven't atoned."

Claudia looked at Richard, who looked sick.

"What'd you do to me?"

"It's okay, Richard. Those marks on your arms, all those blood draws in your apartment, your blood purchased your forgiveness."

Edward reached into his pocket and pulled a syringe with a plastic cap over the needle. He pulled the cap off and turned his gaze to Claudia.

"My God, Edward. How many times have you used that needle? How clean is it, really? Not to mention the tips. They go bad, get distressed, their points break off, the shards can shred veins, cause bleeding, cause clotting. It can kill them. They're small already..."

"Claudia, if you can believe me, you too can be one of my disciples and know the truth, and the truth can set you free."

"Edward, listen..."

"No, Richard, you're not listening. The Lord is coming to smite the world with a curse. Before that happens, he has sent me to turn the hearts of the children of this world back to the fathers of the faith. Back to the belief that their blood brings forgiveness of sins and atones for their souls. I am including you in my mission. You, Claudia, Krystal, even Tom, you will be the Elishas to my Elijah calling. The disciples to my John the baptizer. In time, even the disciples to a...greater calling.

"We are the wise, but the foolish too can be saved. First, everyone must shed blood. For forgiveness of sins and atonement of souls. I have spilled my blood. Richard, I have your blood given at your dining room table through this needle. I have Krystal's blood given in the bathtub in her apartment through this needle. This needle has redeemed the souls of children throughout this hospital. Now it will redeem you, Tom. And you, Claudia. We will have your blood, for your good, one way or another."

38

Officer Arthur L. "Whitey" White came to the hospital looking for his girlfriend, Lila Collins. Whitey and Lila had been dating for seven months, and for Whitey it was love at first sight. They had made plans the day before to meet in the cafeteria for lunch. Whitey had been in the cafeteria for forty-five minutes, and Lila wasn't even answering her phone. He knew she was important and her job was as chaotic as his, but it wasn't like Lila to miss a planned date, no matter how short. It was also not like Lila to ignore messages from Whitey. The previous day, she assured Whitey she would hand off the days duties to her team and take an hour just for them.

The Franklin Hospital cafeteria wasn't on any food bloggers' top ten list of most romantic lunch spots, but when Whitey and Lila got together, whether at the hospital cafeteria, the police station break room, or the Blazing Sun Steakhouse high atop the city in the twentieth story of the twenty-story Elite Hotel, the tallest building in the skyline, the world faded away, and it was them and only them. Now, Whitey stood in the doorway of Lila's office, and she was not only nowhere to be found, according to Indiana Powell, she may be in danger.

"Tell me again, why is Lila in danger? And while you're at it, why weren't the police called if you think a murder took place by someone who could still be here?"

Whitey's concerns made sense in hindsight, but now wasn't the time for regrets. Lila Collins and Addison McCray were in danger, and Indy needed Whitey, your mother, and I to help her find them.

Indy filled Whitey in again as quickly as she could while being as thorough as possible, a gift given by her time following Lila into patient rooms. Everything was lining up to a point, right until the line went off a cliff and vanished in the wind.

There had been an uptick in deaths in the hospital. It was assumed to be a temporary uptick that would soon level off, but Lila had her suspicions that something was up. She couldn't prove it, and with nothing to go on, there would be no inquiries.

"After Chloe Miller died this morning, Lila asked a simple question. Why did Chloe's mother say there had been more in the room than the night nurse when her chart showed nothing of the sort?"

The simplicity of the question was why not even Lila thought to ask for a police presence, even if only from Whitey. The events of the morning turned up a couple of names.

A nurse named Claudia O'Dell and two IV team members, Richard Mercier and Edward Falcone.

"We split up this morning to get this all done a little easier so we could get back to our rounds sooner and relieve the unit that took over this morning. Lila went to find where Tom took Chloe after he left. Tom is the body transporter and would've taken her to the morgue. Lila was planning to call in a favor and be present for the autopsy. Addison was looking into the nurse logs to find a pattern, if one existed, and she found Claudia O'Dell. I went to the head of the IV team to get cooperation from the team. We have questions, and they have answers. Doctor Kirschner sent a message to the team and said he'd make it discreet. I found that Edward Falcone and Richard Mercier's names were linked to the nights Claudia worked the night shift most nights over the last few months, and Claudia was a nurse for every kid who has died recently. Addy went for a walk to cool off after getting worked up. Now Lila and Addy are both missing, and Addy's smartwatch told us she's hurt. I don't know where to start to look."

Indy was increasingly exasperated and was looking to Whitey for input while trying to not run out of the room blindly after her friend.

"Did you see the message Doctor Krisher sent to the IV unit earlier?"

Whitey's face was on full cop mode. His brow was furrowed, his lips pursed. In short, every stereotype in every cop drama was being played out in real time in Indy's small office. Honestly, I was trying to not chuckle and was thankful for the inadvertent moment of unintentional humor.

Indy responded, "Kirschner, and no. I took him at his word. Was that a mistake? If I'm to blame for this because I was too trusting of a senior administrator..."

Whitey responded, "I wouldn't say it was a mistake. Don't take that on yourself, Indiana. But if your timeline is accurate..."

"It is."

"It begs the question of why his message is a juncture point."

The three others in the room sat silently waiting for officer Whitey to continue his thought. Surely he didn't assume everyone knew what a juncture point was, did he? Joey glanced at Indy, who glanced at me.

"I'll go," I said. "A juncture point?"

"The point in time of a critical circumstance that changes everything on the other side of it," Whitey spoke with the assumption everyone was still on the same page, though multiple pages had been in play for a while now.

"I knew that, but they looked confused. Go on."

Chloe, I was again thankful for the task of trying to not laugh. Joey was not as thankful and flashed me her best 'what is wrong with you?' look. It was like all those times when we heard the unintended joke and knew your mother did not. I looked around for you, to share that familiar look, but you weren't there.

Whitey continued, "The three of you were all present and working on a task. Doctor…" He glanced at Indy like an elementary student seeking approval from a teacher. "Kirschner sent a message to his team, and now two of the three doctors are missing. That's a juncture point. Right now, we don't have anywhere to look and would simply be running around like children in a corn maze if we go out looking for them. We could split up, but if there's something bad happening, that would be a mistake.

"We need a direction to go in. Addison was going to blow off steam, and Lila was going to the morgue. Unless Addison has a specific place she goes…" He looked again at Indy, who responded with a shake of her head. "Then I say we head to the morgue and go from there. If we can find out what that message said while we're on our way, that wouldn't be a bad idea either. Make sense to everyone else?"

Eight eyes in the room, and none knew where to look. The one thing we all knew was we couldn't stay here. Whitey needed to find Lila. Indy needed to find Addison. Your mother and I needed to find out whether or not someone took our daughter from us before her time was truly up.

All eyes converged at once and an unspoken union solidified.

In that moment, the quartet of people in the room, connected by the day's events both witnessed and unseen, made a silent pact. We all knew we would be willing to fight together if fighting was necessary, even die for each other if the need arose.

39

Indy brought us to the staff elevator. As the only member of the party who actually worked in the hospital, she was our best bet on getting to where we needed to go with a bare minimum of meandering.

Our group looked at the elevator's call buttons and stood silently. It seemed to be a game of chicken, with each one seeing how long they could wait until someone else would make the first move.

Whitey lost the game. "We were going to the morgue, correct?"

"Of course," Indy replied. "But you see, the interesting thing about going to the morgue is...I've never been there. I have no idea where it is."

I groaned twice, once in response to Indy's reply and again when Joey elbowed me in the ribs for the first one.

Whitey spoke again. It seemed as if with each successive statement aboard this elevator, his voice would include more condescension.

"Forgive me if I'm wrong, *Doctor*." The emphasis on the word "doctor" made Indy's nostrils flare. "But don't hospitals put their morgues in the basement? Something about the inherent cooler climate underground keeping the need for electricity and refrigerant at a lower level than if they were above ground?"

It sounded reasonable. Smart, even. But the way it was said made the rest of us in the elevator feel like someone had insulted our mothers. He's lucky granny Miller wasn't there or he would've had to go outside and find a switch.

Indy smiled and matched Whitey's tone. "Of course."

She pressed LL, the button for the lowest level in the hospital, or so all of us on board thought.

40

The elevator came to a stop. The bell dinged, and the light under the LL button went off. Indy led our group off of the elevator into the landing outside of the emergency room with all the confidence of an employee who had only ever known L1 to be the lowest level in the hospital. She had never needed to visit the morgue. After all, she dealt with the sick. To be sick, you first needed to be living.

Indy opened the door to the emergency department, and we followed her inside. Indy had done rounds in an ER for a six-week span during clinicals in med school. It was then she decided she did not want to be an emergency department doctor. Some people thrive in chaos. It replenished them, recharged them. It could be the thing that made them feel like they're truly alive. Indy thought those people would be better off on a motorcycle or hanging off the sheer face of a rocky cliff than in scrubs and a gown with a stethoscope draped around their neck. Then again, who would be there to mend them once they fall?

The ER at Franklin Children's Hospital wasn't like the one Indy had done her time in. That one had meaning to its shape, order to its chaos. When the remodel came to the lower level here with the purpose of upgrading the emergency department, there were still the issues of working around the building's very old bones. So instead of one central hub with hallways branching out, they had split the department in thirds, each with its own main station, the three working as cohesively as possible through a busy main desk that had access to each department's main board and scheduled as necessary. The work got done thanks to the ingenuity and care of the staff. However, the wait times were the longest in the region thanks to the layout of the space and the system they were forced to employ.

Indy was sure the way to the morgue would appear in one of the three emergency wings. She confidently puffed out her chest and held her head high like a doctor on a mission — which she was, but not the type of mission usually undergone by doctors in hospitals — so no one would think to stop her, and by extension the group, on her way through. Time was of the essence.

Hall after hall, room after room, our group followed Indy while dodging scurrying nurses and power walking doctors seemingly unaware that other humans walked these halls too. The sights and sounds of the emergency room reminded the group of two things. First, none of the four wanted to spend any more time in this environment than was necessary. Second, if our missing friends were in any condition similar to some of these kids, they needed to be found as soon as possible.

We passed a room on our right that had its door propped open, hopefully for ease of access for someone — a nurse, a janitor, someone from FEMA's disaster relief team — to enter by. There was an adult standing in the corner of the room with her hand over her face like she was cosplaying Heather from the Blair Witch Project. The floor was covered almost in its entirety with vomit, as if he were conducting an experiment where he had been attempting to tie dye the laminate floor with a green and brown swirl.

Around one corner, we had to suddenly stop and juke like NFL running backs hitting the hole to avoid the trail of tar-black stool coming from the overrun diaper of the four-foot-tall girl with the long blonde hair trying, rather unsuccessfully, to make it to the bathroom. Her mother apologized as though there was anything at all she could have done to avoid the mess.

There was the ear-splitting scream of the older teenage girl with the knee she dislocated while wrestling with her friends at a sleepover that seemed to be in a competition for highest decibel produced by scream with the young teen boy two halls over who had been bench pressing with his buddies when the load got too heavy for his young bones to handle, his forearm breaking at the growth plate and the heavy bar fracturing two ribs on the landing. That solidified my reasoning not to lift weights. Cardio only for this guy, Chloe.

Joey and I started the expedition through the emergency wings looking into each room at the parent or parents there with their children, and by the end of the third wing we walked the halls with our heads down, not making eye-contact with anyone, clutching each other's hand as we walked, our eyes focusing on the feet of Indy and Whitey so we didn't get separated from the group.

One room in particular hit us with a pair of punches to our solar plexuses. Looking into the rooms in the emergency room and seeing small preteen girls sitting sick on the hospital bed was a reminder of the start of our journey in this building almost two weeks ago.

However, this particular room was like a window into our past. There wasn't a huge sample size of interracial couples in Franklin, so when we saw a small girl with a white daddy and black mommy in the second wing, it was a cold reminder that we had brought our little blessing to a room like the one we were looking in, but unlike the probable outcome for that little girl, ours was lying cold in the morgue we were trying to find. It was right about then when a thought struck me. We wouldn't be able to see you once we got there...would we?

41

"Doctor Indiana, do we need to ask for directions?"

Indy's face scrunched like she had taken a bite out of a lemon. Or a pickle. She hated pickles. She had no idea what Lila saw in Whitey.

"If we don't see it soon, we will. I want to follow up with Doctor Kirschner first, since we're down here. It's around this corner."

Indy saw the doorway to the imaging hall and tried to not show the relief she felt at the moment. She had noticed your mother and I becoming visibly distraught the farther we walked through the emergency department and was glad to get us out of that environment.

Joey, happy to be leaving the emergency department, thought back to the conversation in the office upstairs and asked, "Indy, didn't you say this doctor had been in the hospital a long time? He would know where the morgue is, wouldn't he?"

"Potentially. Some hospitals use their morgue for autopsies, so their doctors would use them in that case. We use the operating rooms for those, and as far as I know, we always have, with the exception of during the worst of Covid. But some hospitals don't even have morgues. They send their dead to the local funeral home straight from the room…"

Indy stopped herself and spun around. Whitey had to catch himself so he wouldn't run into her. "Joey, I'm so sorry. I'm rambling about this, and you guys…"

"It's okay, Indy." Joey smiled. "What's done is done. I asked, you answered. It's fine. Continue, please."

Indy hugged Joey.

The gesture caught your mom off guard. The sentiment of the moment and the affection shown from the doctor, who was herself on the verge of tears… I thought it was crazy, but Joey had always said she could smell the onset of tears. What was it with this floor making everyone relive things they were trying to suppress for a few minutes? For twenty seconds, the ladies allowed themselves to break. I placed a hand on each woman's shoulder and closed my eyes. Even Officer Whitey put his hands in his pockets and lowered his head, remembering that his duty to serve and protect included serving as a means of helping the grieving during their times of distress. It seemed likely that too often he forgot.

The women broke their hug and wiped their eyes.

"Indy?"

I couldn't seem to lift my face from the ground. I could feel the tremble in my voice.

I lifted my head, and the change in elevation pushed the swelling tears over the brims of my eyelids.

"I need to ask you... We had been here for almost two weeks. Chloe had been getting better, hadn't she? Were we really on our way to going home? Wasn't she..."

Your mother clung to her husband like moss to a tree. We knew that separately we couldn't handle any of this. We were quickly learning and being reminded that together we could keep our heads above water. I could feel my breath already regulating.

Indy had no such shoulder to lean on. The ones she had always relied on within the walls of this building were currently missing.

She did her best to gather herself, the way her mentor Lila had always done before entering a room, and addressed the couple the best she could.

"We believed so, yes. All outward signs we observed from Chloe herself told us she was improving. Any inward signs we had available to us, the labs we were drawing, the sights and sounds we could attain with our instruments, all pointed to the same conclusion. We were discussing discharge."

She took us by our hands and lifted her eyes to meet ours. "When this morning went the way this morning went, it devastated us too." She took great care to accentuate each word that followed. "That's why we're here. To get answers. For Chloe."

The three of us squeezed the hands we held as each took a deep breath. A cleansing breath. We released, and Indy turned to her left.

"Doctor Kirschner's office is just ahead."

42

"Doctor Kirschner?' Indy called as she gently pushed open the door to the old doctors office. It had been a couple of hours since she had last been in his office, and she wasn't sure if she expected him to still be there or not. Her questions were quickly answered at the sight of Doctor Kirschner sitting behind his desk in his black ridgeback executive office chair.

"Doctor Jones! How pleasant to see you again so soon! Is there something else I can do for you this morning? Assist in an expedition to a foreign land, perhaps? I only have so many Nazi-fighting years left in me, after all."

Indy and the old doctor shared a hearty laugh that went directly above Whitey's head like an air show down at the fairgrounds. When Doctor Kirschner noticed me standing in the doorway, his laugh slowed to a slight chuckle until I nodded my appreciation for the joke, an "all's well" for the old doctor he greatly appreciated.

"I was wondering if I could take a look at that message you sent out after I left, Doctor. My boss thought it best if we were completely prepared if we do need to talk to anyone on the team today, if that's alright with you."

Indy wasn't even aware she had turned on a measure of Southern belle charm, folding her hands in on each other and smiling while her eyelashes batted away.

"Oh, I see no harm in that. It may be quicker if you come around the desk and look for yourself."

Doctor Kirschner scooted his chair out of her way and stood in the corner, giving the young doctor plenty of room.

Indy's smile quickly and visibly faded away once she saw the message that went out to the IV team, which included Richard Mercier and Edward Falcone.

Indy knew in that moment, felt in the marrow of her bones, that something terrible had happened to Lila and Addison. She couldn't know what, where, or when, but reading that message solidified the why.

"Is there a problem, Doctor?" The old man in the corner behind Indy asked.

Indy closed her eyes to steady her breath. Her chest was beginning to noticeably heave, and she needed Doctor Kirschner to stay oblivious. Who knew what other ways he could put us all in harm's way unknowingly?

"No, doctor. Nothing wrong at all."

Whitey could tell from the voice of the woman that the antithesis was true. Something was very wrong indeed.

Whitey stepped forward to draw the old doctor's attention away from Indy, giving her a chance to get herself together. "Doctor Kirschner, Officer Arthur L. White. I'm a friend of Doctor Powell here."

Doctor Kirschner stepped forward to shake the extended hand of the police officer standing in his office and wondered for the first time why a policeman and two regular looking folks were walking around with the young doctor.

"I was wondering if I could ask a question, sir. It would settle a discussion I was having with my partner the other day. He says hospitals all have morgues. I told him morgues are only in funeral homes. There's a coffee and doughnut riding on this, sir." Whitey laughed his best work laugh, even though he hated the "doughnuts are for police" stereotype.

Doctor Kirschner pondered the question seriously for a moment longer than anyone thought he should. I wondered if perhaps your mother and I should turn and go, that the doctor was going to start asking questions we couldn't answer, but his face lightened up, and he smiled at Officer Laurence.

"Officer, that is actually a great question, and one that I'd wager would confound many people not in health care. Probably even quite a few who are, I'm afraid. The fact of the matter is that both of you are right, and both of you are wrong. There is actually no industry standard for the matter. Some do, some don't. As far as I'm aware, there is no rhyme or reason to which ones do and which don't. I'm not sure what that means for your doughnut decision, I'm afraid."

"I suppose it'll have to be a draw then. Thanks for answering as best as you could, Doctor."

Whitey signaled Indy with his eyes to go ahead and leave. Her heart was in her throat, and she had a million questions for Doctor Kirschner, but she listened to the silent judgment from Whitey. He let her pass in front of him and head into the hallway. After a smile and nod of appreciation, he turned to follow Indy out, but before closing the door, he stopped and turned back toward the inside of the office. I was betting he learned that move from Columbo more than from the academy.

"Oh, Doctor Kirschner, just one more thing. Does this hospital have a morgue?"

Doctor Kirschner approached his black ridgeback executive chair and sat in it while he answered the officer's question.

"Actually, we do. This hospital is quite old, one hundred and fifty years or more, I believe. Once upon a time, and for many decades in fact, the morgue was quite heavily in use. When I was a young doctor, I heard of the occasional cremation that even took place, though I haven't heard of one of those in some time. I haven't been to our morgue in many years. To my knowledge, no one has since the renovations. We do still store bodies down there for the funeral homes though."

"Down there?"

Whitey wore his confusion like a robber wears a mask to a bank heist. It seemed to catch Doctor Kirschner off guard.

"Pardon?"

"You said you still store bodies 'down there' for funeral homes? Where is 'down there' if we're on the lower level?"

"Oh, we're on a *lower* level, Officer. However, we're not on the *lowest* level. There is a basement level underneath this one. The morgue is the only thing still in operation down there. The entire rest of the floor is an antiquated relic, probably a quite disheveled one at that. Much like myself, I'm afraid. Once I retire, I'll be put out to pasture like the offices, storerooms, and whatever else once occupied that space. Why, the only person who even needs to go down there would be Mr. Tom, the head of patient transport, unless he started allowing the rest of the team to do corpse transports, which frankly I think he should. It's a little off-putting to keep such a delicate thing all to yourself, in this old man's opinion."

Whitey smiled at Doctor Kirschner and thanked him for his time. He even promised to bring him a coffee and doughnut sometime to show his appreciation.

43

"Indy, what did the notice he sent to the IV team say?"

"Indy? Hey, guys, I think something's wrong with her."

"Indiana, are you in there?"

"Take that arm. Let's set her down. There we go."

"Indy? Indy?"

We hadn't made it far from Doctor Kirschner's office before realizing something was off with Indy. She was moving with the group, but not like the Indy from the emergency department. Her head was down, her gaze was vague, and she was totally unresponsive.

If we could have heard the world from inside her head we would've known she wasn't with us at that moment at all. The noise of the world had been reduced to an indirect hum that flooded from all around her, and she could see nothing but the darkness around her and the spots that filled her vision. Truth be told, Indy was dancing with a full-blown panic attack, and it was starting to take the lead.

Joey ran ahead to a vending machine in the next hallway and brought back a bottle of water, which Whitey placed on Indy's cheek before resting it on the back of Indy's neck. I had knelt down beside the seated doctor and was holding her hands together with one hand while gently stroking her arms with the other.

Indy blinked and softly said, "He killed them."

The rest of the group rushed to her side, all kneeling to get their eyes and ears in direct correlation to hers while asking her to repeat what she had said.

She looked at us, each individually and then somehow all at once. "He killed them. He killed us. The doctor... He was... My God, we talked about... He was supposed to be tactful. That was the word he used this morning about his message. 'As tactful as I can be,' the senile old man."

Indy grabbed the water bottle from Whitey and took a long drink.

"Indy," Joey said while Whitey took a visual assessment of her vitals, always working. "What did the message say? Why do you think he killed them?"

"He didn't kill them himself, but his message...and we can't find them. There's no way... They know."

All at once, Indy stood up and spiked the water bottle on the ground like she had scored the go-ahead touchdown in the big game. She looked at the group wide-eyed and frantic, and she managed to make a whisper come across like an angry yell at the same time, exclaiming to the group, "They KNOW."

Indy looked around for an open room, and finding one and looking inside to check it for occupants, motioned the group inside before stepping in herself and closing the door.

"He spelled out plainly, with absolutely no tact, that an investigation is under way by a team of primary doctors looking at recent child deaths and the potential for correlation by IV team consults. I mean, he laid the whole thing bare on the table to the exact person, or people, who would be guilty if we're right. That went out to the entire IV team, which includes Richard Mercier and Edward Falcone, the two IV team members who may have been involved with recent child deaths. And he said a team of doctors were looking to talk to them about it. If we're right, they know, and if they saw Lila and Addison coming, they are already dead."

"This is taking too long. We need to get down there yesterday," Whitey said to the group. "Upstairs, I wasn't sure about this whole thing, but it's getting pretty clear something is up, and it's bad. Who has an idea how to get down there? We hit the lowest level on the elevator, but it brought us here."

I spoke up, "Didn't the doctor say some guy named Tom took the kids down there? Could we call him or page him or something?"

"I could, but who knows how long he would take to come up here? If you haven't gathered, Tom is...very Tom."

"Where do the bodies go after the morgue?"

Everyone turned to look at the mother whose child was currently resting in the morgue. Joey had known that tomorrow would be funeral home day, but if your body was currently down in the morgue, she wondered how you would be getting there.

Whitey answered first, "Do you mean location? Where do they go? The funeral home takes them—"

"No, I know where they end up," Joey interrupted the officer, who wasn't used to being interrupted but let it slide. "I mean, how do they get from the morgue to the funeral home? Where in the hospital do they go? Surely that Tom guy doesn't bring them back up here and wheel them out the front door."

44

"Thanks, Larry."

Whitey hung up his phone, slid it back into the pocket of his crisply starched, and ironed slacks.

"That was Larry. He owns Bob and Sons Funeral Services over on West Virginia Way. He said—"

"A guy named Larry owns a business called Bob and Sons?"

You know, Chloe, I was beginning to figure out how much Whitey hated to be interrupted, but I couldn't hold this one back. I couldn't stifle the smirk when Whitey glared at me either.

"Bob and Sons has been in business for forty-five years. Larry is technically one of the sons. Bob retired a few years back. The other son, Bobby, didn't want to take ownership. He wanted to work—"

"Wait, so Bob owned it, named it after himself and his sons, and when he retired, Bobby didn't take it, which would've kept the name accurate, provided he had sons, I guess, so the other son Larry took it. So instead of Larry and Brother, it's still Bob and Sons, even though it's neither owned by a Bob or Bob's sons, plural?"

Joey smacked me on the arm before Whitey would have a chance. "Ignore him. Please continue."

If looks could kill, the day's body count would've gone up at that moment.

"Gladly. Larry explained that when a body is coming to them from Franklin Children's, they bring a transport van—"

"Van? Not a hearse?" Joey interrupted Whitey this time. She was instantly mortified. I sarcastically smacked her on the leg. "I'm sorry. Whitey, you were saying?"

"Hearses are only used for funerals, not general transport. Since the casket is a purchase made after the body has generally been moved already," Indy responded with her head down. When she raised it, she saw the tension from Whitey at having been interrupted more times in the last minute than the last four months combined. "What? It's true... Sorry, you were saying?"

Whitey took a deep, cleansing breath and continued, "They bring a transport van to a freight elevator somewhere in the service port of the garage. There's a bell he rings, and that Tom guy brings him down to get the body. Call me crazy, but I say that's our in. If there's another level to this place, maybe Lila and Addison got down there somehow. Apologies for my lack of tact here, but if there's already a body down there from earlier today, maybe a ring on that bell will be enough to get us a ride down to the morgue."

45

On the lowest level, Claudia and Richard stood next to each other against the wall, in front of the "Never Give Up" poster, and faced Edward and Krystal from across the room. Tom stood off to the side, one hand in his pocket and the other scratching the stubble on his neck.

"Edward, we need to talk about this some more. You're blindsiding me here. It's been a long night, and I think we all need to go home and sleep some things off."

Claudia was trying to hide the desperation in her voice. She was not doing a great job of it.

"She's right, Edward. This was more than we ever talked about, man. Let us think this one over for a little while."

Richard thought back to all the times he sat with Edward, in Edward's apartment or Edward in his, and talked about their jobs and the pact they had agreed to. It wasn't even Edward's idea. It was Richard's. Now in the moment, his head was swirling, and he was having a hard time remembering who said what and when. In any of their conversations, or the group sessions with Krystal, had any of this redemptive blood stuff come up? Surely it had and he missed it. Richard felt as small as a church mouse and hoped he wasn't running out to get eaten by a snake.

Edward stepped forward in front of Krystal, who was smiling and watching him like a schoolgirl who finally admitted to the class she had a crush on the popular boy. Not only had a crush, no. They've been together for a while. She felt Tom's eyes burning a hole through her more fervently than usual.

Edward spoke, "Richard, Claudia, I know this may seem like much. The timeframe here is a little advanced, admittedly. We planned to build you up a little more before letting you in. You need time to grow in your faith and mature. I understand that and do sympathize with you, but we are in it now. The wise must be ready to do the work of the bridegroom to prepare the foolish, and the children must return to the wisdom of their fathers. Blood must be shed for the forgiveness and atonement of souls lest judgment come upon the world.

"Now, even this morning, this very hour tares have had to be plucked from among the wheat, and now there is work to be done. They have to be bound together to be burned."

That sent chills down half of the spines in the little hidden room. Krystal had been studying the same passages as Edward for the last several months. Richard and Claudia grew more unsettled with each passing moment, tears forming in each pair of eyes.

He turned to Tom and stepped toward him, drawing the man's attention away from Krystal for the first time since she stepped into the room.

"Tom, that means you have a work to do. I would prefer to finalize your atonement first, but I'm afraid we'll have to put this particular cart before this particular horse, just this once, as time is of the essence. There are tares waiting to be burned. I need you to start the cremation oven."

46

Tom looked at Edward, then at Claudia, then back to Edward. He was waiting for a punchline that never came. His dream of having a room full of good friends was quickly becoming a nightmare. Tom hated nightmares. They reminded him of his childhood bullies, both outside his home and inside.

Edward knew he sometimes had to wait for Tom to respond to questions or requests, but he hadn't anticipated Tom not responding at all.

"Tom? Tom, I need you to go start the cremation oven now. Time is short, my friend. There is work to be done."

"What did you do?"

The soft voice filled the room like the first waters in the storm surge that caught the unsuspecting victims off guard, thinking the tide was only rising before being swept away. There was a fire in Claudia's voice that was peeking out from behind the nerves and apprehension. Soon it would rage, if it wasn't first quelled.

Krystal stepped forward to take charge of the situation with the young nurse before it developed into something that would be harder to control. Plus, if she took the initiative with this, it would leave Edward free to deal with Tom. Krystal knew Tom could be a handful to deal with.

"Honey child, nothing's been done that didn't have to be done."

Claudia's eyes snapped from Edward to Krystal with such force it seemed to cause Krystal to stumble slightly. Krystal had heard the theory of how a butterfly flapping its wings could cause a storm to blow on the other side of the world, but here she was only feet away from Claudia's eyes. To Claudia, however, they were worlds apart.

"You. I don't even know who you are. I've cried to you. I've laid open my soul to you. I've listened to you when I needed advice, and you've opened your arms to me when I needed a friend. But this? All of whatever this is? This isn't about saving people or leading people to salvation or redemption or whatever. This is Netflix-documentary-level cult leader and serial killer bull..."

"Claudia, I hear you, and I..."

"That's the problem, Krystal! You don't hear me. You don't hear Richard, and you for sure don't hear Edward, or you'd be the one leading the charge to shut him up! You—"

Claudia stopped suddenly, her face showing the levels of betrayal she was feeling. Betrayals on a personal level, sure, but she suddenly saw the faces of the parents who had been in the hospital over the last five months then confronted with the task of burying their children. Children Edward had been *redeeming*, a work done with her help.

Claudia continued, "You helped him. That's your story. You bought his spiel hook, line, and sinker a decade ago, and when you got here, you gave all your progress and hard work away to fall back into it all over again. You...you knew what he was doing to those kids. How could you look their parents in their eyes? You counseled them, Krystal."

Tears ran down the multicolored face of the girl who eight months ago had no friends, five months ago had best friends, and at this moment didn't know who was a friend and who was the devil himself.

"You're right. I knew." Krystal grabbed the stool on her left that had been occupied by Richard earlier but had been empty since her entry into the room and held it out to Claudia. The shadows cast by the lampstands in the corners of the room showed a picture that looked like a bridge between two towers. A bridge was being extended from the chaplain. She had hope Claudia would accept it.

"I saw in you what I saw in myself. A lost little girl. That's why I asked Edward to invite you and Richard to my group.

Because I once was lost, but I have been found. We found you and wanted to bring you into the fullness of all you could be, baby. I was there for you because I could see all you could become. I counseled you so you could know that forgiveness could be found, that hope could be found, that you are not broken and are not worthless. You are strong, and once you found yourself you could lead others. Honey, all that is true. I know it because I've lived it.

"Edward is who he says he is. I've seen it and know you have too. He didn't hurt those kids. He redeemed them. That's what I told their parents. Weeping only lasts for a night, but joy will come in the morning, because those babies are saved by the blood, and I have seen the blood that they have been saved by. You can see it too. Maybe that's what you need, Claudia, to see the blood."

Claudia went to stand from the stool she had collapsed her weary body on, but Richard stopped her. He placed his hand on her shoulder and stood in front of her.

"See the blood? Edward, what is she talking about?"

Edward kept his eyes on Tom and, placing his hands on Tom's shoulders first, said, "Tom, the oven, now. Go. I'll come to you in a minute."

Tom glanced around the room. Since he was a child, he was uncomfortable in rooms filled with tension. He felt it with his parents, he felt it with his counselors, and he could feel it now. He wanted to be with his friends but was confused as to whether that was where he was anymore. Tom nodded and left the room.

Edward turned to the group and addressed Richard.

"You know what she's talking about, Richard. You gave your blood to be..."

"I didn't give you my blood, Edward! I was letting you practice your job! My God, man, what were we even doing these last few months? Who... What are you?"

"I was testing you. And I was training you. All those years ago when it was made clear to me who I was meant to be and what I was meant to do, I knew there would be others who would come along and help me redeem the world. Krystal came first. The others she came with are God knows where. They've likely gone apostate like that old man, Creed. But Krystal showed me the complete picture. We needed others, missionaries in a sense. Then came you and Claudia.

"This place is special, so full of life but an example of death at the same time. Where better to begin the redemptive plan of God to turn the hearts of the children to their fathers? It's a special calling, but it's yours, Claudia. I wanted to bring you both in fully from the start, but thank God for Krystal. She came to me as the angel of the Lord came to Elijah and counseled me as I redeemed her. She told me to bring you along slowly. She saw your doubt was strong.

"We have been bringing you to a place of fulfillment but did not know the day or the hour, and behold. As it happens, today is the time of harvest. Today, I have had to separate tares from among the wheat, and now they must be burned so we can continue the work before us. For now, I think Claudia needs a minute. Let us leave her to her thoughts and reconvene in a little bit. We have tares to burn. Richard, Krystal, come with me."

Edward backed out of the room and gestured for Krystal to follow him. Krystal walked out of the room into Edward's arms, greeting him with a kiss. Together, they motioned for Richard to follow. As Claudia sat with eyes wide open and mouth agape at the prospect of being left alone, Richard mouthed an apology to his friend and walked out of the room. Edward closed the door, the girl with the patch on her face still seated inside, and locked it behind them.

47

Richard felt like he was in a fishbowl. The world was upside down. He didn't think he was walking in a straight line and wasn't even sure where he was walking to. Over the last eight months, he had gotten to know four people very well. Now he was sure he didn't know at least two of them and was very sure the one he wanted to know the most would likely never look at him the same again.

He had been asking himself lately if he had really fallen for the girl who had removed her N95 mask on the elevator to reveal the most unique and beautiful face he had ever seen, and until two minutes ago he believed the answer was yes.

Two minutes ago, however, he had walked out on her and watched as she was locked in a room by a man who apparently believed himself to be the next Elijah, Moses, or John the Baptist, he was having a hard time keeping up, from the Bible and who had not only lied to him and used him to help gain access to children in the hospital that he wouldn't have had otherwise, but he had also stolen his blood? What was this life?

Still, he found himself walking away from Tom's room where Claudia was locked inside by herself and following the man who claimed to be redeeming the world, one child at a time, and the chaplain who believed and enabled him.

He had two questions burning brighter than the rest of the treasure trove of questions racing around in his mind. One, did Edward really have his blood, and what did Krystal mean by "you could see it?" Two, what did he mean by removing tares? Weren't those weeds? Wasn't April too cold for weeds? And burning them in the...cremation furnace?

They stopped in the hallway outside of a closed door. Richard already felt uneasy, but something about the way that hallway smelled had his stomach knotting up. Edward whispered something in the ear of the chaplain, who had been feeding whatever thoughts he had expressed to her when they were kids. She nodded and smiled at Richard then went down the hall and turned the corner out of sight.

"Richard, I know it's been a lot to take in this morning. I need you to know we never wanted any of this to come out this way. But the Lord works in mysterious ways, and we have to be ready in season and out of season, so here we are working through the situation we find ourselves in. Now I need your help. Behind this door is a problem I was forced to solve. Now I need you to help me get it to Tom and get rid of it. It's time for the tares to burn and the chaff to be blown away."

"Edward, I don't know what any of that means, man. What I do know is the girl I've been falling for is locked in a room right now, and she thinks I've been tricking her so you can do whatever it is you've been doing."

"And we will go back to her! We will go back as soon as we're done here. And, Richard, might I add I think you and Claudia will be just fine. She understands the call but needs a moment away to let her mind settle. To rest. I have no doubt she'll run into your arms the moment we return, which will be as soon as we're done here. Now wouldn't that be a great thing?"

Richard sighed. "Okay, alright. Let's do whatever this is."

He heard a strange noise coming from the darkness up ahead. It was a rumbling that started off small and was gradually intensifying in both volume and speed, as if a herd of wildebeests had broken free from the African plains and were rampaging this way. His eyes darted between the darkness and Edward, who didn't seem to mind the approaching thunderous herd. All of a sudden, from out of the darkness came Krystal, pushing an old rolling computer cart. One of the wheels was spinning sideways while the other three held the weight of the steel frame.

"All I could find."

"It will do," Edward responded and opened the door. The smell of rotten sewage mixed with copper hit Richard's taste buds moments before his nostrils. He recoiled from the smell, but the taste was worse.

"In here, but we have to move fast. There are two bundles that must be burned."

48

Claudia sat alone in Tom's room. At this time yesterday, she had been living her best life. She loved her job, she loved her friends, and she was beginning to feel she loved one in particular and had hoped he felt the same. Today, she wondered if any part of her life wasn't a lie.

She ebbed from hurt to furious and back again, each emotion containing a need for tears, though they flowed differently depending on which side of the tide she was on.

She was playing the last eight months of her life over again in her mind, letting the reels rewind and play again when the tape ran out. Nothing made sense, but surely there was something that would put it all in order.

Yesterday, Richard and Edward were her friends, and Chaplain Jenkins... *Call her Krystal, Claudia. She's forfeiting the right to be called chaplain*. She was on her way, though she had been more of a friend than anyone but the two IV nurses had been in years. And Tom, well, was more of an acquaintance. She hated to make someone into an outcast after spending so much of her life as one, but it was hard to accept Tom as anything more than that. Was that terrible? Maybe she did need saving.

That's crazy. Get out of my head, Edward, she thought to herself.

Yesterday was too close. She told herself to go further.

This ordeal began with the pact. It was stupid, and she knew she shouldn't have gone along with it, but had it felt so bad at the time? Sure, she had her reservations, but was there any indication this was where the road would lead? Was there ever any indication of where a road could lead? Every bend in the road looked like the end, but still it pressed on until it wasn't, the next bend hid the "Under Construction" sign, and off the road they went.

Claudia was stuck on Edward's demeanor today. There had been a definite shift. A little while ago, he was still Edward, until he wasn't, like the road. Something happened that sent him past the construction sign and over the edge into the abyss. He went from giving her that same spiel about "needing practice" to preaching some sort of cult crap about blood and redemption. Something happened when they took their break. He seemed to admit that. Harvest time was now, and he had to pluck the tares and accelerate the plan? Her granddad was a farmer and King James Bible thumper. She knew tares were both weeds and unbelievers. Did someone call him while we were out of the room?

She needed clarity and didn't know how much time she had to get it. They could come back through that door at any moment, and unsurprisingly she was the only one who needed to bleed today. Well, that wasn't the way it was going to go.

She reached for her phone. Maybe someone could find their way down here and get her out of this room before Edward came back, but the empty pocket of her scrubs reminded her that her phone was in her backpack, and her backpack was in the room on the other side of the locked door next to Richard and Edward's, where they left them before coming in. No phones allowed in groups. It was a rule they all followed. Maybe "no bloodletting children" should be adopted to the rulebook too.

Claudia put herself back in that place in October when her new friends proposed the pact. It was indeed all about blood, but why?

"To help the children, Claudia," "Sure it's a little iffy now, but think of all the kids in the future who will benefit," "This is a temporary measure for a permanent solution."

They told her it was about the job. They needed to do their job better, and this was a small enough and old enough hospital that they didn't have the resources they needed, so they *had to* do it this way. Whose idea was it anyway, Richard or Edward's? Edward talked the most. When it was the three of them, he always did. It was when Krystal was around that he clammed up. Why was that? So he wouldn't say too much too soon?

Claudia had enough of trying to figure it out. Edward was crazy, Krystal was crazy, and they were feeding off of each other. Richard may or may not be in on the crazy, but she was not and would not be. They had fooled her. Taken advantage of the sad girl who showed them the patchwork girl behind the mask. From that point on, he knew he had her, like he knew he had Tom. She watched him play Tom from the minute he met him.

This would not continue. She would not be his lifeline anymore. When he came back, she would tell him. Or maybe she would show him.

49

Tom did as he was told on a day-to-day basis. It was how he maintained calm in his life. No one had reason to treat him poorly if he did what was asked of him. He learned that early on. When he got the chance to work primarily around recently deceased kids, he took it. The dead didn't make demands.

Tom spent a lot of lonely hours in the basement of the hospital. He got to do things he ordinarily wouldn't get to do, things like finding a room behind a room and arranging the first in a way to fully obstruct and hide the second.

Things like organizing Edward's vials in his own storage room. He was going to move them soon to their own hidden place, but they were safe for now. Tom hadn't seen anyone in the basement that he didn't give an elevator key to since he took the job as head of the patient transport unit.

Things like lying in the refrigeration unit meant for the bodies. It really was like a cot in a walk-in freezer. He had been late for several pickups because he had fallen asleep in the freezer, so he had to stop lying in them or they might take his job, and that thought scared him almost as much as the thought of disappointing Edward.

Things like turning on the old cremation oven, even though it hadn't been in official use in decades, and seeing what would burn up and what wouldn't. So far, everything Tom had put in had turned pretty much to ash.

Surely Edward's weeds would too.

Tom had been smart about using the oven. He was proud of how smart he had been. The oven used gas to heat itself. Tom figured if he was turning the oven on some this month and not again for a few months in a row that someone would see the gas bill and come asking questions. So for the last few years, Tom would turn on the oven once a month. He used it as an incinerator for his trash. Yet another way to make sure no one knew he was living down here. Edward was lucky enough that the day he asked was a few days before trash day for old Tom. Once he got the oven lit, he planned to get his trash to burn with Edward's weeds.

Tom stopped and thought about the moment he saw the chaplain walk into the room. That thought was interrupted with the memory of watching his friend Edward kiss the chaplain. Tom opened the door to the oven to check the heat, which struck his face in the same way the kiss had struck him. He could still feel the sting and had wondered if they could see a mark left by the blow of the betrayal.

At that moment, Tom had a vision of Edward's body among the flames in the heart of the oven and wondered how long it would take to come back a pile of gray ash. It only took an hour for the dead opossum he found in the parking lot. Although Edward was a lot larger than an opossum.

50

By the time the guys from the IV team had approached the room that currently both held Edward's blood collection and the body of Addison McCray, her blood was not the only thing that was once inside her body that was now on the floor under her body.

When Richard walked through the door that Edward had opened, his mind flooded with the possibilities for what the origin of that smell was. His preference, if you could call it that, was that a family of something from the rodent family, opossum, or some such thing had somehow made its way inside and gotten trapped. Maybe they starved or cannibalized themselves. He didn't know if that was even a possibility but nurses weren't animal specialists. Whichever happened, surely that smell would be something animal control would've been more qualified to handle.

As he stepped farther past the threshold of the room, he saw the shelving units that took up most of the space, he saw the steel desk that was missing a leg, then he saw the missing leg on the floor. What he saw next stopped him in his tracks. There was a foot in what appeared to be a women's shoe, connected to an actual leg, a bare human leg. There was a pool of something that had formed under the leg. He couldn't see what it was but could sure smell it though. The shadow had a reflective quality that told him it was liquid of some sort. He looked back to Edward and Krystal, who had crossed the threshold themselves, pushing the cart Krystal had found into the room with them, and Edward motioned with a nod to go on.

So far over the last eight months, every time Edward advised Richard to go on with something, it had typically seemed like a good idea, but looking through the hindsight of today's revelations, they all had invariably been bad ideas. This was no exception.

Richard put his head down and continued walking deeper into the dark room. The leg had a match. He hadn't seen it at first because it was splayed out at an angle that told him the person it belonged to wasn't on the floor intentionally, unless they had a circus performer level of flexibility.

The legs came together at the panties of their owner, exposed from under the skirt that was flipped up and over the woman's waist. Her lower half was facing up with her legs at opposing angles like the hands of an analog clock, but her upper half was lying face down. Her arms flailed to the sides, and her hair was strewn about from her head.

It appeared as though she had been spun around by a whirlwind and dropped haphazardly on the floor when the twister moved on. Her body likely slumped flat as her muscles relaxed, which had also caused the ungodly odorous pool under her waist and legs.

Whatever killed her did so quickly and violently to put her in this position. Richard got close enough to make out the flowers on her dress in the darkened room and saw the contrasting splash of dark color in her light-blonde hair. It reminded him of the wrestlers he saw on TV when he was a kid who kept their hair color light so the blood would stand out.

The woman was face down with her head in a puddle of its own. The smell was so thick Richard was sure he would still be tasting it long after the day was done.

He heard the thumping and squealing of the cart being pushed behind him as he had crossed deeper into the room, but he hadn't heard it since turning the corner and seeing the entirety of the dead woman. *Oh God*, he thought. *I am in a room with a dead woman. Is this what shock feels like?*

From when he saw the first glimpse of a foot, he had felt drawn farther into the room, like he had been caught in a tractor beam. The beam was off now, and the gravity of the moment took over. Richard was standing in a dark room in an abandoned basement of a hospital built in the time of the Civil War looking at the dead body of an obviously murdered woman.

He turned to find Edward and Krystal watching him. If he was being honest with himself, he felt like he was turning around for the last time.

There stood Edward and Krystal next to the steel cart with one bad wheel. Edward was smiling, one arm around Krystal's shoulders. Krystal had one hand on the cart and the other around Edward's waist. She wasn't smiling, but she wasn't running away either. Why wasn't she running?

"Edward, what is this? Who is that?"

Edward stood far enough back from Richard to be able to distance himself. The need for that distance would either be necessary or not depending on how Richard responded during the next few moments. His response would also dictate the need, or lack thereof, for the rusty old scalpel on the cart. Edward had asked her to find two things when they got to the room. A rolling cart for the transport of the bundled tare to be burned and a weapon for defense in case Richard turned apostate and proved himself another foolish virgin with his lamp oil already burned out.

Edward answered, "The kingdom of heaven is likened unto a man who sowed seed in his field, but while men slept his enemy came and sowed tares among the wheat then went his way. When the seed was sprung up and brought forth fruit, so too came forth the tares. The servants of the man asked him, did not thou sow good seed? From where came the tares? He told them an enemy has done this. He told them, 'Let both grow together lest you pluck out the wheat with the tare, but at the time of the harvest, gather first the tares and bind them in bundles and burn them, but gather the wheat into the barn.'"

Edward watched as Richard's face showed the alternating waves of questions, understanding, and confusion washing over him like a shoreline. When moments passed without response, Edward spoke again. He knew time was a limited commodity that was growing rarer with each lost second.

"From the time God showed me the path for my calling on the sidewalk outside the mission on Pine Street, I have been sowing the good seed he has entrusted me with, Richard. But while I slept, my enemy continued working in the dark. Now we find ourselves at the time of the harvest, harvesting for the kingdom of God. No man knows the day or the hour when the Son of Man comes, and though we were aware we were within the proper season, the appearance of the sower's fruit has let us know that today is that time.

"Time for us to go forth to forgive and redeem this fallen generation and by their blood turn their hearts to their fathers and atone their souls. The question is who are the good seed and who are the tares? Krystal is a good seed, bearing fruit that will help the cause of atonement. There are also tares that sought to choke out our fruit. They must be bound and burned. What we must discover is if there are more tares among us. Decide today whom ye serve, Richard. Will you be an angel helper to me, or should you be bundled?"

Richard Mercier trembled with such force the cold sweat that had begun to spew from his pores was shaken from his skin like spray from an aerosol can, painting the floor around him leaving two dry footprints on the ground once he turned away from Edward and walked back toward the twisted body of Addison McCray.

Driving his arms under her torso and hips, Richard lifted her like a forklift would lift a pallet of medical supplies and gently set her body on its final transport, the cold steel cart with one busted wheel. Edward held the door open as Richard helped Krystal push the cart out of the room.

Following Edward's directions, they found the body of Lila Collins — if it had been headless, it would have been less disturbing to see — and added it to the cart. The added weight was beginning to make it difficult to push the three-wheeled unit. Together, they began the journey to Tom, who was waiting for them by the cremation oven, running hot at nearly 1,700 degrees.

51

Richard pulled the cart to a stop outside the swinging double doors that led into the morgue.

"Krystal, can you give us a minute? I need to ask Edward a question."

Edward stood with his arms crossed in front of his chest and replied, "Richard, Krystal is a good seed. You can ask your questions in front of her as you always have. Nothing has changed. Your eyes have just become open to things they had been closed to before."

"That's okay, sugar." Krystal placed her hand gently on Edward's arm and gazed up into his eyes, his hardened expression softening like clay on a potter's wheel as she spun and molded him. "I'll go see if Tom needs any assistance with getting his part ready."

The doors swung open then shut again as the hospital chaplain left the two men in possession of two corpses on their way to the cremation oven.

Edward struggled to maintain the newly softened expression as he looked at Richard. Time was of the essence, and he felt the day dwindling away with so much left undone.

"What can I do for you, Richard?'

Richard felt a bubble rising in his throat, which caught midway, bumping his anxiety up another level. He didn't think he had many more levels until it blew out the top. He could feel his hands trembling, though he felt slightly out of his own body. From the time he mentally bent the knee to his colleague in the storage room, he had felt like he was both outside of himself and trapped within himself. An out-of-body experience that was still trapped within like a prisoner stuck in the hole.

"Claudia. What's going to happen when we get back to Tom's room?"

Richard watched Edward's expression. It was as though he was stifling a storm, maintaining the calm outward expression while the inside was turmoil. He could see it all in the single twitch at the corner of Edward's left eye, then at the slightest tremble of his lip. A calming breath, in the presence of Lila, tamped down those emotions, and he met Richard's eyes with his.

"Claudia is a danger to us all, Richard. I'm a little surprised you haven't seen it. She has been marked from the beginning of time itself. She wears that mark on her face."

52

Tom heard the ringing of the bell that signaled the arrival of someone awaiting delivery from the morgue and instinctively walked toward the freight elevator as he had dozens, maybe hundreds, of times during his years as head of patient transport. It was odd that they were here already for the body of the young girl he had brought down earlier that morning. There hadn't been any paperwork yet, and the patients Tom had gotten lately that Edward had given him pre-warning about sometimes had autopsy requests come before the funeral home release papers came. Not always, but sometimes. A lot of the parents of young kids simply wanted the process to be done, but some wanted answers. And the funeral home showing up before the paperwork got downstairs to Tom wasn't all that unusual either. This was a hospital, after all. Things like paperwork moved slow here.

Tom was almost to the instrument panel for the elevator when he heard the squeal of the double doors to the morgue, so he turned on his heels and went to greet the arrival. He didn't like to let people down, especially his friends, especially those friends who made him feel feelings like he felt back home in the field. Edward was one of those friends, even though Tom wasn't sure why. Before today he hadn't heard Edward say much. He had talked to Tom some, but he had been pretty quiet in most of their meetings. Still, Edward made Tom nervous. Today though, Edward scared Tom. He also made Tom angry when he kissed the chaplain. Tom had pictured doing that himself, not the man who made Tom nervous.

When Tom crossed the threshold from the cremation room to the morgue, he forgot all about the bell from the elevator. There was an angel in his morgue, a dark-skinned angel with thick features and twisted braids. Tom had to remind himself to breathe at the sight of the chaplain standing in the flesh inside Tom's morgue.

53

"What are you talking about, Edward?"

Richard was shocked at Edward's insensitivity pointing out Claudia's white patch and insinuating there was something wrong with her because of it.

"Calm down, friend. I'll explain it, though I must say I am a little disappointed in you, Richard."

Edward had a way of talking down to his friends, and Richard always got triggered when he did it. He was beginning to think maybe he should've taken that condescension as some sort of sign. The fire in Edward's eyes tempered that feeling.

"There are certain evidential truths that bookend the scriptures, Richard. Maybe you aren't the one I believed you to be after all, if you can not see these very simple things. But maybe it's your closeness to the situation at hand that clouds you and blinds you. If we had more time, maybe you would have seen it after all, but the farmer can not know the day or hour when the harvest comes. Maybe you can be forgiven of that, as long as it is not unbelief. Do you believe, Richard? Or are you not as one who has been tried by fire and now shines as the purest gold?"

Richard's head was swimming, and try as he might he could not shake away, blink away, or smack away the cloudiness that persisted in the forefront of his mind. Edward's riddles rang in Richard's head in a way that made him seem far off and close by all at once. Of course he was a believer. He had passed the tests, hadn't he? Wasn't this all a test? Nothing made total sense, but everything made sense. He only had to believe, right?

"Of course, Edward, but I don't completely understand. That's all. Help me understand."

"And with the faith the size of a grain of mustard seed he shall grow to be greater than all the herbs of the Earth. Yes, exactly. Richard, the scriptures contain truths that bookend not only the great book itself but all of humanity. In the beginning, man communed with God until they sinned and were separated. At the end, man was separated from God until forgiveness of sin where we come together with God again. To be immortal as gods, Richard. This is the great joy of faith. This is why I was called to return the children to the fathers and redeem the world by their blood.

"But there is more than joy. There is sorrow. Great sorrows. The first instance of death was murder. Cain rose up and slew his own brother, his flesh and blood, and what happened to Cain? God gave him a mark so that people would know him.

What happens at the end? There is to come a great beast with power to blaspheme and wage war against the holy people and it will conquer them. And it forced people to wear what, Richard?"

"A mark on the foreheads."

Richard felt as though his world had been crumbling for eight months and he never knew it. He had made two friends when he joined the team at Franklin Children's Hospital, two night nurses like him, one on the IV team with him. When he saw Claudia's face exposed for the first time her beauty took his breath away. Now it was his face that felt exposed. His best friend, his confidant, his mentor, was pulling away his outer facade, and he realized in the moment that Edward had been ripping at that facade for months. Peeling away pieces of Richard's unbelief. At least, that was how he felt.

Men like Edward have a way of setting walls around us without our knowledge. Then, when they tear those false walls down, they get us to believe in the "great thing" they've done. That is when they can rebuild, with our full permission, whatever false truth they want. It's worse still when they believe it themselves.

Something inside Richard was tugging on him like a bell keeper trying to toll the bell to warn the villagers of an impending disaster. Edward was tearing his walls down, but thank God for the bell tower that still stood. Richard temporarily silenced the keeper as he dropped to his knees and asked forgiveness.

"Forgive me." He wept puddles of tears onto Edward's feet.

"I already have. You were redeemed with your blood, Richard. You have already atoned, and once is for all. Rise, there is work to be done. Though she bears the mark, all can be saved. She bore the cost of the initial test the same as you, and though she has faltered, she can still be made pure by her blood. If she more than falters, if she rejects, and you still wish to save her, you will have to make her atone. She will not be pure, but she can be free, if you wash her in her blood."

54

If a small explosive had gone off inside of Tom's room, it would be in better condition than it was right now in the midst of Claudia's outburst.

Once the door had been closed and locked, Claudia had begun talking to herself. The room was dark, the cinder block walls and no windows keeping the room fairly, but not entirely, soundproof and without any natural light. He had a collection of lamps, only two worked but there were four in all. Instead of just bringing the bulbs and making a switch when one stopped working Tom would just bring a whole new lamp. He liked the way the lights would cast shadows from the lampstands onto the walls and make him feel like people were in the room with him when there weren't. The shadows made him feel better while he was talking to himself late into the night.

His bed was a single hospital bed he found in the storage room on the other side of the basement. He plugged it into the wall outlet and found out why it was stored instead of used, the mechanics had a fault somewhere and wouldn't raise or lower anymore. He almost brought a maintenance man down to work on it but thought better of it. He thought the man might tell someone about his special room.

There were two chairs and three wooden stools, plus a stack of wooden boxes that had been in the hospital since the Reagan administration. He knew because one had a Reagan '84 bumper sticker on the back side that was torn on one edge where someone had tried to peel it off but wasn't able. Next to his bed was a small desk made of steel. The legs were rusty and in danger of falling off but he thought it made him look important to have a desk in his room no matter how out of place it actually looked.

When small group meetings would happen everyone would find a seat, there was one for everyone, and listen to the Chaplain talk about sin and redemption, separation and reconciliation, brokenness and forgiveness.

Claudia spun around and one of her outstretched hands smacked one of the lampstands that were giving out what little light there was in the room. The light increased. Claudia paused and looked at the lamp. Her grandmother had a lamp that intensified with touch, but she hadn't seen one since she was a young girl. She touched the lamp again, and the light increased. Another touch and the light was gone. Claudia laughed. The sound started out soft and increased in volume and veracity until she was lost in it. She felt like a caricature of herself, drawn in a padded room and hidden by jagged "Ha Ha Ha's."

She gave three sharp taps to the lampstand and snapped silent as though the light had cut off her ability to make noise. She ruminated on the light, more so on the lampstand itself. It had stood in her atmosphere in the little room all morning. It had surely been there during any number of past meetings here in this room, lighting their way and running out the darkness. Yet today it had been dimly lit and simply needed a touch, and neither her nor Richard, Edward, Tom, or Krystal had touched it.

A light that had the ability to expel the darkness with a touch had been allowed to remain dim, and no one seemed the wiser, failing to simply reach out and touch it.

Claudia was not laughing anymore.

She took the lampstand in her hands and swung it at the cinder block wall as though she thought she could create a pass-through in the wall. She couldn't, but she did wreck the stand. The light hung from the broken fixture, casting strange shadows on the walls around her. Tom would've had lots of people to talk to.

Claudia tossed the lampstand aside and became a whirling dervish of destructive energy moving through Tom's room like a tornado in an Oklahoma spring.

Lamps bent and broke. Stools lost not only their legs but their seats, one falling next to the door, a single leg connected to the seat like a giant oblong garden hoe made of wood.

Claudia grabbed one of the chairs and swung it at Tom's desk, one of the rusty legs snapping through at one particularly oxidized end and falling to the ground, followed quickly by the rest of the heavy metal table now with three legs.

Claudia sat on the edge of Tom's bed — if old Tom knew Claudia had been on his bed, he might die with a smile on his face — out of breath and wondering what force had run through Tom's room. She hadn't felt rage like that since her teenage years when she realized without doubt that her lack of friends was directly influenced by the lack of pigment in the patches on her face and belly. Here she was years later, with friends she felt close to who didn't seem to notice her abnormality, yet they locked her in this room to decide. Decide what, exactly? If she was okay with bloodletting a bunch of children, and herself apparently, with whatever that needle was that Edward had. It was no wonder they were dying.

Her eyes fixed on the poster of the frog in the mouth of the pelican, its hands around the throat of the carnivorous bird. "Never Give Up."

She wouldn't. For the kids. For Chloe.

55

"We're sure this is the right elevator?"

Whitey looked at me and smirked, "Do you see another freight elevator back here?"

It seemed like a logical question, but I suppose I did deserve the return burn.

"Okay, boys. That isn't helping," Joey addressed the pair of us guys standing by the motionless elevator but looked only at me before turning to Indy. "Who is this guy again? Why is he the morgue guy?"

Indy was doing everything in her power to keep from pacing around the service lot where the freight elevator was located. She was fidgeting with her badge, the one she tried to swipe on the keypad next to the call button hoping to override the need for help from below, to no avail.

"He's the head of patient transfer within the hospital. Mostly they're the ones who push wheelchairs, or whole beds when it's better for the patient, from one unit to the next. They take them to and from imaging scans, from floor to floor when the patient is moved from one to another, that sort of thing. He'd worked the unit for longer than I've been a doctor. Now he's the head of the unit and made himself the only one on the team to do deceased transports. Strange little guy, but the job gets done."

"And we're sure he's the only way to get from here to the morgue on a level lower than the lower level?"

Whitey had a way of asking questions to people while not giving them any indicator he was talking to them. Indy still didn't know what Lila saw in him, but she could be bossy herself, so maybe she liked a guy who could give it back.

"That's what Doctor Kirschner said, and he's been here longer than anyone. If this is the only way to get there, then we hit the button and wait for Tom."

I broke eye contact with my wife and stared at the ground. I must have looked like I had smelled something rotten.

"Hey." Joey started in my direction before stopping herself. If there was something she couldn't smell yet, she didn't want to step in it. "What is it, babe?"

I was wiping my face with both hands like I had stepped through a spiderweb and was trying to wipe off the web.

"I don't know, but I think I've heard that name today. I'm trying to remember where."

"Inside at the old guy's office, he told us…"

I waved Whitey off. It was a gesture Whitey did not care for, if his expression was any indicator.

"No, that's not it. Man, why do I know that name...Tom...Tom..."

Indy's stomach growled so loud Joey heard it and laughed. She hadn't eaten since before her shift started, and her body was beginning to remind her it wanted food.

"Sorry, ignore my stomach."

Chloe, I clapped so loud it scared the three standing around me, and they all jumped. Even Officer Better Than Me. No one but me noticed Whitey's hand on his holstered gun, which he gingerly put back in his pocket. He probably thought no one could notice.

"I remember."

My eyes, wide and glassy from the fresh mist that found their way out of my tear ducts, found the eyes of my sweet wife. Eyes I had been lost in many times and wished I would again. I'd rather be lost inside her eyes than anywhere close to where I actually was at the moment. To be honest, I'd rather be lost in them right now.

"Early this morning, while Chloe was still..." A hitch made its way into my throat. I took a moment to clear it and continued. "After Chloe had woken up. When I left the room...to go get our food."

Sometimes a smile is not from joy but sorrow, the mouth's way of trying to take the sting off the pain behind it. It was through such a smile that Joey interjected. It gave me a chance to gather myself.

"You always left early so we could have hot food. Winslow, I'm so sorry you weren't there. I hadn't even thought about that..."

Joey's mouth could hold back the sorrow no longer. Her tears betrayed her, and their flow prevented her from going on.

I shook my head as I held my wife's hands. "No, I couldn't have known. Why would today be any different from any over the last two weeks? That's not the point. When I was downstairs in the cafeteria, I met a man named Tom."

Whitey snapped to attention at the mention of Tom's name, and Indy stepped up to me. "You met Tom? Little guy, mustache..."

"Sounds like he dropped out of school before grammar lessons could take, yeah. Tom."

"What'd he say?"

"Think hard. Did he say anything relevant to what we're doing here?"

Once a detective, always a detective. Decorum and tact, we never knew ye.

"I think so. He freaked me out a little. Once I got upstairs...I forgot. We made a little small talk about being in line and how the day would be and you know, whatever. Shootin' it like strangers do. Then he said he was in the hospital because he had a delivery or something... no, a pickup. He said he had a pickup to make in the hospital. Said it wasn't the cheeriest job, but it was work. Something like that because I told him to try and find some joy in it. What got under my skin a little was what he said in response to that. He said, 'Oh, I'll enjoy it. It's just that no one else will.' Said it real vacant-like too. But it couldn't ve been Chloe. I heard her monitor stop when I got to the door. That was a good ten, maybe fifteen minutes later. Was there anyone else this morning or last night maybe who...needed transporting?"

Indy began to melt from the way we all looked at her. She knew the answer already. It was her job to know that answer. That didn't mean she was prepared to give it.

"No, there was no one else last night or this morning who would've needed Tom."

Whitey felt his body begin to tense up like it always did before chasing someone through a parking lot or subdivision. It was almost that time. He was sure of it.

"That means ol' Tom already knew. Maybe he knows we're here." Whitey turned back to the elevator and pressed the call button a second time.

"Hey, Tom! Come out and play, you piece of—"

Everyone stopped and stood at attention. The elevator had begun to move.

56

"Hey, Tom!"

Krystal let the swinging doors coming to a close behind her before making her way over to Tom. From the time she had reconnected with Edward and began studying the scriptures through his guided view of "special revelation," she had known a day like this would come sooner than later. Time was short, and there was work to do. Neither Edward nor Krystal had planned for today to be that day, however.

She regretted not getting Tom to show her around the morgue — or the cremation oven — but to get Tom to give her a proper tour meant she would have likely had to be alone with him in the basement, and she still wasn't ready for that. She knew the way Tom looked at her. She could feel his eyes on her at random intervals throughout the day when they would be in the same hallway in the hospital or when she walked in with the rest of the group during regular meeting times, and she could feel it now. It was like being in a cartoon where the dog looked and saw a T-bone steak instead of a cat. Krystal had no interest in being Tom's meal today or any other day.

Tom watched the chaplain saunter over to him, her hips swaying out a rhythm that seemed to hypnotize him. He had to remember to close his mouth, or he might drool on the floor.

Tom walked out of the stone room with the heavy door mounted in the wall, an entrance to a fiery furnace King Nebuchadnezzar would have been proud of, and grabbed a folding chair from its place by the refrigerated unit. He set it out and motioned Krystal to it. If Tom had one social skill, it was manners for a lady. Tom would never be the one to not give a seat to a woman, especially one with the ability to steal the words from his mouth with a look.

Smiling, Krystal sat in the chair Tom placed in front of her. She didn't fail to notice his hand lingering on the seat back long enough to press up against her backside as she sat.

"How are you, Tom? Did you get that job done Edward asked you for?"

As much as Tom liked to stare at the chaplain he sure had a tough time looking her in the eyes when she was looking back at him. He looked every way but forward when he replied to her.

"Yes'm. I got the furnace turned on. It's been 'round a long time, ya know? Prob'ly older than I am now. They dun use it no more, but I fires it up from time ta time. Keep it ready 'n case they ever do."

"Mmm, that's good of you, Tom. I do hope everyone upstairs notices all the good you do here. You're a good man. Tom? Could you do me a favor and look at me? I need to talk to you before Edward comes in. That's good, thank you. Could you kneel down here? Let me look at you, hun."

When Tom was a young man, he liked stories. He wasn't a great reader, wasn't even a good reader, which was why he took so long sometimes to get things done around the hospital, but when he was younger, he would get his mama to read to him. He liked the ones where the outcasted boy would be chosen by a deity figure for a righteous quest. His favorites involved a sword and a mystical lady. He most remembered the lady in the lake who granted the sword of truth to the young man who would free the land. Kneeling down in front of the chaplain, he felt like that boy about to receive his commission from a holy lady for his righteous quest to save the world. That was what Edward kept talking about anyway. Saving the world.

Krystal put her hands firmly on Tom's shoulders. This was no time to be gentle. She needed his full attention.

"Listen close and listen well, Tom. Today has been...weird. Maybe not the start of it, but now it definitely is. I'm sure you can feel it, but I need you to prepare yourself. It is about to get weirder. There are things happening that are hard to explain and harder still to understand. But I only ask you to trust me. Do you trust me?"

It wasn't the ministry of presence Krystal was employing by drawing Tom in close to her, but she hoped the proximity would help hold his attention. It had been difficult enough to give messages to the nurses over their time together the past few months to get them ready for the end time. They could reason better than Tom. She just had to get Tom to go along, by whatever wiles she had available.

"If you dun't know that I do by now, then I dun't know whut ta tell ya, Chaplain. I brung ya to my home here and do whatere it is ya ev'r need. I mean..."

"Yes, you do, sweetheart. Oh honey, you have a heart of gold and I hope you know it."

"Oh, I know it alright."

Krystal lowered her head when she failed to stifle the laugh that bubbled genuinely from her soul. It was the kind of laugh that shook her whole body up and down in the chair. It made Tom blush.

"I tell you what. I wish more people could know you well. I mean that. Listen, Edward and Richard are outside those doors. They are going to wheel in a cart we found in another room down here. What is on the cart needs to go in the furnace. That's why Edward had you turn it on. This is important, part of God's plan. If we had more time, I'd show you, like I show you during our group time. There are things bundled up to burn away. Can you trust me enough to do this, even if you may not want to?"

Tom thought back to his childhood, running through the muddy corn field up the hill from his house where the other kids were playing war. When he wasn't under fire, sometimes catching crossfire from both sides, he would sometimes be brought in and given instructions by one of the teams. "Run around and get them from the rear, Tom." But they always expected him, and he'd catch it in the face. "Lay in the mud under the old tree, Tom. Wait for my signal." But the signal wouldn't come, and he'd crawl out from under the tree all chigger bit with ticks in his underwear and no one to be found until the next day when he heard their cries and laughter ringing down the hill from the field above. For a moment, he thought maybe Chaplain Jenkins was telling him something that was going to get him hit in the face or left alone, but only for a moment.

Maybe he should've let the moment linger a while.

The double doors burst open, and Tom saw Edward and Richard pushing and pulling a metal rolling cart with three good wheels and one bent wheel spinning without touching the ground despite the load the cart was under. On top of the cart, it looked like two people were taking a very awkward nap. There was a lot of blood, and Tom thought it smelled like the portable bathroom that had been in the service lot at the top of the freight elevator last summer. That smell reminded Tom that someone had pressed the call button recently. He looked at the chaplain, who was no longer smiling but instead gave a somber nod at Tom. He thought he could hear her telling him it would be okay.

"Come on, Tom. Help us now. We can't do this without you. If you don't help us, this can't get done."

Tom looked at Edward, who was letting Tom know how imperative he was to the success of what was happening. The holy lady had given him a righteous quest. Instead of a sword, he had his furnace. Instead of vanquishing evil, there were two bodies that needed to go inside.

"Tom, please." Richard looked into Tom's eyes.

Tom rose and led them to the furnace.

Once the job was done, Edward surveyed his disciples. Krystal wiped her eyes, a temporary weakness Edward would forgive, for now.

"Tom, take a minute and clean the cart for me, then meet us back in your room. We have to go talk with Claudia."

Richard, upon hearing the name Claudia from Edward's lips, lowered his head to the floor. He pressed his fingers into his closed eyes until he saw light from beyond himself, blinding him even though his eyes were shut. Once he was sufficiently sure there were no tears to greet the open air, he opened them and told Edward he was ready.

The three of them left Tom in the stone room, the double doors swinging shut behind them. He went to the steel cabinet in the corner and found an old spray bottle of cleaner of some sort. He assumed it would be an industrial cleaner by the placement alone. Before he could spray a drop, his thoughts were interrupted again by a bell. Someone was ringing for the elevator again. This time, no one walked in to stop Tom from sending the elevator car to the loading dock.

57

Edward stopped just inside the door to the storage room that hid the locked entrance to Tom's room and motioned for Richard and Krystal to close the door and face him. Walking down the hallway, Edward had realized that by this time, he, Richard, and Claudia had been awake for over twenty-four hours. The surge of adrenaline that came with the playing out of the end-of-days harvest around him had Edward flying high with no indication he would be able to come back down anytime soon. Earthly creations needed rest, but not Edward, not now. He was feeling the full extent of the calling on him, and he was invigorated. It was as though he had a power cord connected to a never-ending supply of electricity.

He also knew that although his disciples carried a similar calling, theirs was still lesser, and they would likely be feeling the draining effects of the day. Until now, when he would give to them from his special supply and invigorate them with power from on high to finish the work set before them. Yes, it was time.

Edward began with his head down. It took a moment for Richard to realize he was speaking at all.

"No man knows the day or the hour. Isn't that right? How could we know the mind of God? Except I did know, really. That is why we are here, because I had been prepared whether in season or out, and here we are in the season of harvest. God was speaking, and though I still see through the glass darkly, I do see through the glass, moving everything into place, though I could not see it."

Edward looked up and into the faces of his two closest friends and disciples. "But now I see. I was given a calling years ago. Through the blood in my eyes, I saw the vision, and through the ringing in my ears, I heard the voice of the angels telling me what I was to do. Redeem, by the blood. Forgive, with blood. Atone, through blood. The scriptures are plain. I learned them from a man who could not see them for himself. Even he fell away. He was foolish. He let his lamp burn out, but not you.

"I was called to fulfill the promise of Malachi. John the baptizer fulfilled a part, with his disciples, and now I fulfill a part with mine. He brought back the hearts of those fathers to their children, and now we will bring, are bringing, back the hearts of the children to the fathers of the faith. We have taken their blood and forgiven them their sins. Left them atoned, and for what purpose? They were destined to leave this world, many of them, and now to a new kingdom. They look to judge us for saving the world? They are foolish and are the tares growing up among you, the good seed. That is why now at the harvest they had to be burned. So we could be free to go about our fathers business.

"This calling, the call of Elijah the prophet, God's prophet preparing the way for the second coming, a coming that is now at the door..."

Edward looked seemingly through the shelves stacked in the way of the door to Tom's room. He lingered on the door before turning back to Richard and Krystal.

"Jesus came with three callings. Son of man, fulfilled. Son of God, fulfilled. Son of David, not yet but he is on his way. Between those, he will arrive *in* his people to prepare the way. Do you see?"

Richard looked at Krystal, her countenance was simply shining through the pores of her skin. He wondered if the same could be said of him, were his pores effervescent with shimmering glory, or was that the gooseflesh rising from the message he was hearing?

"The Elijah of this day is the lord Jesus Christ, do you see? Not man. God almighty. See? He stands before you to root out the tares and burn them, to raise up disciples and lead them, to turn the children to their fathers, and to redeem the world through atonement in blood.

"Now, there is one more choice to make, and it is not mine and not yours. It belongs to the one on the other side of that door who bears the mark upon her face. I have sought to redeem her, as I have redeemed each of you, but her mark has fought for her. God put a similar mark on Cain so none could destroy him. The beast is now putting similar marks on those he has claimed, but they cannot stand before the God of this age.

"If she will not choose righteousness, if she will instead choose against the will of God, she will face God's wrath. It is written, 'As it was in the days of Lot, fire and sulfur will reign down on them from heaven, so it will be when the son of man is revealed.' I have revealed it to you, my disciples, today. So it is written, so shall it be."

Edward stepped forward so that Richard and Krystal were close enough to smell the fire in his eyes. He grabbed each by the nape of their necks and drew them to him.

"Let those who have ears to hear, hear what the spirit is saying."

Richard heard the voice of the chaplain, the voice he had come to know as the voice of reason in the whirlwind of his life, speak out, "Thus saith the Lord."

58

Anticipation flooded your mothers and my minds, as well as that of Doctor Indiana Powell, while waiting for the freight elevator doors to open. Whitey was too busy running potential scenarios for what may transpire in the moments after our arrival at the bottom of the elevator shaft.

The bell sounded again, the abruptness startling me out of a daydream, the resulting gooseflesh on my arms causing me to shiver before marching forward into the unknown that awaited us all further below ground level.

The steel door opened, revealing a second door made of steel formed into a cage. Fitting for the mood of our little quartet who all felt like we were entering into a fight with a possibly unknown entity.

Whitey steadied his focus on the inanimate objects around him. He worked solo and would've left the group behind if he thought we would stay in the service lot. He knew better than to propose such an idea.

"Do we think this Tom guy is a killer or a patsy? It seems to me those are the two most likely scenarios."

Indy responded quickly and coldly before sliding closed the cage doors, "Don't forget about the nurses. That's what led us here in the first place. Do I think Tom is involved? Maybe, I would've said no until about a minute ago, for whatever that's worth. There are as many as three nurses, two men and a woman, who I figure are involved. Whether they're down here or not, I don't know, but someone sent the elevator up. We'll find out soon enough."

"I wouldn't write this Tom guy off so easily. If he knew their girl was dead, dying, or going to die, even potentially, that spells involvement, and believe me when I say, that makes him potentially dangerous."

With the cage door closed, our group stood still and looked around the freight elevator. Thick blankets hung on the three walls that made up the car. Whitey grabbed one and moved it aside to reveal a half wall of steel cage, stopping at his belt line and leaving nothing between the inside of the car and the concrete walls of the elevator shaft. He let the blanket fall back into place, and the door to the outside world began to finally close.

Under my breath, I softly sang, as we often did when beginning journeys both large and small, "And awayyy weee gooo..."

Equally soft, I was the only one who heard her, Joey whispered, "You're flingin-flangin right."

The car stopped with a jolt. Indy counted, "One, one thousand. Two, one thousand. Three..."

"Quiet," Whitey said with enough authority to silence a storm.

His hand moved to his holstered department-issued .40 caliber Glock 22, his thumb releasing the strap used to keep the firearm secure, while his legs readied themselves for a sprint. Whitey was preparing himself for anything that could be waiting on the other side of the doors that were taking entirely too long to open.

"Oh, wait," Indy said as she stepped forward to open the cage door. "Maybe it needs this first?"

"It shouldn't..."

The outer doors were the latest thing to interrupt Whitey as they opened with a bell and a squeak that an oil can would be hard-pressed to fix.

Standing before them was a short, balding man with a mustache and well-worn blue scrubs.

"Hiya, folks, I'm not riddy for ya yet, beins I hadn't got yer paperwork, but if ya show me your..."

Startling as realization took hold, Tom took two steps back away from the tall man with his hand on a gun that looked to be holstered, though the top strap was definitely unbuckled.

"Are ya from the funeral home, mister?"

Tom looked away from Whitey, and Whitey's gun, and noticed me standing next to one of the pretty doctors he'd seen upstairs when he made his transport runs, the one with the glasses and curly hair that Tom thought probably felt like a cloud on a summer evening in the mountains. "Don't I know you, mister?"

I stepped forward, letting go of Joey's hand and moving further between her and Tom.

"We aren't from any funeral home. And we met this morning in the cafeteria, Tom."

Tom took backward steps that matched the forward steps Whitey and I were taking in his direction. He switched his focus from me to Whitey, back to me, to Whitey's gun, then back to me again. He took a moment with each change of focus to linger slightly on Indy. Tom never took a pretty doctor for granted. A light went on behind his eyes.

"Oh, well ya know I don't think I went ta the cafeteria this mornin', friend. Think ya got me mixed up wit sum'mon else. They say I have a face like that, ya know."

The farther our group got to the center of the stone room, the more confused the looks on our faces appeared to be. The

318

four distinctly different noses crinkled while all eight eyes got smaller until they looked like slits so tight Tom wasn't sure if we could see out of them, and the focus of each member of the group appeared to be off somehow. We were looking down, up, and all around. Finally, a voice came out from behind the seemingly random black man from the elevator who said he knew who Tom was. He was so focused on me that he didn't see Joey standing there. You could tell immediately Tom thought she was very pretty. He even blushed.

"What's that smell?"

"Tom," Indy, the doctor with the round framed glasses said, "Is that your lunch or something? It smells like...barbecue?"

The aroma of smoked meat hung in the air like a fog you weren't aware you were driving through.

Tom backed out of the stone room and across the threshold into the open area of the morgue, taking full advantage of the distraction provided by the smell of flame-broiled doctors.

Whitey turned his focus back to Tom and, noticing the little man enter a different area away from the group, pulled the matte black Glock from its holster.

"Stop right there, buddy! That's plenty far enough."

Tom froze fifteen feet from the double doors that separated the morgue from the hallway that led to it.

Whitey's sudden command brought the group's attention from the sickeningly sweet and smokey air to the .40 caliber handgun that rested, fully loaded with fifteen rounds in the mag, in Whitey's outstretched hands that were pointed directly at Tom.

A commotion arose from the trio behind him. Indy's voice was the first that stood out from the rest.

"Whitey! You can't shoot that down here! What if the bullet ricochets? And think of the sound. I don't want to go deaf today."

"You're thinking too much, Doctor."

Whitey was done with such pleasantries as first names. This was the Officer White Show, and the lights were saying it was go time.

"This man is either responsible for the death of their daughter and God knows how many more of the kids he's brought down here, or he knows who is. So how about we..."

"Shut up, Whitey."

That snapped him out of his hyperfocus and back to the space he was occupying in the basement morgue. Whitey turned and looked from under a singular raised eyebrow at the man God almighty chose to be your daddy. A fact I thank God for, Chloe. And I wasn't even looking at Whitey. I could not possibly have cared any less about Arthur White at that moment. I was standing next to the morgue freezer, my eyes on the handle of the first unit. Joey stood behind me with one hand resting on the small of my back, the other covering her mouth.

"Excuse me? What do you think you're—"

"I said shut up, Whitey."

My hands were tented together and pressed against my face.

Sweet girl, the bond between a father and his child was one he could not anticipate before becoming a father, and one he could not explain after. You learned your child's voice. You became accustomed to their smells, both good and bad. But beyond the physical things, there was born a metaphysical connection wherein you could sense the presence of your child. Being near them filled you. They were, in fact, created with a single strand of your very DNA. You exist as a part of them. You didn't carry them, you didn't feed them, and you didn't birth them, so the connection that gets talked about, justly, goes to the mother who did those things; but they were still a piece of you. The bad ones chose to sever that bond, a decision the good ones simply could not comprehend.

I like to think of myself as a good one. Or I was once. I hope I could be again.

I could feel a piece of myself on the other side of that cold, stainless steel door.

All eyes present were on me. More specifically, all eyes present were on the single outstretched black hand that was beginning to reach out for the handle of that door.

All eyes except for Tom's. He saw the attention of everyone in the room, particularly the man holding the gun that had been pointed at him but was now sagging down and to the man's left, and made the quickest decision he had ever made within the walls of Franklin Children's Hospital.

Tom ran.

The sound of Tom bursting through the double doors of the morgue was loud enough to bring everyone back to the reality of the moment. Whitey cursed and ran out after Tom. He was followed through the door closely by Indy. Joey, tears gently running down the slight creases on either side of her nose, wiped her face with one hand. With the other, she balled her hand into a fist containing a bunch from the back of my shirt. Feeling the weak tug on my back, I let my hand fall off of the handle and come to a rest on my pant leg. I turned toward my wife and embraced her.

We wept.

The embrace lasted only for a moment until the sound of a single gunshot reverberated through the empty space like an explosion in a quarry blast zone. Forgetting momentarily about the body of our daughter in the freezer behind us, we ran out of the morgue. We ran toward the gunshot, toward our new friends, toward the man we believed may be responsible for your death, and toward the man who actually was.

59

Claudia was bleeding. Somehow during her outburst, she managed to cut herself on her left forearm. Now instead of a white patch like her face and belly, there was a streak of bright red, more of a trickle than a stream, tracing a bloody trail from forearm to wrist. The last thing she wanted to do was show Edward her blood. God only knew what he would do at the sight of it running down her arm. She shook her head at that thought. God wouldn't know. God had left Edward a long time ago.

Claudia looked around the dim room for something to clean up her arm. Tom had a small box inside his closet that he used as a laundry hamper, though Claudia saw no evidence that Tom did any laundry. She considered using a small washcloth to wipe her cut but quickly thought better of it. The thought of whatever was on that cloth wiping across a fresh wound left her nauseated. She dry heaved once before gathering herself and continued looking.

Tom's closet was at once both simple and a mess. Years of uncleaned dust hung in the air, threatening her airways like dancing in a field of ragweed or rolling in a pile of fallen and dried up leaves. A series of boxes stacked on top of each other was the extent of his organizational system. Claudia opened a series of boxes to find something to clean the blood off her arm. A first aid kit would be like finding a treasure chest, with bandages instead of gold doubloons.

After a series of uninspiring boxes, one contained receipts that appeared to all be from the cafeteria upstairs suggesting poor Tom never left the hospital, Claudia found one with surgical do-rags that looked like they were from the 1980s. Tom must've used his free time to explore the long forgotten basement like Indiana Jones in a remote jungle or desert. As old as they looked, they also looked clean enough so she removed one and used it to clean off her arm. *Okay, Edward, nothing to see here. No blood for you.*

Claudia closed the box and slid it back into place, bumping another box with her elbow and causing it to fall. She knew time was running short. Surely Edward would be back any minute, but curiosity got the better of her, and she opened the box.

Inside were an assortment of empty collection tubes nurses use when drawing blood. She padded through the empty vials and noticed one different from the rest. It had a label wrapped around it. Not one of the official ones with full name, birthdate, room number, etc. This one was a blank sticker with a name written in black sharpie. Andrea Yarborough.

Claudia dropped the tube back into the box and covered her mouth with the hand that held it, feeling like she may throw up. Andrea Yarborough was a nine-year-old patient on the fourth floor. She had been there only three days. How close was Edward to Tom? Was Andrea the next patient marked for "atonement?"

Claudia fought back the tears that were starting to form behind her eyelids. She was a part of this. He couldn't have carried out his plan without her blessing and her help. She closed the box and was about to put it back when she saw something poking out of the box that had been under this one. Placing the tube's box aside, Claudia guided the next box to the dirty floor of Tom's closet and picked up what was poking out of the top. A patient bracelet.

Claudia threw up in her mouth. The name on the patient bracelet was "Chloe Miller." She knew there was only one point when Tom could have gotten your bracelet into that box, when Edward suggested they all leave the room for a bathroom break, and the thought of Tom being either fast or sneaky sent chills down her spine.

Beneath Chloe's patient bracelet was a collection of patient bracelets. Some red, some green, each floor having its own color-coding system. Claudia looked at one. Devyn Samuels. Claudia was her nurse two months ago. Another. Emerson Paige. Claudia had her three weeks ago. She was funny. She would squeak every time Claudia had to stick her for lab draws. She probably squeaked when Edward stuck her too.

Claudia heard someone talking outside the door, and the voice was getting louder. Edward. She could tell he was ranting about something to someone. She assumed it was probably Richard, and maybe Krystal and Tom too. Claudia hurriedly put the boxes back in the closet after tucking the bracelets back inside. She moved to the door of the room and listened with her ear pressed against the wood. Something about fire and sulfur. Claudia had no intention to stand around and find out who or what Edward planned on burning. If Richard wanted to follow Edward down that path, he could face the same fate. It was out of her hands now. She thought she knew Richard, thought she knew the chaplain, but what she thought she knew had nothing to do with the contents of the boxes in Tom's closet. Those told her nothing was what it seemed.

Claudia would not be caught unaware.

Claudia bent down and grabbed a broken pole from one of the lampstands.

It would have to do.

The talking had stopped, and the silence made time seem to stand still. Claudia adjusted her grip on the tarnished brass pole while pressing herself as flat as she could against the wall to the side of the door. She felt like she had been waiting there for hours even though barely ten seconds had passed. All at once, something outside the door began to move. Whatever they had used to lock her in Tom's room was being removed. She steadied herself with one more breath. A cleansing breath.

The door opened, and Claudia stepped forward, the pole cocked back over her shoulder like Mike Trout's 32.5 ounce Old Hickory baseball bat. She closed her eyes, turned her hips, and let her hands fly. She didn't open her eyes until she felt the broken copper pole smash into its intended target.

Home run, Claudia.

60

Whitey had been in a handful of foot chases in his time as a police officer. Typically, they involved people both younger and faster than him. Tom was neither. Point to Whitey.

Those chases all tended to happen on fairly neutral ground: the parking lot and side alley of the CircleK, the backyards of the local well-to-do neighborhood, etc. where no one had home-court advantage. This was in the basement of the hospital, essentially the outer courtyard of Tom's house. Point to Tom.

Lastly, while most of Whitey's official foot chases happened in the late evening to overnight hours, they were mostly all outdoors while at least the moon was out and often there were streetlamps of some sort. This was the dark and dingy forgotten basement level of the hospital, where lights were few and turns were many. Point to Tom.

Whitey burst through the double doors, leaving the morgue with the force of the football team captain running through the banner at homecoming.

What he didn't know was the layout of the hallway on the other side of that door. Whitey anticipated the morgue coming at the end of a long hallway with plenty of room to catch his footing and continue in his pursuit of the little man with the head start.

That assumption was incorrect. Point to Tom. Whitey was quickly falling behind.

The hallway actually ran lengthwise, perpendicular to the doorway. Whitey found out the moment he burst through the double doors and stumbled at full speed directly into the wall five feet away.

"FREEZE!" Whitey shouted with the air left in his lungs after denting the paneled wall with his shoulder. Years of dust fell in a cloud around him, causing him to draw back and sneeze in a roar that may have been heard upstairs if the ER had been quiet that day. If he hadn't sneezed, Tom may not have been able to reach his room, at least not without leaving a bloody trail from that first hallway outside the morgue.

Whitey had raised his firearm, his shoulder screaming through the firestorm brought on by the fresh dent it left in the wall, and fired a single shot down the hallway.

Indy was coming through the door when the gun went off. Screaming at the explosion in front of her outstretched arms, she recoiled first before shoving Whitey back into the wall and following it with two chopping smacks on his back.

"I could've ran into that! Who taught you to do that!"

Indy's question was not a question but an indictment of both Whitey's training officers and Whitey himself. It was followed by a string of profanities that not only rivaled the volume of Whitey's sneeze but also helped to bring her heart rate down.

She stopped and thought of Addison, who was not simply a colleague but a dear friend. She realized that in spite of the reasons why she was in this basement in the first place, she hadn't thought of Addison since before Doctor Kirschner's office. She had become preoccupied with getting here to this space and finding not only answers but finding her friend.

She was thinking of Addison and Lila when we shoved the double doors open again, the force blowing the burnt smell of overcooked meat into the hallway.

Whitey already had another head start on our trio as he tried desperately to not lose Tom in the dark maze-like hallways. With each new turn, Whitey could feel himself gaining ground until a new corner emerged or new obstacle appeared in his way. One hall was lined with wheelchairs, another with gurneys old enough to have carried patients who voted for the first George Bush, when he was still a vice presidential candidate with dreams of taking over the big-boy desk once Reagan's second term ended.

It seemed to Whitey that he was running into more of these that should've been possible. He had decided when he first laid eyes on Tom that he wasn't smart enough to make evasive maneuvers during a foot chase. Whitey hadn't counted on Tom's years of running from people like Whitey, people who wanted to hurt him.

61

To Tom, that was all Whitey was, another tall guy who wanted to hurt him. Tom knew where he needed to go but didn't know if he could get there in time. He had no intention of letting the big guy with the gun get his hands, let alone his gun, on him. Rocks and dirt clods were one thing. Guns were another entirely, and even old Tom knew that. No, there was too much down here going against Tom for him to let that happen. If the man only wanted to arrest him, Tom was pretty sure the things he had done for Edward would get him in trouble. Storing his empty collection tubes for him, storing the full ones while finding a safe place for them, even keeping the bracelets of the kids he brought down. He knew he shouldn't be doing that, but he did it anyway. No reason, he simply liked it. He felt connected to them. He liked being part of something bigger than himself, even if no one else would understand.

It sure seemed like the man didn't understand.

That was why Tom knew he had to get to his room. Why his room? That was where Edward would be, of course. He would protect him. Why, look at everything he'd done for him. First and foremost, he befriended him when no one else did. He also brought more friends. Because of Edward, Tom regularly had four friends all in his room at the same time. Sometimes the girls even sat on his bed. He knew they did. He would think about it after they'd gone.

Edward also included him in his work. Work that seemed very important. Tom didn't really understand it, but Edward was so passionate about it. Passion was always just, as Edward said. He had even forgiven Tom. That made Tom one of Edward's closest friends. He called him a disciple. That was good too. He had heard that word as a boy in church. Jesus had disciples, and they were good. Most of them anyway. And now Edward had disciples. This time all of them would be good. Tom was sure of it.

It felt like they were running forever, but wasn't that always the way when you were going someplace for the first time? What felt like an hour was only minutes.

Tom could see the doorway to the room that hid his home. He was almost free. Although the door was closed, he thought he could hear angry voices inside. Tom thought about who could be in his room. The only people down here, except the new visitors running after him which he let down himself, were friends. His friends. Why would his friends be angry at each other?

62

When Tom had first found the door that led to what is now his room, he thought it would have led outside. At the back of the storeroom crowded with metal shelves, obstructed by both the presence of the shelving unit and the absence of good light, was a wooden door that seemed wholly out of place for the basement of a hospital. Made up of vertical slats of wood held together by horizontal metal strips fastened with rivets, the door looked like it belonged outside leading into a groundskeeper's shed. Tom assumed with no further thought that the door was originally intended for that use but brought inside to hang here simply because the builders were a door short. Whatever the original intended use for Tom's room, groundskeeping tool storage or quarantine of some mid-century ailment, the room was as secure as it was hidden from the world.

Edward slid back the bolts that currently kept Claudia locked in solitude and prepared to enter. He pulled the door open, pausing a moment with it still in his hand. Richard behind and to his right and Krystal behind on his left, he quickly surveyed the dimly lit room, illuminated by lamps in the corners of the room. When they last saw the room it had more light, something had happened to bring the total of working lamps from two to one. Edward paused and shifted to his left. Placing his hand on Richard's shoulder, he ushered his disciple to enter the room ahead of him, which Richard did without giving it a moment's thought.

Richard stepped through the door, never seeing the brass pole swinging at his face from behind the wall on his right. The pole hit his face in a line that fractured both his right cheekbone and the bridge of his nose. An eighth of an inch higher or to the right, and it would have hit his eye directly on the pupil, likely rupturing the globe. The brass pole bent from the force of the swing, splitting a line diagonally across Richard's forehead.

He screamed out from the pain of the blast to his face and fell forward to his knees. Claudia had swung the pole from the lampstand with as much force as her body could muster. The inertia she had put into motion carried her into Richard's path, where she fell over her fallen friend, dropping the pole on her way down to free her hands to break her fall.

Edward leapt into the room over the falling pole and fallen disciple. He reached out to Claudia as she scrambled to regain her footing and pushed her farther off balance, the woman flailing to the ground.

Behind him, Krystal scooped up the bent brass pole and joined her lover, her professed lord at this point, at the side of the fallen woman who was formerly a friend to them all. Krystal held the pole in her meaty hands, wielding it like the Sword of Excalibur, its sharp broken tip pressing at Claudia's throat. Claudia didn't need the chaplain to say a word. Her eyes told her that if she so much as flinched wrong that pole would pierce her throat like a vaudeville sideshow act gone wrong.

Edward turned on his heels and stormed toward the door and back again, pacing like a bull ready for a fight.

"I chose you!"

He was looking at no one in particular while he continued pacing, though Claudia knew exactly where his wrath was being aimed.

"I chose you! You were chosen for this from before the world was made!"

Edward turned and dove at Claudia. It took all the strength left in her to remain where she was. Between Edward and the sharpened pole Krystal had pressed against her throat, Claudia felt completely out of options.

"I believed in you, Claudia. From the moment we met, I believed you to be one of my disciples. You were the entryway to the beginning of the work set out for me. I thought I was to be as John the baptizer, preparing the way of the second coming of the Lord as he prepared the first. Until I met you. You were why it all lined up. You were the key to it all. Everything fell into place with you, Claudia. I was not only the messenger. I was to be the redeemer. I was to be the way to forgiveness, repentance, and atonement for this wicked generation. I needed my John to prepare the way for me...and that was *you*."

Edward grabbed Claudia's face in his hand, jerking it past the outstretched jagged tip of the pole in Krystals hand, leaving a nick in Claudia's neck that began to run with a small trail of blood. He pulled her to him as the blood pulled his attention. He wiped it with his hand then smeared it across her cheek where her white patch began. The red formed a barrier between the light-brown skin of her cheek and the white patch that cut across her face.

"You were to be my John. You opened the way for me, proclaiming my coming to the children who needed to be redeemed, though you knew not fully what you did. But I did. Krystal did. Tom did. Richard would have known very soon, but you... You clouded things when you took off your mask and showed yourself for who you really are. As Christ had a Judas in his first coming, so I have a betrayer. I am the embodiment of his return to this Earth, Claudia. And you who were to be my John, you bear the mark God put on Cain after he murdered his brother. The same mark the beast puts on his servants. You are a harlot, Claudia! The mother of lies and deception! I chose to test you to give you a way back from the darkness to redemption, to cover your mark with your blood, but you have chosen this day whom you will serve! And now judgment will come upon you with fire and sulfur from heaven above to be bound and burned here below like those who burn already!"

Edward's exclamation was accentuated by the sound of an explosion that rang through the hallways of the basement and into the room where Richard crouched, cowering by the bed on the opposite side of the room, a trail of blood leading from where he had knelt on the floor over to where he now sat with his face in his hands.

Claudia pulled Edward's attention back to her blood-smeared face. "You're insane. You're all insane. Kill me now, Edward! Whatever you're going to do, do it! I deserve it for letting you into those rooms with those kids! You and your little followers, Krystal and Tom. He has his box of trophies in the closet. What do you two have, huh? You psycho freaks! Do it! Do it now!"

"YOU DON'T TELL ME WHAT TO DO, YOU BEAST-MARKED WHORE!"

Edward stood to his feet and grabbed the pole out of Krystal's hands. With both of his hands, he raised it over his head like a logger raised his axe.

Before he could bring the pole down on Claudia, he was startled by a crashing sound behind him. He turned to see where the sound was coming from when Claudia, seeing an opening and taking full advantage, raised her size-six sneaker and sent it with the force of a woman's desperate last effort to avoid certain death into the crotch of Edward's black scrubs.

He hit the ground as she scrambled to her feet, pushing over the chaplain and scurrying to the corner of the room as another explosion rang out, this one closer than the last and accentuated by bits of concrete mere feet from where she now stood, spewing out from the wall and spraying over that side of the room.

No one needed to see Whitey's gun to know what that explosion was.

63

Tom's legs could've given out with any of the final steps he took as he sprinted, the final paces to his storage room. The thing that kept his feet under him and his head held high was the promise of a savior from the madman who was closing in behind him.

Whitey was not slowing down. He had been preparing his entire life for this. When he was a child, he sat at his grandfather's table and heard stories of the pursuits — trumped-up pursuits, according to his grandmother — his grandfather went on to catch bad guys. His eyes wide with wonder as he hung on his grandfather's every word.

When he was a young man, he would sit beside his father on the well-worn couch in front of the family television as his dad would rest his weary body and regale his son with the heroic exploits of the day that had left him so weary and worn.

He thought about his father and grandfather as he gained ground on Tom during the final stretch toward the room Tom was entering. *Go ahead and box yourself in, Tom. Make it easy on ol' Whitey, why dontcha?*

Indy, Joey, and I were right on Whitey's tail. We had gained ground with every obstacle, since it was Whitey who was surprised and had to throw aside the objects in his way. That cleared the path for us bringing up the rear. Seeing Tom run into a dark room let us know the race was almost over. Whitey could get his man, and maybe we could find what we had been looking for since just after eight o'clock that morning. Indy could find her friends, or find out what had happened to them, and we could get some answers about the last night you were alive.

Tom opened and sped through the door, crashing headlong into the storage shelves that were waiting in the dark. He no longer had the strength in his legs for any sort of evasive action. Tom was little more than a wrecking ball on legs at this point. He scrambled to his feet, his hands and legs bruised from the collision with the metal units. His legs screamed at him as he begged them to last a few moments more. Tom approached the threshold of the door to his personal nirvana in the same moment Whitey approached the threshold of the door to Tom's storage room.

Whitey again raised his gun, and while a chorus of shouts rang out from behind him, he pulled the trigger.

Whitey was breathing harder than he was when he fired the first time, but he did not sneeze. His legs and lungs burned more too, but the fire in his shoulder was only a smolder. His aim was not perfect, but it was better.

The .40 caliber slug hit Tom in his left shoulder. The impact spun him to his right like an unbalanced, mustached top, depositing him on the floor to the right of the entryway to the room. Concrete dust was in the air as the bullet went right through Tom's scrawny shoulder and impacted the stone wall across from the open door.

Whitey came through the door with his gun drawn while he surveyed the room. In the corner, grasping a golden lampstand like she was trying to hide behind it, was a five-foot-tall woman with golden-brown curls pulled back in a ponytail and fresh concrete in her hair like little barrettes. Her skin was light-brown, but she had a white patch that ran diagonally across her face like a slash. There was blood smeared on her face, and more trickled down her neck.

To his right, curled in a seated fetal position up against an old hospital style bed, was a man whose face was wearing a crimson mask. He had a gash that ran from his cheek clear across his forehead. There was a trail of blood from his head to a spot inside the door.

To his left, closer to the opposite wall, were a man and a woman. The woman, short, stocky, and dark, appeared unharmed. The man, bald and bearded, was in obvious pain while he held himself with both hands.

All around the room were signs of struggle, signs of war. Chairs, stools, boxes, lamps, even an old metal table now on three legs, were broken and tossed, like the room had somehow trapped a tornado from the Bible Belt.

From behind Whitey came three more bodies into the increasingly crowded and dimly lit space.

Doctor Indiana Powell entered first, her white Keds no longer white after running through the decades-old dirt of the basement she didn't know existed in the hospital until roughly an hour ago. She surveyed the room with the looks of horror and anticipation. She did not see Lila or Addison, but she did recognize the chaplain seated on the floor next to the nurse holding his crotch. She was about to speak when the final members of the party entered the room, saying, "Oh my good and gracious God."

Winslow and Josephine Miller, you know us as Dad and Mom, entered the room dimly lit by one working lampstand casting rays of light through the cloud of dust that hung in the air.

We looked around the room and did not see the broken furniture. We did not see the blood on the floor. We did not see the poster of the frog in the mouth of the pelican, holding on for dear life, with the caption "Never Give Up" in big, bold letters.

We did see the chaplain who had introduced herself twenty-four hours ago with a Christian prayer in the room with you and who had counseled us outside the hospital in our grief mere hours ago.

We did see the golden-brown curls of the masked nurse who had cared for you, our daughter, on multiple nights over your final weeks alive on this earth.

And we did see the bald, bearded man who had come into your room during the night shift when the nurse said she needed a consult from the IV team.

64

Silence fell on the room like a weighted blanket. Dust was still hanging in the air from the impact of the bullet that tore through Tom's body and lodged in the wall. Blood was drying as a third tone on the skin above Claudia's shirt collar. It ran from the new crevice in Richard's face and poured from the hole in Tom's shoulder.

Richard held his broken face in the corner while struggling to see through the blood in his eyes.

Tom was in agonizing pain, a lightning bolt alive and dancing in his shoulder as he struggled with consciousness from both the shock and loss of blood.

Claudia, Krystal, and Edward stared silently, mouths agape, at the couple they most recently knew from room 513.

Claudia stepped out from behind the lampstand.

"Mr. and Mrs. Miller?"

Tears formed in her tired eyes as the levee began to break in her soul.

"Claudia?"

Joey stepped out from my shadow with the mention of the name of your nurse and took my hand, side by side.

Though one may be overpowered, two can defend themselves.

Edward spoke from the floor through grimacing lips, the pain in his crotch now a dull ache, the fire subsiding but the damage done, "Claudia, don't you…"

"You shut the hell up," Whitey said as he raised his gun, still with thirteen shots in the mag, and aimed it at Edward. "Let the girl talk."

"Mr. and Mrs. Miller…"

"Winslow and Joey."

Claudia's face fell to the ground. She wiped her eyes and tried to gather herself before raising herself back up and continuing.

"Winslow and Joey, I'm so sorry for…everything…"

Her body moved as though she wanted to come to us, hug us and beg forgiveness, but she couldn't. The air between us was dense and repelled her like a magnetic pole repelled a charge of similar polarity. Her legs were heavy, her feet a part of the floor. She stood unable to move.

"Claudia," I said softly, aware of the negative charge in the air that seemed capable of igniting at a pin drop, "Just tell us what happened. We deserve to know."

"We all deserve to know." Indy's voice quivered, referring to the three-person doctor team that had started looking into the night nurse team hours ago. The doctor team that was down to one, the others roasting into ash several corridors away.

"The man bleeding from his face by the bed, that's Richard. This one holding himself, that's Edward. They're on the IV team."

"I said STOP!" Edward started to stand, but Krystal put both hands on his shoulders to hold him in place.

Whitey raised his left hand to reinforce his grip on the Glock 22.

"Last warning, the next bullet will be for you if you interrupt her one more time. Try me."

Edward seethed at Whitey, staring at him like he was measuring something inside of him, before settling into his seat on the floor when the measurements added up to something he decided he didn't want to test.

"Eight months ago, I started my job here. Totally new, fresh out of college. I didn't know anyone. I haven't had friends or even acquaintances since middle school, when these began to grow."

Claudia pointed to the patch on her face. A bloom of white slashing across tanned, golden-brown skin. She lifted her scrub top to her ribcage to show the matching white slash across her toned stomach for the first time in her young life.

"I don't leave my apartment in a crop top, sports bra, or anything remotely cute that might show that. I also don't leave my apartment without a mask. If you look close, you'd still see it peek out of the top, but no one looks close. No one looked until after I started here and met these two guys. We became friends. Work friends, but friends. The only ones I've had since my patches grew. Then one day I forgot about hiding my face. I pulled my mask off like I was all alone, but I wasn't. They were there. I was mortified, but they didn't even notice. Or I thought they didn't."

She glared at Edward. If superpowers were real, she would've killed him in that moment, whether she meant to or not.

"We spent all of our time together and an increasing amount of it with her too, the hospital chaplain. We met and talked. We vented, counseled, and got counsel. She'd open her Bible and teach us. It was nice. I trusted it. I trusted them. I loved the job. We help kids. I love my kids. I'd do anything for them, to help them, to protect them. Or I thought I would."

Her voice began to crack. If not for the charge in the air, maybe someone would have approached her, but no one did. No one moved.

"Five months ago, Richard and Edward came to me with a request. It was Edward's plan, but he made Richard ask. I think everyone could tell how close I felt to Richard. It seemed dirty, but I trusted them. He said they wanted to be the best nurses they could be for the kids. Franklin isn't a big fancy hospital in a big fancy town. We don't have some of the things the big hospitals have. I mean, they don't even keep up the basement. No one but us has been down here in decades, and that's only because Tom gave us keys to the elevator or it'd be just him.

"University hospitals, the nice ones, have cadaver labs. Surgeons get to practice on actual bodies. Researchers use them. You can even use them to practice your IV sticks. Some newer hospitals have labs with artificial cadavers where you can poke over and over again. We don't have any of that. So when they asked me to get them into the occasional patient rooms, I could at least see the merit.

"I wouldn't do it unless the kid *needed* to be poked. Labs, an IV, that sort of thing. Policy is that we only call the IV team once we've tried multiple times and had another floor nurse try as well. All I was doing was calling them before making the kid go through the extra steps. I was saving the kids from extra pokes, or that's what the guys said. It made sense. But since it was off policy, it had to be off record. I texted them instead of doing an official call. It felt wrong, but not too wrong, you know? But then kids started dying."

Claudia couldn't hold it back—she broke down. Indy wanted to go to her, but the disgust of the situation held her back. Your mom and I had an arm around each other, bracing for the impact of the climax we knew the story had. Edward and Whitey had their eyes locked on each other like lions from opposing tribes who found themselves at the same watering hole. Krystal and Richard sat motionless, staring off into space. Tom did the same.

"It wasn't all of them. If it was, I would've stopped. I should've stopped anyway. Edward was constantly in my ear telling me it was a coincidence. I was a floor nurse, I would see ebbs and flows in patient deaths during my career, this one just happened to be happening now. I believed him, even though I didn't. I trusted him. He was my friend. They all were.

"Then today, we came down here after our shifts last night. We do that sometimes, to debrief and talk before getting some sleep. While we were here, they got a message from their boss. Some doctors were investigating the IV team. We knew what it was about. That's when all hell broke loose. Something broke inside Edward's fractured mind, and he showed himself for what he really is."

Indy was sobbing, quiet sobs but heaving. Everything she feared about that message from Doctor Kirschner was confirmed by the nurse standing in front of her.

Edward's eyes were burning, his mouth beginning to snarl. Whitey's finger was itching as he tapped it to remind Edward to stay silent. Claudia had to finish her story.

"It was all a plot from Edward. The whole damn thing. The plan was a front to get me to say yes so he could get in the rooms. He thinks he's some prophet or something, maybe thinks he's God in the flesh. He thinks he's redeeming the world one child at a time by taking their blood. I think he's been using the same old, broken, dirty needle on all of them, and it's killing them. Something in the blood or clots from the damage or something. I don't even know. But *he* knows and *he* thinks he's holy, and they're all *in on it*!"

Edward had enough. He stood and brought Krystal up with him. Whitey started to pull his trigger but waited for a better shot. The woman was in front of the guy with a crazed look.

"I don't *think* I'm God, Claudia. I *am* God, tabernacled in human flesh, you DEVIL! KILL HER AND SILENCE THE BEAST ONCE AND FOR ALL!"

Edward's shout echoed throughout the cave-like room, while confusion swirled like a windstorm around them. Claudia's final revelations were mind-numbing, but Edward's final exclamation was the candle on top of the cake.

Krystal exploded from her place in the room toward Claudia like an Olympic sprinter from the starting blocks. Whitey tracked his aim on the short woman who was lunging with a crazed attack on the woman with the patch on her face. He fired two shots.

When Edward's voice had reached its crescendo, Richard began to stand. He saw through the red tint of his bloody vision as Krystal began to lunge at Claudia, who barely had time to begin to backpedal. Richard shot out of his spot by

Tom's bed at Krystal. He wouldn't let her get to Claudia. Not today.

Whitey's first shot hit Richard in the upper back to the right of his spine. Lower and it would have hit his lung, to the left it would have severed his spine, higher and it would have hit a major artery. Richard dropped to the floor.

Whitey's second shot hit Krystal in her chest. It didn't need to go higher, lower, left, or right to hit a major part of her body. It hit her heart directly. She went down in a heap. The sound of the shots made Indy, Joey, and myself recoil from the events of the room. The exploding concrete from the wall opposite Whitey made Edward and Claudia cover their faces.

Nothing could have caused Tom to recoil from the sight of the chaplain being shot and falling lifeless to the ground.

A wildfire exploded within the bleeding little man. He picked up the first object he could find within his reach, the broken leg of the metal table next to him. Three feet of rusted steel settled in Tom's hand like a battle axe, its L shape sharpened by years of oxidation and capable of great damage in the wrong hands.

In his current rage, Tom's hands were the wrong hands.

He stood behind and to the right of Officer Arthur Lawrence "Whitey" White. If your mother and I hadn't sprung back with our hands covering our ears and faces, maybe we could have stopped Tom, but maybe not. Tom reared back with the force of fifty years of teasing, taunting, and turmoil and brought the steel leg of Tom's old table down at Whitey's neck like a lover scorned. Whitey killed Tom's love, and Tom felt he had no choice but to reciprocate.

The leg came down with the sharp side of the L shape directly onto Whitey's neck, where his shirt collar ended and his neck began. It sliced deep into Whitey's flesh, stopping only when it hit the bone of vertebrae. Tom nearly cut Whitey's head clean off with that rusty steel table leg.

I looked up and saw the steel table leg in the torso of the officer who had helped bring me to the basement. A fountain of red sprayed from the severed artery in Whitey's neck as he collapsed dead on the floor. I grabbed Tom from behind and slung him down by the bed. Until moments ago, I believed that little man had killed my daughter, and now he had killed the police officer whose body was falling to the floor to the tune of Indy and Joey's harmonizing screams. Tom tried to stand, but his head rose into my upward-swinging foot. The kick lifted Tom from the floor and sent him back onto his bed, bleeding and unconscious.

Claudia grabbed Richard by his outstretched hand and pulled him up. She yelled at me to turn around, "Your daughter's killer is still in the room."

All eyes turned to Edward, who was standing in the corner facing the crowd with fire in his eyes and lightning on his lips.

65

"Look around, Claudia. You did this!" Edward howled from the corner, positioned like a doomsday prophet on a New York street corner, ready to pronounce judgment. The difference between them and Edward was that only one believed himself to be God incarnate.

"None of this had to happen. Krystal. That cop. The two in the furnace. No one had to die today!"

At the revelation that yes, the smell of burning flesh had been the two missing members of her team, Indy collapsed in on herself in a ball on the floor next to Whitey's body and wept.

"No one had to die today?"

Joey spoke for the first time since entering Tom's room.

"No one except your half-breed daughter, but you should be thanking me. I saved her soul before death came for her. She stands atoned by the blood I drew out of her."

"Half what?"

It was as though I was standing in the doorway, watching myself and everyone else in the room. I saw myself begin taking steps away from Tom's unconscious body toward the man who proclaimed judgment on my baby girl. Joey extended an arm to stop me, before stepping into the center of the room herself.

"Say it again. Tell me again what you did and why. I want to know exactly what psycho revelation you've been spewing to these people before I kill you."

Chloe, throughout the history of the world, many threats have been given to many people. None have held more weight than the one levied by Josephine Miller to Edward Falcone in the basement of Franklin Children's Hospital.

"God created this world pure before the woman, created by Satan himself, poisoned the bloodline of humanity. Cain's mark, the one shared by the followers of the beast, was not the only one humanity was cursed with. The burnt skin of Ham was placed as another mark, and when the bloodlines mix, why that's a half breed, lady. But I have come to redeem the world. I was called and chosen, bought with a price. I shed my blood to become reborn, God incarnate in flesh upon this Earth to turn the hearts of these children back to their fathers and to SAVE THEIR WRETCHED SOULS! Krystal understood that! I redeemed her myself. God even prepared her for our union by removing her ability to spawn offspring, knowing his future incarnate home could never produce a half breed like your daughter.

"Everything that had happened until this morning was in the mind of God from before the foundation of the world, and now it has been tainted because of the evil one who stands before you with the beast's mark upon her face! Now fire and sulfur will reign down on all you who seek to impede the will of the—"

A gunshot went off that produced a red spray of rock and dust from beside the "Never Give Up" poster on Tom's wall. Edward fell to the floor, his life extinguished. When the dust settled and the ringing began to subside in their ears, everyone looked up to see Indiana Powell with Whitey's Glock 22 in her outstretched and shaking hands.

The explosive crack hit Tom like a defibrillator paddle to his chest. He rose from his blood-soaked bed and saw his lord lying dead on the floor and a gun in the hands of the doctor lady who helped chase him from the morgue. Tom shoved past me and ran toward Indy, but Claudia picked up the broken wooden stool, two legs snapped off leaving a seat with two legs like a bent wooden shovel, and swung it at Tom. The broadside of the seat cracked into his face. When his head bounced off the hard, dirty floor below him, Tom lost consciousness for the last time.

I helped your mother carefully take Whitey's gun from Indy's hands. Joey held the two pounds of polymer, gunpowder, and lead in her hand and looked at the lifeless body of the man who murdered her daughter. She raised the weapon and aimed it at the mass that moments ago had been so full of hate that it seemed to vibrate with condemnation and contempt meant for the whole world, past and present.

I saw the pain in my wife's eyes, pain I could feel in my own as well. It burned from deep within my soul and bubbled toward the surface in a way that, if left unbridled, could consume the world around me, likely taking me and my wife with it. Seeing Joey's hands shaking under the weight of the firearm, and not only the firearm but the weight of all that would come with pulling the trigger, I placed a hand on the one that held the gun and softly spoke to my wife.

"Two are better than one, because they have a good return for their labor. If either of them falls down, one can help the other up..."

As the gun lowered, Joey spoke, "But pity anyone who falls...and has no one to help them up."

Joey's hand relaxed and allowed the weapon that had ended the life of the man who took her daughter from her to slip from her fingers and fall to the floor. I embraced my wife. Both having fallen throughout the events of April 18th, we each held the other up and pitied the ones who had no one to help them.

Richard, still bleeding but managing through his pain, removed the radio from Whitey's chest and used it to call for help. He told the responding lady on the other end that four people were dead and he was injured. He asked me how we got to the basement then relayed the information about the freight elevator to the officer on the other end. We left Tom's office as a group. Before leaving, Claudia got the boxes out of Tom's closet. She removed your bracelet and gave it to Joey. She left the rest in the box on the floor.

***

When the group entered the morgue, we stopped by the freezer. I placed my hand on the door but did not open it. Instead, I bowed my head as your mom took my hand. Seeing us with our heads down and eyes closed, Indy, Claudia, and Richard stopped and did the same. Showing respect for the innocent loss that had started the course of events that morning, which had ended less than a day later with the largest single-day body count the small town had seen in fifty years.

We passed into the stone room that held the entrance to the freight elevator. Before pressing the call button, Indy looked to her left at the door to the cremation oven. The large red light above the door went off.

Indy wept.

66

Dear Dad,

It's me, Chloe.

I've come to learn over the passage of time since my final day that people often wonder whether the loved ones who pass on can see how life continues after they're gone. As you can probably tell by now, I saw everything that happened after I died. Watching life go on once you're gone is different than experiencing it while living. It's like you already know all the backstory and everyone's motivations, like the dirty glass you were looking through to see the world has suddenly been taken away.

I've seen everything that's happened since. Both the events of the day to the times after, including the conversations you've had with Claudia, Richard, and Indy, and the conversations you haven't had with Mom. I even got to read your letter as you were writing it, and I tried as I could to piece in the missing places where you couldn't have known what was happening or where.

Dad, if you can hear me, I'm okay. Tell Mom I love her. I love you too.

I can remember the feelings from the moment I was able to take my last breath until the moment I closed my eyes for the final time, but barely. What is clear is the love that I felt from Mom as she was trying to do everything in her power to help me.

And I know that you think you missed my last moments, Dad, but you didn't. You heard that beeping from the machine, but so did I. I had a few seconds with you at the door.

I remember them clearly. The room was getting dark, and I faintly remember fear. It was strong. But then there was a light. It wasn't the only one. There was one in the room, but it was off to the side. This one was coming in the door. When you got there, it was blinding. The last thing I knew in life was the overwhelming light of your love coming into the darkness of my death. It calmed me. It led me home.

When I opened my eyes again, I was standing in the hall of the hospital, fully dressed with no stab wounds, IVs, or monitors. I was watching everyone go by.

I wanted to come back into the room to comfort you and Mom, but something wouldn't let me in the door. Maybe the place of our death is the one place we can't re-enter once we're gone. Or maybe the air was just too heavy.

I began to walk. I saw things. I heard things. Terrible things. None of the terrible things compares to what I see hanging around you when I look at you now. There's a dark cloud around your head like clouds on the peaks of the tallest mountains. The trauma and grief are overtaking you. You are not the daddy I knew. If you aren't careful, you're in danger of never being that Winslow Miller again, and it isn't fair, dad. Not to my memory, to Mom, and not to my sister. Faith deserves to have the same daddy I had. You have to remember who that was. Most of all, you have to let April eighteenth go.

It's been two years now. You guys had tried staying in the home you raised me in, but your pain was too much to bear on a daily basis. You would turn a corner expecting to see me sitting at the table doodling in my art book only to see an empty chair. Walk down the hall toward my room to call me for dinner to see an empty bed still made up from before they took me to the hospital.

Mom swore she could hear my video games in the night, like I was still huddled under my blanket playing Animal Crossing or Fortnite instead of sleeping, but when she'd go in, of course, there would be no one there.

You sold our little house and bought another on the other side of town. You didn't tell the realtor about the sounds Mom heard. You tried but never could hear them.

This house sits inset on a hill, the driveway sloping down to the garage on the side of the house that entered the basement on the left side. You like to back down the drive so you can pull straight out, but Mom never does. So on the morning of August third, you instead had to back up and out of the steep drive.

Twenty minutes later, the white Corolla is sitting in traffic two miles from the hospital, Faith is crying, and it is ten minutes to noon. The news stations and the email from Indy had said the ceremony would be starting promptly at noon.

"We're going to miss the ceremony."

"They aren't going to start without us."

"Why wouldn't they, Wins? We don't have anything to do with this?"

"Of course we do! They wouldn't be remodeling the basement if it wasn't for what happened, and we were part of that."

"Yeah, but they aren't saying that. We aren't part of their story. The 'Lila Collins & Addison McCray Memorial Wing' in the newly remodeled basement is for two doctors who were murdered by a lone night nurse before being cremated in the oven by his psycho follower, who he then killed, and who was himself killed by hero cop Arthur White, but not before killing his lover and threatening the other nurses. They found Edward guilty posthumously with the testimony of the survivors. There's no mention of the children, his trophy room with vials of blood, or Tom's collection of bracelets. Hospital administration wanted no mention of the children's deaths, which would be a PR nightmare for such a small town organization. Officially, there was only one child harmed by the rogue nurse, and that is only because her unnamed parents were found among the survivors. They've buried our involvement ever since, which is fine by me. Indy invited us on her own. That's it. And now we're gonna miss the whole thing because of this traffic!"

Dad is shaking his head and checking his mirrors before whipping the car onto the sidewalk, "Nope, not today!"

They ride the sidewalk one hundred feet to a small, freshly paved parking lot across the street from the east side of the hospital. It has a new chain-link fence that borders two of the sides of the lot, the other two sides made up of neighboring brick buildings currently undergoing renovation as part of a city initiative to revitalize the downtown section around the hospital.

"Grab the stroller while I get Faith out of her seat. We're making it if we have to melt in this heat to get there. Who needs a parking garage these days anyway?"

Winslow, Joey, and Faith Miller, my Dad, my Mom, and *my sister*, walked up the sidewalk along the front of Franklin Children's Hospital. A small crowd had gathered in front of the main double doors that made up the entrance to the hospital, where a ceremonial yellow ribbon had been tied between two temporary columns. The columns stood inside a pair of concrete benches. Mom and Dad looked at the bench to their right and smiled. There was a tear in Mom's eye.

"Twelve-oh-five. Told ya."

Mom returned the smile and elbowed Dad as only a woman in love could do.

It's twelve-fifteen, and the crowd has grown to a couple dozen, generous for a Monday at noon. Dad and Mom are standing to the right of center and are making their way toward the front of the crowd, rubbing shoulders with local news stations busy getting footage for the five o'clock news. Finally, the doors open, and a small group begin to walk out and line up in front of the yellow ribbon. Mom and Dad were doting on their new baby girl when the first speaker began. The familiar voice caused their attention to leave my sister and shift to the ceremony.

"Good morning. Well, I suppose maybe 'good afternoon' is more appropriate."

The crowd gave a courtesy laugh as Doctor Indiana Powell addressed them. Her attention was on the cameras currently aimed at her. When she paused to allow the laugh to ring, she glanced around the crowd. When she saw Dad and Mom, who was now holding Faith in her arms and giving her her noon bottle, she broke her official decorum and smiled with a wave. The couple reciprocated, and Joey held Faith a little higher so the doctor could see her better. Indy clasped her hands to her face and took a single step back to take a breath — a cleansing breath — before resuming her practiced speech. She removed her hands from her face, and her smile beamed so bright it lit up the heavens as she choked back her tears.

"We apologize for the delay. We had hoped to start at noon but had a slight situation we had to attend to. Nothing too big, but duty does call as life goes on here in the hospital.

"Two years ago, I experienced the darkest day of my life, both personally and professionally, when a deeply mentally ill nurse took the lives of two doctors. My two closest friends at the time. Lila Collins and Addison McCray. Lila was the head of a team of doctors made up by herself, Addison, and me. Their deaths have impacted me personally and our community as a whole. I stand here today as the head of my own team that I strive everyday to lead with the class and grace of my mentor and friend, Lila Collins.

"Two years ago, hospital administration looked at the circumstances of those tragic events and decided, rightfully in my opinion, to take some ownership of the events and then to make changes. A construction project began in the summer of that year, and we are here to unveil the fruit of the labor of the men and women who came together to make that project a reality.

"Ladies and gentlemen, I present to you the Lila Collins & Addison McCray Memorial Unit of Franklin Children's Hospital."

A tarpaulin that had been covering a sign to the right of Indy that Mom and Dad hadn't noticed when they walked up was removed to reveal the sign underneath. There was also one on her left, but it remained covered. The sign displayed the new name for the basement level of the hospital. The doctor's memorialized names forever signaling that the basement level will never be left forgotten again, where idle spaces could become the devil's playground.

Looking to their left at the new sign Dad and Mom spotted a figure at the back of the crowd. There was a woman with wavy golden-brown hair pulled back in a loose ponytail, her face partly covered by a mask, the white patch that contrasted with her tanned olive skin peeking out at the top edge of the mask. The couple waved. After a moment when they thought she would remain stoic, Claudia finally lifted a hand and waved back. It was hard to tell, but they thought they could see the edges of the mask raise slightly, perhaps indicating a smile.

Indy spoke again as the applause died down, "Now, may I introduce to you a special guest for one more announcement before we cut the ribbon and you can get back to your busy days."

More courtesy laughs, mainly from the news crews.

"Please welcome from the Wayside Sojourner Mission down the road, Pastor Richard Mercier."

67

Dad and Mom were looking at each other with questions on their lips they didn't want to ask but needed answers to. At the back of the crowd, Claudia took a single step forward before stopping and lowering her head.

Richard stepped out from behind a line of doctors and nurses and hugged Indy before taking her spot in between the spectators and administrators. He had on khakis and a buttoned-down shirt left untucked. It was probably made to be left untucked judging from the way it fell to his belt line and no farther. It was a far cry from the scrubs Mom and Dad last saw him in. He had a scar that ran across his forehead and extended beyond his right eye to halfway down his cheek. It was still red enough that it almost matched his hair. Claudia could see it from where she stood in the back of the crowd.

"My name is Richard Mercier. Two years ago, I was a nurse here in the hospital. At the time, I was a friend to what I know now was a deeply disturbed man who had been corrupted by delusions of grandeur and doctrines that were frankly so shockingly false that I'm ashamed to have ever been associated with him in any fashion. I saw a picture once of a frog caught in the mouth of a predatory bird. The frog had its hands on the throat of the bird and the sign said "Never Give Up." When we get caught in a snare, suddenly it can be easy to see the enemy and to know how to fight back. Too often though, the devil who roams like a predator seeking vulnerable souls attacks not suddenly but gradually. I have often wondered about that frog and whether he would have been able to fight back if his assailant had drawn him into the safety of a pot and gradually turned up the heat until it boiled. I think not. I am thankful that there are those around us who, when they recognize their fellow man boiling, choose to never give up on them and will risk their own lives, even laying them down, to knock the pot over. I stand here today free from that man who was able to ensnare me because of people who chose to not give up.

"After the events of April eighteenth, 2024, I handed in my resignation and walked away from this place. Though free from the pot, I could still feel the residual heat and had no more desire to stay in the place I had allowed it to overtake me. And I wasn't the only nurse who left. One of the best friends

I've ever known did too. We walked away not only from this place but from each other. I miss her. I wronged her then and hope she knows how remorseful I am. I hope she can one day find it in her heart to forgive me.

"Over the last two years, as construction has changed the bottom level of this place from it's dark, dirty, and confusing corridors to the light, clean, open spaces that will soon be filled with teams of doctors and nurses in the new imaging wing on the west side and the new wing we'll talk about in a moment on the east side, I too allowed my heart and mind to be torn down to nothing and slowly rebuilt.

"You'll notice here in front, an empty wheelchair. Three weeks ago, the world lost a great man who would have been here this morning had he not been called home by the God he served for many years. He coached me out of the state I had found myself in and led me to the place I stand here now, as the pastor of the mission he began years ago. Out of the Wayside Sojourner Mission, I carry out the task commissioned once by Jim Creed to show the love and mercy of God to the youth of our dear town. I have seen how the wrong hands can mold people in the wrong way. I will not allow hands such as those to mold our children anymore."

More applause, though not as much out of courtesy but appreciation. Rumors of Edward Falcone have swirled since echoes of his cult of personality had risen in the days following

April 18, 2024. Officially, he had only been an unhinged nurse, but word of his message had swirled through the community like a poisoned fog from a Stephen King novel.

Here stands a man determined to dissipate that fog and defend the community from it. A man who wore the mark on his face that bore testimony of what would come from Edward's hateful doctrine and doctrines from those like him.

"I bet you're all wondering what's under this tarp on my left. You've seen the sign for the new Lila Collins & Addison McCray Unit, the official name of the newly renovated bottom floor of the hospital. I've actually been asked to unveil the name of the east wing of the unit. In the east wing will be a state-of-the-art training facility for doctors and nurses young and old, new and experienced to work on and perfect their craft for the benefit of patients of the hospital for decades to come."

Mom and Dad's eyes caught the eyes of Indy, who could barely hold back the tears from streaming down to her face, heading for the smile on her lips. They looked to see if Richard had a similar expression but saw him focused to their left at the masked woman at the back of the crowd. Claudia had her face in her hands. Her shoulders heaved as she sobbed, her mask becoming a wet mess of tears from above and snot from within.

"Ladies and gentlemen, I present to you..."

This time it was Dad and Mom who took their faces in their hands. If Mom hadn't placed Faith in her stroller after finishing her bottle, she may have been in danger of dropping her.

"...the Chloe Miller Medical Training Wing."

The tarpaulin covering the new sign fell to the ground, unveiling the most beautiful sign they had ever seen.

Questions would be asked by reporters today why the name of the new unit was what it was. The simple answer to be given was that the administration wanted to remind its employees of their job as caretakers of children, so they chose the name of a former patient. That was all, nothing to see here. Most reporters would let it die there, except for one newspaper reporter who was planning a lengthy piece that described the events of April 18, 2024 in excruciating detail, using unnamed sources.

Richard and Indy felt the story should be told correctly at least once.

After the unveiling of the sign, Richard went back behind the crowd of administrators so the proper people could get their photo-op in the papers.

Indy was telling Mom and Dad how she assumed they wouldn't mind if my name was immortalized as a beacon for good. No one would be able to say there wasn't a proper avenue for training ever again. Not at Franklin Children's

Hospital anyway. As they talked, Dad lifted Faith out of her stroller and held her in one arm. With the other, he took Mom's hand in his and held it to his chest. The cloud around his head was breaking apart and lifting away. He looked happy. My sister drifted off to sleep, content in the arms of the daddy she deserved.

Claudia stayed in the back of the dissipating crowd. Richard remained at the edge of the doctors hobnobbing with reporters, getting their politically correct version of events leading to this unveiling in all the papers and on the evening news.

The former friends locked eyes. Richard smiled before pointing to the scar running across his face and shrugging with a small chuckle.

Claudia removed her mask and allowed it to drop to the ground. She wiped the tears from her face, her own scar a patch broad and white, covering a slash of her face from her left eye to her right jawline. It appeared to be slightly bigger than before.

Claudia smiled as the breeze grabbed her mask and blew it away.

THE END

Authors Notes

There are a number of real cult leaders whose teachings have left a trail of dead bodies in their wake. The question becomes whether they were intentionally doing things to physically harm their people or were they so indoctrinated by their own false teachings that they truly thought they were doing something good, but that thing had bad consequences? Sometimes it's difficult to tell. What we can tell is whether their words are dangerous cult speak. If they are we can run before the harm comes, intentionally or otherwise. If you hear anything from a preacher that sounds remotely like Edward, that's your sign to run.

In the summer before my daughter turned 13 she got sick. Really sick. Long story short, we spent 8 out of 10 weeks in a hospital room at our children's hospital. I was walking back to our room with my wife and my breakfast when I had a thought, "What if something happened while I was gone?"

Nothing had, but I soon took ownership of those thoughts and wrote them down. This book is where they went.

Our experience with the staff was nothing like this. Our nurses were great and many of their names (including Joey and Chloe) are in this book. My daughter is well and living with ulcerative colitis with no issues since that stay. My wife and I have been together 23 years, as of this writing, and I love her more each day. Our other child isn't younger, he's older and has always been a great brother and son.

Lastly, my love of reading was instilled by my mother. She passed away after complications from chemotherapy and breast cancer. She was able to read the first draft of this book. I'm glad she did, though I wish she could've held the finished book.

Life turns on a dime, sometimes. Appreciate what you have while you have it. Thanks for reading.